DIVIDED WE STAND

BOOK 3 IN THE DIVISION BELL TRILOGY

RACHEL MCLEAN

JOIN MY BOOK CUB

If you enjoy this book, you can join my book club to get the companion stories set on the opening day of this novel for free.

Please see the end of this book for full details.

Thanks,
Rachel McLean

Catawampus Press

catawampus-press.com

FEBRUARY 2022

THE STATION SHOULDN'T BE THIS QUIET.

It was rush hour. Bodies swarmed around Jennifer as she attempted to find her platform. But the people passing her were silent, the hush of New Street Station overlaid with a patina of unease. It was as if everyone was waiting for something to happen.

She stopped and looked up at the departures board. Had she missed something? Was there a security alert?

But the screens were quiet, announcing nothing more than the times of trains. And the crowds passing her looked calm, moving quietly through the space.

Only something was wrong, a tautness in the air that made her flesh feel cold.

She reached the top of the escalator, the one she always used to get home. It was blocked. She shrugged and shifted to the next one along.

At the bottom of the escalator, she peered across the track towards her normal platform. It was boarded up. She checked the screen; this wasn't the right platform either, no sign of her train on the list.

She pulled her thin jacket closer and wished the shoes she'd picked out for court weren't so tight. The escalator going back up was broken and roped off. She headed further up the platform to the stairs. She just wanted to get home, to Yusuf.

She emerged onto the station concourse and paused to get her bearings. At this end, a big chunk of the station was boarded off, reminding her of the year the new station had been built, the sweaty underpasses and dim corridors that had passed for the concourse in those days. Now the station was a gleaming beacon of welcome to Birmingham, a vast temple filled not only with ticket offices and departure boards, but cafes, shops and restaurants.

She approached the hoarding, hoping to find a sign that would explain things. It was decorated with nothing more than graffiti and the scuff marks of hundreds of passing shoes.

She found her train and headed towards the correct platform. She felt numb, tired from her journey from Oxfordshire, where she'd been incarcerated in the British Values Centre. Just this morning she'd been in Yonda Hughes's office, being told that she'd earned her release. And just yesterday she had been drugged for her Celebration ceremony, required to prove her loyalty to the state in front of an audience of over a hundred fellow inmates.

She passed a woman struggling with two heavy suitcases and three small children. She wore a black headscarf and looked hot and tired. She was muttering to the children, trying to persuade a boy not much older than Jennifer's own son Hassan to carry one of the suitcases for her.

The boy snapped back at his mother, who looked like she might burst into tears. Jennifer stepped forward.

"Can I help? You look like you've got a lot to manage."

The woman's eyes widened. "No, no. Please. I'm fine."

"Are you sure? It's no trouble."

"Leave her alone. She shouldn't be here anyway."

Jennifer turned to see a young woman watching them. She wore a bright red suit that made her skin look yellow. She wore a look of disgust.

"I'm sorry, I don't think—" Jennifer began.

"Leave it," said the first woman. Her youngest child, a girl of about eighteen months with a chocolate-ringed mouth and tangled hair, started to cry.

The woman in the red suit turned to her. "Get out of here. We don't want you here."

The other woman looked up through her eyelashes but said nothing. She pulled the little girl out of her pushchair and started making shushing sounds.

"Please," said Jennifer. "Leave this woman alone. She's doing you no harm."

"Yeah, right. The sooner they all go home, the better." She marched off, her heels clipping in the muffled quiet.

A crowd was gathering now, people hanging back but staring nonetheless. Jennifer looked back at them, isolated with this woman and her children in a ring of surveillance. Was this how things had got, while she was away?

She thought of her oldest son Samir, and the racist taunts he'd received at school. The way he'd retaliated and almost got himself expelled. Even then, the head teacher had sided with the racists and not with her Muslim son. She'd been entertaining a dim hope that she might find him back at home when she got there, and not in prison or detention. Judging by the atmosphere here, that would be unlikely.

She turned back to the woman. The girl had stopped crying and she was lowering her into the pushchair. Her big brother looked scared, gazing back at the hostile crowd with huge dark eyes. Maybe they were her constituents. Maybe she could help them.

But her arrest had stripped her of her parliamentary seat; she had no constituents now. She wondered who had taken her place, whether her successor would be sympathetic to this woman.

"Where are you going?" she asked.

"Home. Manchester." The woman's eyes fell. Jennifer looked again at the children, not envying their mother the ordeal of getting all the way to Manchester.

"I'll get you a porter," she said. "You need help."

The woman looked up. "No. I'm fine. Please."

"OK. If there's—"

She was interrupted by the air behind her stirring and a sharp, guttural sound. The woman threw her hand up to her face. A glob of spit had landed on her cheek and was running down towards her chin.

Jennifer span round, hot with anger.

"Who are you?" she shouted. "Leave this woman a—"

"Bloody terrorist. Go home, bitch!"

A man stood a few feet from then, glaring at the woman. Jennifer was expecting a stereotypical thug; young, rough round the edges. But this man looked like anyone you'd sit next to on a train journey home. He wore a faded black suit and a red and white tie over a pale blue shirt. He was her age maybe, with grey wisps around his ears. Jennifer stared at him, lost for words.

The crowd behind him was starting to break up. A few people drew forwards, whether to offer support or consider attack she couldn't tell. But most were moving away; checking watches, glancing at the screens. Hurrying home.

She spotted a policeman, possibly the reason the crowd had broken up. She felt her chest lift.

"Excuse me," she said. "This woman needs your help."

The policeman looked her up and down. She'd had her own clothes returned to her, the ones she'd been wearing when she'd arrived at Bronzefield Prison, but they hung loosely. She wore no make-up and her hair was a mess of tangles and sharp grey roots. He'd never guess she'd been a local MP until just four months ago.

He bent his head to his shoulder and muttered something into a communications device. Then he raised an eyebrow.

"How can I help you, madam?"

She pointed back at the woman. She had her arms around the middle child now, a boy aged about five. He was wailing. His big brother stared at him with a look of resignation.

Beyond her, the man in the suit was retreating; he'd be gone soon.

"That man over there," she said. "In the black suit and the red tie. He spat on that woman. Called her a terrorist."

"And?"

She turned back to him. "What do you mean, *and*?"

"If the police got involved every time people called each other names, we'd be overrun."

"He spat at her. That's assault."

The policeman shook his head. Jennifer looked back to see the man disappear onto an escalator.

"Please," she said, resisting an urge to pull at his arm. "He'll get away."

"And what do you expect me to do?"

She frowned.

"It's a hate crime," she said, remembering all the debates

in Parliament. Back when she'd been a government minister. Before she'd brought down her own government. "He needs to be arrested."

The policeman gave a heavy sigh. "Alright, then."

"Good."

"I'll talk to the woman. I'm not going after the man."

He approached the woman, who was still holding her son. The older boy had his hand in hers now and was watching the people passing. He looked scared.

The woman looked up from her children. Her eyes widened. The older boy drew back behind his mother.

"Now," said the policeman. "You need to get out of here. Leave the station, please." The woman nodded. She picked up the larger of her two bags, which was leaning against her leg. She muttered to her children.

"Hang on a minute," Jennifer said to the policeman. "She's done nothing wrong." She looked after the man who had spat; he was long gone. "There was a man. He spat at her. It's him you should be telling to get out of here, not her."

"It's alright," said the woman. "I don't want any trouble."

Jennifer put a hand on the woman's arm; she flinched and Jennifer pulled back. She thought of Maryam, the way she would twist her hair around her neck for want of a headscarf. Bel, and the way she would moan and mutter her way through group sessions.

But this wasn't the British Values Centre. This was New Street Station, not much more than a mile from the borders of her old constituency.

This was wrong.

"Has she broken the law?" she asked.

The policeman sighed. "No, but—"

"But nothing." She hesitated. "You can't force this woman to leave the station if she's done nothing wrong."

"It's alright, honestly it is," said the woman.

"But you have to get to Manchester. How are you going to do that if he makes you leave the station?" She looked up at the Departures screen; had she made the woman miss her train?

The woman shrugged and hurried away. As she moved towards the exit, people stared at her, not hiding the hostility in their eyes.

When Jennifer had been sent to prison, there had been hostility towards Muslims. But nothing like this.

She turned to the policeman. He was moving away from her, ignoring the woman and the people who glared at her.

"Why did you do that?"

"Madam, I really don't think—"

"Don't madam me, please. I don't understand why you told her to leave, and didn't go after the man who assaulted her."

"Assault is a bit of a stro—"

"He insulted her, he used racist language, and he spat at her. Isn't that a crime anymore?"

The policeman scratched his head. He looked towards the boards that separated them from Jennifer's usual platform.

"You're not from around here, I assume," he said.

"I am. I live near Spaghetti Junction. I used to be..." She stopped, not wanting to tell him who she'd been.

"Then you'll know about the bomb."

"The bomb?"

"Right here. New Street Station. Three months ago. Hallowe'en."

She felt herself deflate. "The bomb."

"Sixteen dead, over two hundred injured. Including kids. And two of my colleagues. Surely you know about it."

She nodded.

"Well, you should know that it's safest for people like your friend there to stay away."

"But that's ridiculous. It wasn't her who planted the bomb."

He narrowed his eyes. "No one planted anything. Suicide bomber. Muslim woman, pretending to be pregnant. The bump was a parcel of plastic explosive. Surely you know this?"

"Of course I do. I still think—"

"Either way, it's safest for us all if Muslims stay away from here, for now. For their own safety, as much as anything. Now if you don't mind, I've got things to do."

Jennifer thought of Yusuf. Was he affected by this? Had he become a pariah in his own city? And what about Hassan?

She had to get home.

"Thank—" she began. But the policeman was gone, dealing with a group of young women who looked like they'd had too much to drink. She frowned at his back and looked towards the exit. The woman and her children had disappeared.

She shivered. The easy familiarity of arriving back in the city had left her and she felt only dread. She hurried towards her platform, eager to be home.

CHAPTER TWO

JENNIFER TRIED NOT TO LOOK INTO THE NEIGHBOURS' windows as she approached her house. They would all know where she had been. They would be surprised to see her. She wasn't in the mood to talk.

She kept her head down, hoping that her longer, undyed hair would be enough disguise. She rummaged in her bag. It didn't contain much: the keys to the house and her old London flat, her wallet, her phone – dead, as she'd discovered when trying to call Yusuf from the train – and a pack of tissues. Her parliamentary pass had been confiscated on arrest. She wondered if she'd be allowed back in there. If she'd be able to see her old boss John Hunter, Leader of the Opposition. Would he be the first to visit her, or would he stay away?

Or would it be the Home Secretary Catherine Moore who got in touch first? She ran over their meeting at the British Values Centre; Catherine's cool professionalism, her reluctance to help. But then Jennifer had been put forward for Celebration, and released. Catherine's doing, surely?

The house was only six doors along. She stood on the

pavement, staring at it. Remembering the last time she'd been here, not long after Samir had disappeared. Before she'd discovered him hiding in her London flat.

She took a deep breath and clenched her fists. Mark – Dr Clarke – had said that Hassan was with her mum, but then she couldn't believe anything Mark said. He might be in there, in the house. Would he welcome her back, or would he be wary of her? Four months is a long time, when you're twelve.

She looked at her watch; 6.30pm. She imagined them all inside. Hassan in his room, doing homework after half an hour of arguing with his dad about it. Yusuf downstairs – doing what? What shape had his life taken in her absence?

She looked at Samir's window, at the front of the house, and felt something claw at her stomach. His room would be quiet and dark. The same posters on the wall as when he had run away in September. The same piles of school books mixed with political tracts. No laptop; that would have been taken away by the police.

She closed her eyes, pulling on a smile, and stepped onto the driveway. Her car stood where it always had during the week, waiting for her to come home and use it. She wondered if it had moved in the last four months, and if it would start. An unfamiliar car stood in front of their house, on the street. Yusuf's normal place, but it wasn't unusual for it to be taken by someone using the nearby station. His could be anywhere; their road was a popular parking spot.

She was at the front door now. She raised her hand to knock, then reconsidered. She opened her bag to pull out her keys.

She found the right key and glanced round, worried the neighbours might be watching. A curtain moved in the house opposite. The Danburys. Someone was watching her from an upstairs window. Mrs Danbury – Susan – was friendly, but they had never been close. She lived with her adult son. Was it him, behind that curtain, or his mum?

She shook her head and willed herself to stop being paranoid. All those cameras in the centre had got to her.

She put her key in the lock then thought again and knocked on the door just before turning it. She waited for the rumble of feet pounding down the stairs or the sound of Yusuf shouting for one of the boys – just Hassan, now – to get it. Or maybe with Hassan busy with school work, Yusuf would answer it himself.

She hoped so.

She waited for the door to open. Her key was still in the lock; she let go of it and left it hanging.

There was no sound. After thirty, forty seconds, her keys had stopped moving and there was silence.

She licked her lips. Maybe they hadn't heard her. She knocked again, louder this time.

She put her hand to the key and counted to ten. When the door still hadn't opened, she turned it, feeling her skin grow cold.

She eased the door open.

"Hello?"

Nothing. She opened it further, taking in the familiar scent of home. It made her want to laugh and cry at the same time.

"Hello?" The door was fully open now, but there was no sound from inside.

She turned to see the curtain in the window opposite move again. She frowned at it, then berated herself. She stepped into her house and closed the door.

She padded into the kitchen and put her bag on the

table, the familiarity of the action feeling odd. There was no sign of cooking on the hob, no smell coming from the oven. No dirty dishes waiting to go in the dishwasher.

She sniffed the air. She stood still and listened. Nothing.

"Hello? Its me, Mum. Jennifer. I'm back."

She waited for someone to come down the stairs or emerge from another room. She remembered all the times Samir had stormed up those stairs, the times he had shouted at her for not understanding what he was going through, for being too sympathetic to the powers that be. For being naive. Why hadn't she worked out what he was doing? The truancy should have been a red flag, but they'd been so caught up in everything that was going on in the family; between her and Yusuf, and at Westminster. It wasn't until Catherine had warned her that she'd even considered the possibility of her son being in trouble.

She picked her bag up and dropped it again on the table, then clattered around the kitchen opening doors, slamming a mug onto the counter. This was useless.

She headed for the stairs, pushing the living room door open and checking inside on the way. It was empty, with all the toys piled neatly in the baskets either side of the fireplace.

She stomped upstairs, calling all the way. There was a chance they hadn't heard her. Maybe Hassan had taken to wearing headphones while he worked.

She caught movement out of the corner of her eye and turned to see Hassan's door open. She put a hand to her chest, relieved. A cat shot out and darted between her legs, running down the stairs. It was small and ginger. Unfamiliar.

She smiled and pushed the door further open.

"Hi love. I'm ho—"

But the room was empty. The desk had magazines and school books piled on it as haphazardly as ever, and there was a half-drunk glass of orange juice sitting on the bedside table. The duvet was crumpled into a heap.

She picked up the glass and sniffed it, then recoiled. Hassan was a messy boy, his room always littered with books, toys and stale food. Going in there was like a trip to IKEA; you always came out laden with glasses and crockery. But this glass had been there at least three days. Yusuf would have taken it to the dishwasher by now, if he hadn't managed to browbeat Hassan into doing it.

She resisted the urge to slump onto the bed, and made for her own room. When she opened the door, it was dark; no sign of Yusuf.

They weren't here.

She leaned against the doorframe. She realised she was shaking.

Stop, she told herself. *Calm down.* This might not mean anything.

She dragged herself back downstairs. Yusuf had a small desk in a corner of the kitchen, normally piled with paperwork and reminders to call constituents. It looked much as it ever did, if a little tidier.

She sat at the kitchen table, leaning her head on her arms. She'd spent the entire journey from Oxfordshire to New Street imagining their surprise at seeing her, and playing over what she would tell them. Especially Hassan. They'd lied to him about Samir's disappearance, something she would always regret. What would Yusuf have told him after she'd been arrested? What did he know about Samir, and his whereabouts? Come to think of it, what did Yusuf know?

She had to find them. Her mobile was in her bag. She knew where the charger would be.

She took the stairs two at a time and made for her bedroom. She switched on the light. The bed was made and the curtains open. On her bedside table was a book she'd been reading months ago, her reading glasses on top of it. There was an empty glass there, as if waiting for her to come home.

On Yusuf's side, there was a small pile of books and a pencil case. He liked to read council reports in bed and annotate them with pencil. But the usual pile of paperwork was missing. By this time of day, he would have emptied his work bag and placed everything he needed there, ready for bedtime. Yusuf was a creature of habit.

She told herself to stop worrying – if he was late home, he wouldn't have been able to empty his bag yet – and opened her bedside drawer. Sitting in it was her spare phone charger. The other would be in her London flat.

She stood up. What had happened to her flat? Had her office kept it going, still paid the rent? Was Penny, her old agent, even working there anymore? Maybe they'd shut it up, or transferred it to her successor. If she was going to get to John and Catherine, use their influence to get Samir back, she'd need a London base. She'd need to find a way to get into the House of Commons, now that she didn't have a pass.

That would have to wait for another day. Now she needed to track her family down, or at least the rest of them. She plugged the charger into the socket and then her phone and placed it on the table, checking to see that it was taking the charge. Then she sat down on the bed, letting her mind go blank.

CHAPTER THREE

This was nothing like the group room at Burcot Park.

It was smaller for a start, not much bigger than Rita's old attic bedroom. It had no windows and was lit by a single fluorescent tube that flickered constantly. And where there should be a door, there were bars, and a guard standing outside.

It did have one thing in common with that room: the cameras. Two of them in the corners, peering down at the inmates from above. Rita's place was diagonal to the doorway, directly facing one of the cameras. She tried not to look at it.

There were just three other women in her with her, and the counsellor. The counsellor was a slight, middle-aged woman who looked ready for retirement. Her skin was grey in the artificial light and her eyes were ringed with dark shadows. In different circumstances, Rita might have been sympathetic.

The chairs were different too. Instead of being made of orange plastic, they were metal. Rita had been told that if she didn't behave, an electric shock would run through the chair. Just a light one, designed to give her a fright. But an electric shock nonetheless.

So far, Rita had behaved herself.

This was her third session. There were no one-to-ones as far as she could tell. Instead she'd been brought here to sit with different companions each time. And have the same questions asked of her.

Each time, the whole program was required of them. All six steps. If they got that far without being reprimanded. No one she'd seen had transgressed sufficiently to get a shock, but the threat was always there. It gave the room a heaviness, like a cloak draped over them. It felt like an eternity since she'd left Burcot Park. Since she'd spotted Jennifer standing by the road, hailing a cab.

So Jennifer had got out. She'd passed her Celebration. Had she done it by the rules, or had she found a way to cheat the system, like she'd planned? Dr Clarke would help her, she'd said. Rita doubted it.

They were working round the group of four, one step at a time. In the first session Rita had tried to remember the women she'd been placed with, expecting to see them again. But the group had been different each time, so she'd given up. There was one woman in the group she'd seen before. But with so many faces swimming in front of her, and her mind foggy, she couldn't be sure.

"No," snapped the counsellor. "Try again."

The woman next to her – a tall, white, well-built woman in her early forties – sucked in a breath and tried again.

"I distributed leaflets that told lies about the government."

"And?"

"I printed them. I wrote some."

"Better. And who did you harm, via this activity?"

"The people who I gave the leaflets to."

"How?"

The woman had her eyes closed. Rita wondered about the content of those leaflets; would she ever have seen one? Ash used to bring them to the pub sometimes. Leaflets and flyers about what the government was really doing to stop terrorism. Whole families deported, including grandparents and toddlers. Sympathetic public officials being dismissed for no reason. Dawn raids that hit entire districts of Muslim homes. Some of it got into the news, but not all. And she couldn't be sure what was truth, and what propaganda. Enough to make her doubt.

The woman continued. "I told them lies. It would have changed their opinion about things."

"In what way?"

The woman looked tired. She had a bruise above her right eye and her wrists were red. Had she been beaten, too? Rita hadn't suffered at the hands of the guards here – not yet – but at Burcot Park they'd locked her in a basement bathroom and beaten her for noncompliance.

"They might have joined a group. Become terrorist sympathisers." The woman's voice was dull, as if she was reciting the words by rote.

"Interesting. So do you see how you harmed more people? Not just the people who read your leaflets?"

The woman looked up. "No."

The counsellor's look of encouragement left her face. "No?"

"No. I don't."

The woman looked wary. She pulled her handcuffed

wrists as far from the chair arms as she could, shifting in her chair.

"Don't shock me, please. I'll say what you want me to. Tell me what you need me to say."

The counsellor stood up and leaned over the woman. "That's not the point, Jenkins."

"Sorry?"

The other three inmates, Rita included, were staring at the counsellor, at the tiny, grey-haired woman intimidating the imposing woman many years her junior. They all knew they would be next.

Jenkins sniffed and lifted her hand as if to wipe her nose. Then she remembered it was attached to the chair arm.

"Please. I don't understand the question."

The counsellor shook her head, looking around the group. "This isn't good enough. You have to mean it." She thumped her chest with a clenched fist; Rita thought she might bring on a heart attack. "It has to come from the heart. From you. You've all been in low security facilities. Cushy hotels. Hedge Hill isn't like that. Learn that, if you want to pass."

Jenkins was leaning back in her chair now, beads of sweat running down her face. Rita bit her tongue, hating herself for being glad it wasn't her going through this.

A buzzer sounded, then a clicking from the doorway. The counsellor looked at her watch. There were no clocks here and Rita couldn't be sure if it was day or night. Her cell had no windows and she'd only glimpsed daylight a few times when being led along the corridors to the group room.

Did the outside world know about this place? Was it legal?

The counsellor exchanged some muttered words with

the guard outside who pulled the barred door open. Rita guessed that click had been the sound of the lock being released. So the guards didn't have control over the locks. That meant the people in charge didn't trust them. Could Rita use this to her advantage?

"Move. Back to your cells." The counsellor, who hadn't given her name as far as Rita could remember, picked up a wooden stick and prodded each of the prisoners with it, herding them out of the room. Cattle, Rita thought, thinking of the way cows were treated in her parents' childhood home of Delhi. So sacred that you weren't allowed to move them on if they took up residence in the middle of a busy road junction. It often caused gridlock. What would her parents think of her now, just one of so many hated British cattle?

CHAPTER FOUR

JENNIFER WOKE TO FIND HERSELF TWISTED ON TOP OF the bed, her phone in her hand. She shrugged her shoulders to release the tension and yawned as she checked her watch.

Nine o'clock. Two hours had passed.

She went to the doorway, listening in case they had come home while she slept. The house was still silent. There was a chance Yusuf had put the kids to bed and then crept back downstairs, oblivious to her return.

In the kitchen, her bag was still on the table. Nothing else had changed. The living room was empty. She pulled her tired limbs upstairs and pulled the charging lead out of her phone. Miraculously, it had come to life.

Who to ring? Yusuf's mobile first.

She found it in her contacts and hit dial. She put the phone to her ear.

There was silence. Not a ringtone. Her phone was dead. No signal.

She jabbed at it a few times, turned it off and on and then held it to her ear again.

Nothing.

It had been cut off. The bill was paid through her parliamentary office. Which no longer existed.

She'd wasted two hours, and made herself groggy and bad tempered in the process. She considered the landline, but they'd cancelled it only a year ago, realising that they didn't use it.

She sat back on the bed. Maybe she should just go back to sleep and wait until morning. If Yusuf was at his mum's, he would soon be back.

She let herself slump to the bed again and pulled the duvet up over her legs. Then she stood up. She wasn't in prison now; she should at least get undressed.

She took off her watch and placed it on the bedside table. She crossed to the window to close the curtains, pausing to look across the street. There was no movement opposite now; the Danburys' curtains glowed orange in the dark.

Maybe Susan would help her? If she had a landline, she might let Jennifer use it.

She grabbed her watch and slipped it onto her wrist. Susan worked at the local hospital, as an administrator. Her son – she realised she didn't know what her neighbour's son did. Or even what his name was. How bad was that?

Hopefully nine pm on a Tuesday night wouldn't be too much of an intrusion.

She slipped her shoes on, grimacing at the leather pinching her toes. She slipped downstairs and opened the front door.

Outside, the night air was bright and fresh. The Expressway hummed in the background, lights visible over the rooftops at the bottom of the street, furthest away from the main road. It was a constant presence here, and a reminder of the terrorist bomb that had devastated the city two years ago. She thought about what the policeman had told her, the bomb at New Street. She would have to investigate that once she'd fund Yusuf. People might need her help.

She hurried across the road, glancing at the lit windows of the houses on either side of her destination. Above her, there was a CCTV camera on a lamp post, currently pointing at her own house. She didn't remember it. Was the state watching her family?

The camera whirred quietly and shifted direction, peering at the house next door to hers. No wonder all those curtains were closed.

She hurried up Susan's drive, relieved to see two cars parked. She rang the bell. Would Susan be surprised to see her, or had she already been spotted?

The door opened and her neighbour smiled. She didn't look surprised.

"Jennifer. Good to have you back." There was a pause. "How are you?"

"I'm OK thanks. Considering."

She stepped from foot to foot, wondering if she was going to be asked in. After a moment she realised not.

"I know this sounds weird, but have you seen Yusuf lately?"

Susan looked past Jennifer towards her house.

"Hmm. Not since the weekend, I don't think." She turned back into her house. "Tom! Have you seen any of the Hussains lately?"

A sound came from within and Susan shrugged. She turned back to Jennifer.

"Sorry. I think I saw him on Saturday. Taking your little boy – Hassan, isn't it? Not so little now. Taking him somewhere."

Jennifer nodded. Listening to her neighbour talk about how much Hassan had grown in her absence made her feel raw.

"They didn't say where they were going?"

"Sorry. Are you back for good? I hear they've – they've elected a new MP." She blushed and looked down at her shoes. They were scuffed.

"Oh. Yes, back for good."

There was an awkward silence. Susan was a probably trying to think of the words to get rid of Jennifer.

"Can I ask you a favour?"

Susan frowned. "Go on."

"I need to use a phone. To speak to Yusuf. Let him know I'm home."

"Oh."

"And mine isn't working."

"Oh."

"Er, could I possibly use yours?"

"Oh. Oh, I see." She looked into the house, then back at Jennifer. She still didn't invite her in. Then she glanced up at the camera. It was facing away from them now, towards the top of the street and the bus stop.

Susan lowered her voice. "Come in." She grabbed Jennifer's arm and pulled her inside, slamming the door shut. Her eyes were on the camera the whole time.

Jennifer watched her, seeing the tension leave her face as the door closed. Did she have something to hide? Or was it Jennifer? Was she the thing that needed to be hidden?

Susan sighed. "Sorry. I didn't mean to be rude. But it's just that things are – well, you'll find out. Come inside. Sit down."

Jennifer followed her into a brightly lit living room furnished with a large blue sofa and a battered grey armchair. A young man – Tom, presumably – sprawled across the armchair. He wore jersey shorts and his blotchy, pale pink legs dangled over the arm. It made her think of Samir, the way he had thrown his gangly body over the furniture at home. The way he would again.

"Sit up," his mum told him. He looked up at Jennifer and heaved himself into an upright position. Jennifer wondered if it was he who'd been watching earlier.

"We haven't got a landline anymore," Susan said. "No point. But you can use my mobile. I never use my minutes anyway."

She pulled a phone out of the pocket of her trousers. "Do you know the number?"

Damn. Jennifer had programmed Yusuf's mobile into her phone years ago, and had no idea what it was.

"No."

Could she remember his parents' number? That was in her phone too. She'd left it back at the house. She didn't want to go back, not with the way Susan had looked at that camera. She couldn't be sure she'd let her back in.

What numbers did she know, that she could call? Who might help her, other than Yusuf?

The only person she could think of was Catherine. She could get her via the House of Commons switchboard.

But she didn't need to speak to Catherine. Maybe in a few days, when she'd considered her plan of action, yes. But not tonight. Not without knowing where her family were first. And not until she'd discussed Catherine's visit with Yusuf, worked out what it meant.

"I'm so sorry, Susan. Do you mind if I go home and get my mobile? It's not making calls but the numbers are still stored in it."

"It's not making calls? That's not good."

She blushed. "No." She wasn't about to tell her neighbour why.

She stood and smoothed down her trousers, realising that they were creased and sweaty. She nodded her thanks at Susan and headed for the front door.

It had grown darker since she'd come inside and she could make out the little red light that showed the camera above was operational. Was this something that had been put here because of her or did all suburban streets have them now? In just four months?

She darted home, ran into the kitchen and picked up her bag. Then she remembered her phone was upstairs, on the bed. She dropped the bag, listening briefly just in case, then thundered upstairs. Her next-door neighbours had a staircase on the other side of the party wall. She wondered if they were listening.

Her phone was on the bed. She grabbed it and hurried back to Susan's. She kept her head bent as she crossed the street.

Susan opened the door just enough for Jennifer to get in.

"Thanks." Jennifer gestured towards the living room. Susan nodded.

Tom had disappeared and the TV was blank. Susan took his place in the armchair and Jennifer perched on the sofa. Susan's mobile phone was on the coffee table in front of her.

"Alright if I—?" she asked.

"Go ahead."

Jennifer picked up the two phones and copied Yusuf's number into Susan's. It shouldn't matter that this would leave a record of Yusuf's mobile number in her neighbour's phone. But there was something unnerving about the way

Susan hovered next to her, watching in silence. Jennifer twisted to face away from her neighbour then shifted back, feeling ungrateful. She would only be making sure she didn't use up all her call allowance.

To her relief, the dial tone was instant. It rang out twice and then the voicemail cut in.

"Hello, this is Yusuf Hussain. I can't take your call right now, so leave a message and I'll call you back when I can."

She smiled. It felt good to hear his voice.

"It's me. Jennifer. I'm back home. Just wondering where you are. Give me a—. No, don't. My phone's not working. Just come home, please."

She heard movement next to her; Susan shifting in her seat.

"Can I try another number please? Just the one."

Susan sniffed and looked at the door. Then she nodded. "Of course."

Jennifer considered. Should she call Yusuf's parents? He was probably with them, but then he might not be. If she called them and he wasn't there, they might panic. She'd put them through enough already.

There was only one other person she could think of. She pulled the number up on her own phone. She took a deep breath and dialled.

CHAPTER FIVE

The phone rang out. Jennifer looked at Susan and gave her a wary smile. It came back even more uncertain.

At last there was a click as it was answered. She held her breath, hoping it wouldn't go to voicemail.

"John Hunter speaking." He would be wondering why an unidentified mobile was calling his private number.

"John, it's Jennifer. I'm calling from my neighbour's phone."

She looked up at Susan, whose eyebrows were raised.

"Jennifer?"

"Yes. I got out. Long story. But listen, I'm looking for Yusuf. I don't suppose you've been in touch with him?"

"Sorry, no. Which number are you calling from again?"

"Don't worry. I'll remove this from the memory afterwards."

"Don't be silly, that's not the problem. Where are you?"

"I'm at home. Well, I'm over the road. They let me out. That's all you need to know."

"How? How did you convince them?"

So he knew about the centre. About the Celebration ceremony, and how she'd had to pass it to win her release. Was that because he was Leader of the Opposition, or was it common knowledge?

"Long story. I'll tell you in person sometime."

The living room door opened and Susan's son reappeared. He groaned when he saw Jennifer in his spot. Jennifer moved to the other end of the sofa, her phone still at her ear.

"If you haven't seen him, can you tell me if anything's happened to him? He wasn't— he wasn't arrested, or anything?"

"No. Well yes, very briefly. But then he was released. It was your flat that Samir hid in. The DPP couldn't make a case that he'd been in on it too."

She took a deep breath. "And what about Samir?"

"He was arrested at the same time as you. You know that."

"No. I mean do you know where he is? Have you been told anything?"

"I'm not Home Secretary anymore. I don't know anything about individual cases. You know that."

She thought of Catherine, sitting in Yonda Hughes's office, so calm despite Jennifer's predicament. She *was* Home Secretary. Surely if anyone could help Jennifer, it would be her?

Or maybe not. *You can't leave*, she'd said. *You have to stay here*. But then Jennifer had been fast-tracked, given a chance at Celebration. Twice. Had Catherine had anything to do with that?

She had to get what she could from John, first.

"Can you find out anything about Samir? Surely you—"

"It's not as simple as that."

"Why not? I know you can't officially, but we know—"

"Who are you with, right now?"

Jennifer put her hand to the phone and looked up. Susan had sat along from her on the sofa and was trying to hide the fact that she was listening. Her son had taken the armchair, but he hadn't turned the TV back on.

"You're right. Sorry. I'll call you another time."

"That's not what I mean. Even if you call me on the most secure line in the country, I can't help."

"Come on. This is Yusuf's son we're talking about. Not just mine."

"Things have changed. Since you were sent down. Surely you've heard?"

Tom had stood up. He looked impatient. Susan was shrinking away from him. He might be stringy, but he was almost a foot taller than her. Was she scared of him?

"Please," Susan whispered. "I need my phone back."

Jennifer bit her lip. She would have to find another phone. She'd get a card, pay as you go. Tomorrow. Then she'd start again. It would be fine.

"Sorry," she whispered, her hand on the phone's microphone.

She removed it. "I have to go, John. My neighbour needs her phone back. I'll get my own phone sorted tomorrow. I'll call you then."

"I really can't help you."

She ground her teeth. John was saying this for fear of being overheard, surely. He wouldn't let her down.

"Alright," she said. "If you can't help me, I'll call Catherine."

"Catherine Moore?"

"Yes. I don't know any other Catherines."

"I don't think you'll be able to do that."

"Why not?"

Did he know about Catherine's visit? Had she said something in Parliament maybe, denounced her?

"Why not?" she repeated.

"Haven't you heard?"

"Heard what?"

"Because she's the bloody Prime Minister."

CHAPTER SIX

Jennifer glanced at Susan. She could probably hear everything John was saying.

"She's the *what*?"

"You heard," he replied. "Catherine Moore is the PM now."

"How did that happen?"

She thought over her meeting with Catherine. Time seemed to flow more slowly in the British Values Centre but she was sure it was only a few weeks ago.

"Trask had a heart attack."

"Sheesh. Is he dead?"

A pause. "No. Ill. Retired."

"Yes, but— Catherine?"

"Surprised me too. Fresh blood, I guess. I'm not so sure."

"Hmm."

She glanced at Susan again. Her son Tom was standing next to her, his arm stretched towards Jennifer. He beckoned.

"They need the phone back. I'll have to call you again."

"They? I thought you were with your neighbour?"

"And her son. I'll get my phone sorted tomorrow, John. I'll call you back."

"Right. Good to hear from you."

"Thanks."

"Was it awful?"

She dragged a hand through her hair.

"Not great. Look, I'm going to call Catherine too. There's even more reason to get her involved now."

A snort. "Good luck with that."

"I know you don't like her, but—"

"It's not that. She's worse. Than Trask."

"I don't believe you."

"See for yourself. Read the news. You were wrong about her, Jennifer. You should have taken me up on my request to spy on her back when she was a backbencher."

"We'll see." Jennifer couldn't quite believe that Catherine was as hard-line as her predecessor, the man who had thrust his face into Jennifer's and gloated when her conscience had brought her own government down. Catherine had been her friend for years now. She knew her better than John did.

Tom was next to her, his hand on the phone.

"Give it back, please."

At home, she leant against the party wall. She knew that Samir had piggybacked on her next door neighbour's wifi in the past, dissatisfied with the speed of theirs. They both had BT accounts, and if she could remember her password she would be able to use a slice of their data that was available for sharing with other customers. If that system still existed.

After two attempts she got in, punching the air when the wifi symbol on her phone sprang to life. She went straight to the BBC website.

The headline was about a foiled attack in Glasgow. Six men had been arrested and one shot by police. The police involved were commended for their bravery, as well as a member of the public who'd raised the alarm. No mention of the family of the man killed. They were probably on their way to an airport already, one way or the other.

She resisted the urge to search for her own name and instead typed in Catherine's. One hundred and twenty-three results in the last day alone.

This was going to take a while. She put her phone on the kitchen table, checking it had enough power, then boiled the kettle. There was coffee in the tin and fresh milk in the fridge. So Yusuf hadn't gone for long.

She picked up her phone and mug and took them into the living room, slumping into a chair. It was gone ten o'clock and she was tired. What time had she been woken by the orderlies this morning? It felt surreal to be sitting here in her favourite chair sipping good coffee when so recently she'd been sitting in one of those awful low chairs in Yonda Hughes's office.

Her inbox was full, although the frequency of emails had dwindled over time. There were hundreds from September, when she'd been arrested; hundreds per day, in fact. And then just three today. One was from Yusuf. She scrolled down and realised that there he'd sent her an email every day since she'd been arrested. The thought of him taking the time to do this with everything else he had to deal with made her heart warm.

She opened the most recent one, wondering where he'd been when he sent it.

Hey Jen,

It's a dull, cloudy day today which makes Hassan restless. Yesterday it was sunny so I took him to the botanical gardens to see the mynah bird. He still loves it.

She wiped her eyes and lifted the phone.

Today I'm going to take him to the cinema. Good for rainy days. Then something to eat. Boring, I know.

Hope you're doing ok. Kisses from both of us.

Yusuf x

That was it. No mention of Samir, or of her arrest and imprisonment. She wondered how long he'd tried to get permission to visit her until he'd given up. If he'd been able to visit Samir.

She looked up at the clock. Almost eleven. Tomorrow was a school day, and Hassan needed to be in bed.

She pulled up the calendar on her phone, then realised it was the half term holiday. That was why Yusuf had been taking him out, keeping busy. Distracting himself from the emptiness of a house missing two of its occupants, even if those were the two with the lightest footstep. Samir had spent most of his days alone in his room, while she'd been out from Monday to Thursday, down in Westminster. Not at half term, though. Half term had been special.

But if they'd gone out for the day, where were they now?

MARCH 2022

RITA'S CELL REMINDED HER OF THOSE DOCUMENTARIES she'd seen on TV, travellers going to Tokyo and staying the night in hotel rooms that were nothing more than a sleeping pod. The thought had filled her with dread; it would be like sleeping in a high-tech coffin.

The light had just come back on for the second time. It seemed to have no relation to the time of day.

The hatch opened and a tray was pushed through. There was a thin stew of potatoes and carrots, mixed with a few peas and a pulse of some kind. Cheap food that would keep her alive but wouldn't build up her strength. She didn't care; it was food.

After the empty tray was taken away, Rita lay down and stared at the low ceiling. In the corner, a spider bounced between the walls, slowly weaving its home for the next few days. Company, she thought.

A buzzing sound came from outside and she sat up. A guard peered through the hatch then slammed it shut and opened the door. She waited for Rita without saying anything.

Rita slipped on her thin shoes and shrugged her shoulders to rid them of the ache that had been troubling her. The bruises on her back from the beatings she'd received at Burcot Park would be fading now, turning yellow. Her wrists were red though, from being slapped right here, in the second group session. She'd failed to co-operate and the counsellor had brought that stick out. It was heavier than it looked.

She left her cell, expecting to see other women in the corridor, being herded to their own group sessions. The cells were on the outer edge of the building, in a large wing that smelled of disinfectant and metal. The group rooms were at the other end, in a wing of their own. The cells had windows boarded up on the outside, while the group session rooms were lined with breeze blocks painted in a dirty cream. No windows. She wondered what they'd been used for in the past; solitary confinement?

The corridor was quiet. Only one or two women were out here. In one of the occupied cells, a woman was shrieking the words to the National Anthem. She reached the beginning of the second verse and then fell silent.

Rita fixed her gaze on a woman a hundred feet ahead of her, also heading for the stairs leading down to the other wing. The corridor that linked the wings was the only section of the prison with windows, and she savoured the chance to walk beneath their glare. They may be high in the wall but any glimpse of the sky gave her a welcome grip on reality.

They reached the top of the stairs. The woman ahead had paused for a guard to open a set of doors. Rita felt a finger in her back.

"This way."

She turned to look at the guard behind her. A small

door was open in the wall next to them, one that Rita hadn't noticed before. It was painted cream, the same as the walls, and led to another narrower corridor.

Rita looked at the guard, whose eyes were raised to the wall past Rita's head. She was tall and willowy, with rosy cheeks. She could only be twenty-five years old, at most. What was a pretty young thing like that doing here?

Rita stepped through. She and the guard waited while the door locked behind them. There was a camera above it; someone was watching them, letting them pass. The guard gave her a smile.

"Come with me."

Rita smiled back at her, surprised by this sign of humanity. No one had smiled at her since she'd been dragged away from her group at Burcot Park. How long ago was that: a week, ten days? Two weeks?

She followed the guard through two more doors. Each time, the guard would give her a sidelong glance then look up at the camera and pull her face into an expressionless position.

They reached a door set into the wall on their right and the guard pressed an intercom button. The door opened before she had the chance to speak into the intercom. She shrugged and guided Rita through.

The room was the largest Rita had seen since arriving here, with space for two desks and a bank of cabinets on the back wall. Sun slanted through the window to one side.

A guard sat at one of the desks.

"Hello, Rita." She sounded more like a dentist's receptionist than a prison guard.

"Where am I?"

The guard who had brought her here was staring ahead, avoiding eye contact. Rita had a sudden realisation.

"Is this Celebration? Am I being fast-tracked again?"

The guard at the desk shook her head and opened a large brown envelope, letting its contents spill onto the desk. Rita's eyes widened. Her belongings were there: the outfit she had been wearing when she was arrested in her classroom, her watch. Her purse.

"No, Rita. You're being transferred."

CHAPTER EIGHT

THIS CENTRE WAS QUITE DIFFERENT FROM BURCOT Park.

Sure, this place allowed its inmates a similar degree of freedom. It put them through one-to-one meetings with counsellors. And it had group sessions too, although Mark's first had been quite different from any he'd presided over at Burcot Park.

But where at Burcot Park there had been an initial wariness between the inmates – patients – which tended to work its way up to trust and even friendship, here he'd seen it simmer over into low level violence. On Mark's first night there'd been a fight in the canteen followed by a lockdown, all the men confined to their rooms. Locked in; something he hadn't seen at Burcot Park.

Mark couldn't be sure if this was because it was a men's centre, or whether it came from the top.

Because the governor here was nothing like Yonda Hughes. Mark had dismissed his boss as managerial, believing his clinical background to be better than her bureaucratic one because it was Health Service, not Home

Office. He'd been wary of her, knowing her to be a bully who mistakenly believed she had a heart of gold.

But compared to the governor here, a man called Steve Adams who wore tailored grey suits with subtly contrasting ties and gleaming black winkle pickers, Yonda was a free spirit. A child of peace and love. And not just because of her rainbow of outfits.

This guy hadn't got here via a Home Office career; he was private sector, and he wanted everyone to know it.

On Mark's second day he'd been brought into the governor's office, ushered in wearing his regulation blue jeans and grey hoody, unsure what to expect.

By the time he left, he was equally unsure of what had happened, and what it meant.

Steve had sat back in his cream leather chair, his hands steepled in front of him, and given Mark a look that was part intrigue, part condescension.

He'd welcomed him to the centre, told him to behave himself and work on the program, said *call me Steve* and dismissed him. An orderly called Blue had taken him away, the tattoos that covered his arms matching his name.

Now he'd been here three days, had a one-to-one with his counsellor, and attended one silent group session in which no one had made the remotest bit of progress on the program. And here he was again, in the governor's office.

Did anyone else get asked in here all the time?

The office was empty when he entered. A bleak, featureless space with a bland veneer desk in the centre and a cream fake leather chair behind it. He sat on a low sofa, designed to look smart but actually making his legs itch.

A young woman came in behind him. She gave him a tight smile and sat down on the chair next to him. She was petite, dressed in a cheap red skirt suit and with her face lightly made up. She smelled of lily of the valley. She didn't fit any model he had in his head for a counsellor.

He smiled at her and she nodded back. She looked nervous.

Steve wafted in, waving them to sit. The woman lowered herself to the sofa next to Mark.

"I see you've met Joy," Steve said. He flashed her a grin.

"Not really, no," said Mark. "Hello, Joy."

"Hello," she replied, her voice low.

"Is Joy going to be my counsellor?" he asked.

Steve was going through a briefcase that he'd placed on the desk. He looked up.

"What? Oh no, no. Joy's my assistant. Get us a coffee will you, Joy?"

Joy headed out. She returned with a single mug of coffee for Steve; the *us* was figurative, then.

"Why am I here?" asked Mark.

Steve closed his briefcase. "Thanks, Joy. Great coffee, as ever."

She twisted her lips into a kind of frown. Mark imagined being her and wondered what Meena, his fellow – junior – counsellor, was doing.

Joy took her place again and placed a pad on her lap. Mark looked round the room; sure enough, there was a camera over the door. Why she needed to take notes was beyond him.

"Where were we?" asked Steve. He slurped his coffee and rocked in his chair.

"I asked why I'm here."

"Hmm? What d'you mean?"

"Why am I here?"

"No. Sorry, mate. D'you mean why are you at the centre or why are you in my office? Because if it's the first, then..."

"I know why I'm at the centre. I'm puzzled about being brought to meet the governor twice in three days."

Steve would know about Mark's past. His clinical experience; his transgression not long after Burcot Park opened. Yonda would have told him. Or she might not; she'd covered it up, after all. Turned him into her poodle.

Or maybe Mark was just another inmate to him, another subversive to be processed and spat out via the Celebration ceremony. He tried but failed to imagine the inmates here stamping their feet and cheering at Celebration.

Steve stood and rounded the desk. Mark expected him to perch on it, like Yonda had done in her huge office. But instead, Steve lowered himself to the floor until he was sitting next to Mark.

Mark glanced at Joy; she didn't look surprised. Next thing, they'd be bringing out a beanbag, he thought. Maybe a hot-desking area.

"Why do *you* think you're here?" Steve asked. "That's what I'd like to know."

Mark sighed. "No idea. That's why I asked you."

"Like that, is it? Alright then. I'll start and you chip in when you've got the gist of it."

He paused. Mark focused on hiding his irritation. He sensed Joy doing much the same thing.

"OK. Well, I know you came from Burcot Park. You're clinical, not like most of the counsellors."

Mark nodded.

"Nice place. Countryside, yes?"

"Yes."

"Soft on the prisoners, yes?"

Mark thought of Rita. He'd locked her in that basement cell, desperate to protect himself, to keep Yonda happy. Tim and Roy had beaten her in there, and he'd done nothing about it.

He deserved to be here, but not for the reasons Steve thought.

"I wouldn't say that," he replied.

"Hmm. Not what I've heard." Steve gave him a nudge. "I heard you'd been allowed to get quite close to some of them."

Mark stared ahead, refusing to make eye contact.

"We were encouraged to bond with the patients, yes. To help them with the program."

"Patients. So Yonda's still calling them that."

"I'm a clinical psychologist. I was employed to cure the women. They're my patients."

"Are they, indeed."

Mark said nothing.

Steve stood up. Joy shifted in her chair, tucking her skirt beneath her knees. Her pad was full of scrawled text; Mark hadn't noticed her writing.

"It's a bit different here, you'll find."

"I've noticed."

"Ah. That obvious, eh? Well, I run a tight ship here. Management have got nothing to worry about with me in charge."

Mark shrugged, ignoring the veiled insult to his old centre. He felt an unfamiliar pang of loyalty to Yonda.

"So," said Steve.

"So."

"The reason you're here."

"Yes."

"I want you to do me a favour. Seeing as you're one of us – well, kind of one of us."

"What kind of favour?"

Mark had been in this situation before, in Yonda's office. That time, it had been about saving his job. What would he be saving now? Did he even want to help this man out?

"I want you to keep an eye on some of the prisoners for me. Report back."

"Haven't you already got them doing that in their one-to-ones? In group sessions?"

"Ah, Mark. And there was me thinking you were the perceptive sort."

Another silence. Joy turned the page of her notebook.

"No? Don't know what I'm on about? Maybe I misjudged you."

Still Mark said nothing. Inmate or no, he wasn't responding to insults.

"Shit, mate. Can't take a joke?" Steve shook his head and gave Joy a conspiratorial look that wasn't returned. "Right. Anyway, if you do this, I can help you out."

"Help me out how?"

"It'll be worth your while. Trust me."

"Why do you need me to inform on the other inmates when you've got cameras everywhere?"

"That's not such a bad question. Did you ever look at the footage the cameras caught at your old place?"

Mark frowned. "No."

Steve approached and lowered himself again. This time, he squatted on his heels, bringing his face level with Mark's. He looked into Mark's eyes. His expression had switched from one of a man constantly bullshitting everyone to a man who was worried.

Mark drew back but not too far. He was intrigued.

"Did your boss ever show you any of it?"

"No. Why should she?"

Steve glanced up at the camera then back at Mark. He

threw a tense smile at Joy, who stared back at him, as if willing herself not to look round at the camera.

"Ever see her watching it herself?"

Mark shook his head. "Once." He remembered the time Yonda had appeared in Rita's one-to-one session, after he'd released her from her basement cell. He'd assumed she'd been watching them.

Steve raised an eyebrow. "Really? You saw her watching it?"

"Well, no. I assumed..."

Steve winked. "I'm going to let you in on a little secret."

Mark grimaced. The bullshit was back. "Yes?"

Steve leaned in. "The cameras aren't for the governors. They're for management."

"You're management."

"Not me. Further up the food chain. Bosses at Forval, our illustrious employer. Home Secretary, even."

Mark doubted that the Home Secretary would waste time watching what the inmates of the British Values Centres got up to. But then he remembered Catherine Moore's visit. She'd known more than he expected about his one-to-ones with Jennifer.

Had she been watching him?

Steve was back behind his desk now. He was smiling, an insincere smile that reminded Mark of double glazing salesmen.

"Going to help me then?"

"You still haven't said what's in it for me."

"Jeez. You're not an easy one, are you? Look, come back here tomorrow. I want something from you, mind. Information. Gossip. Anything. Then I'll tell you what I can do for you."

"Why should I help you? I need to know what you're offering."

Steve sniffed. He bent to open a desk drawer and raised his hand to wave Mark away.

"See you tomorrow."

CHAPTER NINE

JENNIFER WAS WOKEN BY VOICES OUTSIDE THE WINDOW. She rubbed her eyes and looked at the clock: 9.30am. How long had she slept?

She shuffled to the window, hoping it wouldn't be Susan or Tom. They'd listened to her conversation with John. Too intently.

She pulled the curtains back. The sun was in her eyes. There was a car parked across their drive. A car she knew.

She thundered down the stairs, not caring that her face was creased with sleep and she was wearing just a battered T-shirt and pair of shorts.

She threw the door open and ran out, ignoring the rough tarmac under her soles.

Yusuf was pulling a rucksack out of the boot: red, with a Pokémon logo. Hassan's. He looked up and gasped.

"Jen!"

She grinned. "Hi."

"You're home!"

He looked round at the neighbours' houses then lowered his voice. "How? How did you get out?"

She shook her head, advancing. "Long story. Tell you later."

He pulled her into a hug, lifting her off the ground. She'd lost weight, she knew. Did it make her look attractive, or just half-starved?

They kissed. His lips were salty and cool. Jennifer felt herself hollow out a little at their touch.

She pulled back, still smiling. "Where were you? Where's Hassan?'

She was answered by one of the car's rear doors opening and Hassan getting out. He looked taller, leaner.

He stopped moving and stared at her. She smiled and approached him.

"How are you, my gorgeous boy? What've you been doing?"

He pulled back and looked from her to Yusuf. His forehead was creased.

"Hey, Hass. It's only me. I'm back."

"No."

He ran past her and into the house, grabbing his rucksack from Yusuf on the way.

Jennifer turned to Yusuf. "What was that about?"

"I'm sorry, love. He's a bit confused. Give him time."

"What does he know? What did you tell him?"

He frowned at her. "Let's go inside, eh?"

She followed him in and closed the door, checking the street as she did so. The TV had been turned on and Hassan sat on the floor in front of it, staring ahead as if his life depended on it.

"I got home yesterday," Jennifer said. "Sorry I missed you."

Hassan said nothing. She turned to Yusuf.

"I tried to call you."

"Sorry. The car broke down. We had to stay in a youth hostel while we waited for it to be repaired."

She turned to Hassan, who'd shifted closer to the TV.

"I bet that was an adventure."

He shrugged. "It was cold. The bed was lumpy." He looked at Yusuf. "You didn't tell me she was coming back."

"Who's she?" asked Jennifer. "I'm right here, you know."

Hassan shook his head and stood up. He gave her a look then moved towards Yusuf. Yusuf reached out and pulled their son towards him. They hugged.

"Sorry, mate," said Yusuf. "I didn't know either."

Hassan looked at Jennifer again, his eyes hard. "I've got homework to do."

"I can help you if you—" said Jennifer, but he was already gone.

She turned to Yusuf. "What was that about? What *did* you tell him?"

"I told him the truth."

"About Samir?"

"Yes. And about you. Well, what I knew anyway. Where have you been? They told me I couldn't visit."

She nodded. "That's not the worst of it." She paused. "Do you know about the centres? What happens there? Has it been on the news?"

"No. What centres?"

She closed her eyes. "It was awful, Yusuf. They gave us drugs, brainwashed us. I had to lie to get out, then I couldn't lie, then... I'm not making much sense, am I?"

She leaned into him. He smelled of wool and petrol. His sweater was soft and familiar.

"Is Hassan OK?" she asked. "He's not at risk of—"

"No. Don't worry. He's just confused."

"This wasn't what I expected."

He wrapped his hands around hers. "Give him time. It hasn't been easy for him either."

She pulled back. "Have you seen Samir?"

His face fell. "No. I've tried, but it's no good. It's like a brick wall of silence. They won't even tell Edward what's happening to him."

Edward was the family solicitor.

"You told me we'd get him back."

"We will."

"You don't sound so sure."

He swallowed. "Well, maybe now you're here, we'll find a way. Two heads are better than one."

"Have you written to the Home Office? Spoken to our new MP?"

"Of course I have. I've done everything."

"Sorry."

She squeezed his hand. He didn't squeeze back.

"I'll get onto it," she said. "I'm sure there's someone who can help."

He looked at her, his gaze level. "I've spoken to John."

"And?"

"He's got no power to help. Even if he wanted to."

"What do you mean?"

Yusuf licked his lips. "He's distanced himself from us. He wants nothing to do with it. After what happened in Parliament—"

"Hang on. This is John we're talking about. Are you sure he won't help?"

"Positive."

She thought back to her phone call last night. His tone had been clipped, not like the John she remembered. She'd assumed it was because he knew she had an audience.

"OK then," she said. "I'll talk to Catherine."

Yusuf dropped her hand. "When are you going to stop expecting that woman to help us?"

"I have to try."

"It'll make things worse."

"How, Yusuf? We've got no idea where Samir is or if he'll ever get out. We don't even know if he's still in the country."

"They'd write to us, if he was being deported. That's the procedure."

"You think they would, with the way things are now?"

There was a sound from upstairs; Hassan leaving his room to go to the toilet. She should go and talk to him, spend some time with him.

Yusuf put a hand on her arm. "Give him some space. Just for today. You've been through hell. You need to process that first."

"We gave Samir space."

"They're not the same."

She widened her eyes.

"They're not," he said. "You know that. Just trust me."

CHAPTER TEN

Rita sat in the back of the police van, listening to the voices outside. They seemed to be arguing.

She sat very still, focusing on the shape of the words. Something about a person called Kochinsky. From what she could tell, Kochinsky hadn't turned up.

The voices stopped. She held her breath and waited for the door to open.

She deserved good news. Since Dr Clarke's thugs had pulled her out of the group session it had been nothing but bad news. Imprisoned in the basement, beaten, forced to watch Jennifer's Celebration. Drugged when she wasn't quiet enough.

She hadn't much liked Jennifer at first. Too eager to please, too pally with the counsellor. But she'd thawed towards her at the end. Jennifer, for all her misplaced trust in the system, had tried to help her. She'd stepped up for her, at risk to herself.

The van's back door opened and a woman peered inside, blinking to see through the gloom. She wore what looked like a police uniform.

"It's just you and me," she said. "That OK?"

Rita didn't see how she could object, so shrugged. So that was what they were talking about – this Kochinsky should have been in the van with them. It didn't make much difference to Rita, shut up back here.

The policewoman started to shut the door then paused. Rita heard another voice, clear this time. Giving instructions. A location. Hillfield. Rita had never heard of it.

She heard footsteps moving away on the gravel, then a moment's quiet. She edged towards the open door. Could she make a run for it?

But this was a secure facility. There were at least two fences between here and the outside world, and probably as many guns. She shrank back into the gloom of the van, shivering.

The door opened again and Rita straightened up.

It was the same woman. "Why don't you sit up front, with me?"

Rita frowned at her. This was probably some sort of trick, designed to test her obedience. She said nothing.

The door opened wider.

"Come on then. We haven't got all day."

Rita looked at the woman. She was small, about Rita's height, with long dark hair scraped back into a bun. Her blue shirt was freshly ironed and her face looked as if it had been scrubbed. She was young; she could get away with it.

"Last chance."

Rita shuffled towards the open door, waiting for it to be slammed in her face. The policewoman would laugh at her.

But she didn't. Instead she glanced away from the van, then beckoned.

"Quick. Please."

Rita slid out of the van. The policewoman took her arm

and guided her to the passenger door. She held it open for her, like a chauffeur.

"In you get."

Rita did as she was told. The door closed behind her and she heard the lock slide into place. This woman may be friendly but she was taking no chances. Rita looked down at the door handle. Could she override the lock? Did she dare try?

The woman landed in the driver's seat with a contented sigh.

"That's better, eh? We've both got company."

Just a few weeks ago Rita would have argued with this woman, answered back. Challenged. She sniffed and said nothing.

The woman started the engine and eased the van towards the first gate. Rita leaned forwards to look around. The prison was modern, with high brick walls and cameras everywhere. Steel spikes topped the walls. The gate ahead of them was made of steel mesh. It clattered open.

The woman opened her window and passed a clipboard to the man in the guard station. She took it back and slid it into the gap between herself and Rita. Rita felt her hand drawn towards it.

They stopped at the second gate and repeated the routine. A red light was replaced by a green one, then the gate slid open. Beyond it was the outside world. Rita looked from the windscreen to her companion, grateful to be up here with a view. She wondered if the windows were greyed out from the outside, if people would be able to see her. Could she get someone's attention?

Don't be stupid, she told herself.

They reached the junction and stopped. The police-woman turned to her.

"I'm Sonia," she said, putting out her hand.

"Rita." After a moment of silence, Sonia withdrew her hand.

They followed unfamiliar roads to the M4. Rita had never driven but she knew that this motorway ran from London to Wales. Neither direction took her home, to Birmingham. Or maybe they would go west, and then take the M5 north?

She felt her pulse quicken as Sonia positioned the van in the road, nearing the roundabout. She was heading for the westbound carriageway.

Rita felt as if she might float off the seat. Could she really be going home?

CHAPTER ELEVEN

JENNIFER KNOCKED ON HER SON'S DOOR.

"Hey sweetie, only me."

She pulled on her brightest smile and pushed the door open.

He was at his desk, schoolbooks open in front of him.

"Hey," she said.

He didn't turn. "I'm not your sweetie."

"Oh. Sorry."

He bent over his work and put his pen in his mouth. He waggled it between his teeth then pulled it out and sniffed.

"Bye."

"Bye? I've only just got back. I wanted to see you, find out how you've been."

"I've been fine."

"Good."

She stepped towards him. His back stiffened. She stepped back.

"I'm sorry, love. About everything that's happened."

He turned. His face was wet. She resisted the urge to run over and pick him up.

"Why did you leave us, Mum?"

"I didn't leave you. They took me."

He wiped his cheeks and said nothing.

"What did Dad tell you?"

Hassan shook his head. "Samir was arrested. He had a girlfriend. She was a terrorist."

"I'm not sure she was actually a terrorist." She thought of Meena, helping her get through her Celebration. She still wasn't sure if she'd been sent to the centre as a spy, or if her story was genuine.

A shrug. "Same difference."

She sat on the bed. He still had his favourite soft toy on the pillow, a stuffed mouse. The kitten she'd encountered the previous night was curled up next to it. She stroked its fur and it shifted in its sleep.

"Who's this?'

He smiled. "Poppy."

"Nice name. How long have you had her?"

"A month. She's ten weeks old. She can go outside in two weeks."

"That's good." She left her hand on the cat's back. She could feel its ribs rise and fall under her fingers.

"She's cute."

"Yeah."

He turned back to his work. "I missed you."

She felt her stomach hollow out. She took her hand off the cat and leaned towards him. "I missed you too. I missed you so much. I couldn't wait to be back here with you."

He turned. "Really? You're not going straight back to London?"

"No. I'm staying here."

"Yeah, right."

"I promise."

"Yeah."

He stood up and left the room. She stared at the cat, waiting for him to come back. She continued waiting.

She felt the house vibrate as the front door slammed.

She hurried to the top of the stairs. Yusuf was opening the front door.

"What was that?"

"Hassan."

"What? Where's he gone?"

Yusuf grabbed his coat. "We don't have time."

He yanked the door open and rushed outside. Cold air gusted in after him. Jennifer stumbled down and stared out.

"Yusuf? Hassan?"

Yusuf was walking back along the street towards her, all but dragging Hassan after him. His lips were tight and he was sweating.

Jennifer grabbed the doorframe. Samir had pulled this trick a few times; had Hassan learned it from him?

Yusuf was struggling to keep hold of him now. He put an arm around Hassan's shoulders and bundled him towards the house. He spoke into his ear and glanced at the houses around them. Nothing moved; no twitching curtains, no doors closing, nothing.

Jennifer drew back to let them in. Hassan gave her a wary look then disappeared upstairs. Yusuf called after him.

"No! I want you down here, where we can talk."

"Maybe he needs some time," Jennifer said. "You told me—"

Yusuf's eyes were blazing. "I'm not letting this happen again."

She said nothing.

⁓

Half an hour later, Hassan had apologised and promised not to run off again. The house was quiet; he'd brought his homework down to the dining room and Yusuf was in the kitchen, sifting through letters from constituents. Every third letter or so he would tut loudly, scrunch the paper into a ball and toss it towards the bin.

"Yusuf, calm down. Please."

His shoulders slumped. "I'm sorry. It's just—it's been hard, without you here."

"That's not exactly my fault."

He stiffened. "No. I know. I missed you. I didn't know where you were. Samir. Hassan's taken it hard."

She stepped in behind him and wrapped her arms around his waist. "I know. Talk to me. Tell me about him. Please."

He followed her to the table. "What is there to tell?"

"Let's start with school. How's he getting on?"

Hassan had started at secondary school in September, just weeks before her arrest.

"Seems to be OK. He told me there are only two other Asian kids in his year. He's made friends with them."

"Really? Samir's year group had, what, twenty? Thirty?"

"It's the new school. Most of the Muslim kids are going there. They've been building links to the mosque."

"Is the council encouraging that?"

"The council is being instructed to." His face was hard. "By Catherine Moore's government."

"Please, don't start that again."

He looked at her. "And they're being made to recite this oath."

"I know." She thought of Rita. Where was she? "I know someone who was arrested because of it. A teacher."

"Someone you met in the centre?"

She felt heavy. "Yes. Rita."

"He misses Samir, you know." Yusuf's voice was low.

"Of course he does." She put her hand on Yusuf's. "We'll get him back. I'll call John again. Catherine."

Yusuf pulled his hand away and stood up. "I need to make lunch."

"Don't worry about that."

"I have to. If I don't look after him, who knows what will happen?"

"Do you blame me? For being away? For getting arrested?"

"No. You were helping Samir. If he hadn't come to your flat, he'd have been on the streets."

"He wanted to go to France, you know."

Yusuf pulled back from the fridge. "What?"

"He had his passport."

"He'd have been stopped."

"That's what I told him. But I think that's where he was going, when they arrested him. After he broke out of my flat."

"I heard about that. He was locked in."

She felt her cheeks grow hot. "That was me. I didn't want him running off again. We were going to fix it, with that debate in Parliament. Me and Catherine." She saw his jaw tighten. She ignored it. "Except then he was arrested, and it all turned bad."

Yusuf closed the fridge door and stared out of the window. Jennifer looked past him to see that the back garden had started to grow wild and the lawn hadn't been cut.

"Did you get to see him at all?" she asked. "After he was arrested?"

He lowered his head, his back still to her. "No. I haven't seen him since the night before he left."

"It was me who saw him last."

"Yes."

Yusuf picked up a packet of tomatoes and crossed to the bread bin. His movements were stiff.

"I have to see what I can do," Jennifer said.

Yusuf said nothing. He pulled a bag of bread put of the bin and started to butter slices.

"Are you OK with that?"

Still he said nothing. He returned to the fridge and took out a pack of cheese, not making eye contact.

"Yusuf, please. We need to talk about this. We need to do this together."

He spun round. His eyes were red. "There's no point."

"I don't see how—"

"You don't understand. That's OK—you've been away. You don't know what's been going on."

"I know there's been a bomb, and that there are cameras everywhere. People seem jumpy. Susan over the road—"

"You went over the road?"

"Yes. I needed to use her phone. Last night."

"Bad idea."

"Why? We've known Susan for years."

"She's white."

"So?"

"I'm not. The kids aren't. They don't trust us anymore. Not since the bomb. None of them trust us."

Jennifer stood up. "But this is Birmingham, for Christ's sake. It can't be like—"

"Do you remember the pub bombings? In the sixties? The IRA?"

"It was before I was born. But my mum told me about it."

"Do you remember how much people in this city hated the Irish after that?"

She shook her head. Since she'd been a teenager, Birmingham had been proud of its Irish community. There were Irish pubs, and a St Patrick's Day parade every year. But then she remembered what it had been like before that, and the stories her mum had told her. She'd worked in a department store. Her best friend was Irish. She'd been sacked for no reason.

"But this is the twenty-first century," she said. "People aren't like—"

"They are. It's worse. Because the government is encouraging it. With the new segregated schools, and the oath, and the rewards for reporting suspected extremists. They even make us recite it before every council meeting now."

"What?"

"The oath. The British Values Oath."

"Shit. We had to recite it in the centre too. And more."

He nodded. "I'm sorry. I know what they put you through. I shouldn't take it out on you. But my parents are thinking of going back to Pakistan."

"They'd never do that."

"Things change. At least they won't be hated there. Won't be spat on in the street."

Jennifer thought of the woman she'd helped at the station. Had she even made it to Manchester?

"You've made me even more determined," she said.

"How so?"

"Forget John. I'm going straight to Catherine."

"You know what I think about that."

"Just let me try. Give her the benefit of the doubt. She risked a lot to tell us about Samir, after all."

Yusuf stopped what he was doing. "Do you still have it?"

"Have what?"

"The note. The note she gave you about Samir. The warning."

She frowned. "I don't see what that's got to do with it."

"It's evidence."

"Evidence?"

"That she broke the law. The Official Secrets Act. Find that, and you've got her."

"I'm not doing it like that. She came to see me, you know."

"What?"

"In the centre. It was her who ordered my Celebration. That's how I got out."

"Are you sure—"

"She's my friend. She'll help us."

CHAPTER TWELVE

THE MOTORWAY FLASHED PAST. RITA STARED OUT AT IT, marvelling at the novelty of the outside world. How long was it since she had seen grass, and trees, and the sky?

The Malvern Hills were looming to their left, dim grey shapes against the pale sky. The day was one of those bright but sunless days when a thin layer of cloud denied the people scurrying beneath the joy of sunshine. But it was good enough for Rita.

The hills were directly to their left now, which meant they couldn't be more than twenty miles from Worcester. Where Ash lived. Not far from Birmingham, and home. Rita sat on her hands, reminding herself that they could be going anywhere. This could just be a coincidence. But as the motorway signs counted down the miles, she felt her heart rate rise.

The policewoman hadn't spoken since inviting Rita into the front of the van. She gripped the wheel in her pink-tipped hands, focusing on the road ahead and occasionally muttering when another driver pulled in front of them or got too close.

As they passed another sign – 35 miles to home, Rita hardly dared breathe – the traffic slowed and then stopped. After a few stationary moments the driver pulled on the handbrake and took her hands off the wheel. She turned to Rita.

"You doing OK?"

"Yes." Rita nodded. She kept her eyes on the surrounding traffic, the fields beyond it. "Where are we going?"

A smile. "Sorry, I can't tell you that. Not too far now though."

Rita could feel her pulse throbbing in her wrists. She put a finger on each and willed herself to be calm. Tonight she could be home. She could contact Ash. If he hadn't been arrested too.

The policewoman – Sonia, Rita reminded herself – reached into the pocket of her door and brought out a chocolate bar. A Twix. She opened the wrapper with one hand.

She waved it at Rita. "Want one?"

Rita had been surviving on institutional food for weeks. She could feel her ribs.

"Yes please."

Sonia pulled a bar out with her teeth and handed the wrapper to Rita, with the second bar inside. Rita stroked the gold plastic, pushing down an urge to swallow the chocolate in one bite.

At last she let herself pull the bar out and took her first bite. It was like velvet on her tongue. She closed her eyes and leaned back in her seat.

"How long since you last ate something decent?"

She opened her eyes again and shrugged. "Weeks, maybe. What's the date, today?"

"You don't know the date?" A pause. "Hang on, nor do I." Sonia laughed and pulled a phone from the same pocket where the chocolate had been. Rita eyed it. Could she steal it, use it to call Ash? Her family? She hadn't spoken to her parents for two years and they wouldn't have missed her, but still.

This woman was being nice to her. Stealing would be no way to repay her.

The traffic started and Sonia dropped her half-eaten stick of chocolate in her lap to take the steering wheel again. They edged forwards a hundred yards or so and then stopped. Sonia groaned.

"I hate the M5."

Rita nodded. She had rarely used it, despite living less than four miles from it. School was a thirty-minute walk from home, and if it was raining, the bus was easier than driving. No parking to worry about.

Sonia applied the handbrake again and picked up her chocolate. She downed it in one gulp, then wiped her lips. Rita was still nibbling at hers.

"Do you want me to make that easier for you?"

Rita looked back at her. "Sorry?"

"The handcuffs. They can't help."

Rita's eyes widened. "Yes. Of course."

She held her hands out, the chocolate in the left one. Sonia pulled a keyring from her belt and stretched the elastic to bring it to Rita's hands. She unlocked the cuffs and Rita felt the cold metal slide off her wrists. She wriggled her fingers then ate the rest of the chocolate in one bite.

"Don't get any ideas though. The doors are all deadlocked."

Rita eyed the passenger door next to her. Did she dare

try it, in case Sonia was bluffing? Or would that just get those cuffs slapped onto her wrists again?

She decided to leave it, for now.

The traffic started to move. Sonia crept forwards, keeping a steady distance behind the car in front.

"So what did you do?"

Rita frowned. "Sorry?"

"What did you do? To get yourself sent here?"

If Sonia didn't already know, there would be a reason. And Rita didn't like to talk about it. She still didn't know who had informed on her, who had told the authorities that she wasn't reciting the oath with the children in her class each morning.

She rubbed her wrists; they ached from the handcuffs but that was nothing to the soreness from the beating in group. She couldn't risk having those cuffs on again. Safest to respond.

"I'm – was – a teacher. I didn't recite the oath with the children. The British Values Oath."

"That all?"

Rita nodded.

"Blimey. I had you down for some kind of terrorist or something. One of the women they rip the headscarves off as soon as they arrest them."

"I'm not Muslim."

"Oh."

"Not that that's relevant, of course." She remembered all those conversations in the pub, the anger at the rising Islamophobia they saw all around them. When it was stoked by the government, there wasn't much you could do to stop it.

"Right," said Sonia. Rita looked at her. A white woman,

working in the police force: of course she would be Islam-ophobic.

Sonia turned to her, taking her eyes off the road for a second. "You think I'm a racist, don't you?"

"I never said—"

"No. But you do."

"I didn't—"

Sonia raised a hand and looked at Rita, more squarely now. Rita glanced at the road, nervous.

"You probably wouldn't believe me if I told you my girl-friend's Muslim, would you?"

Rita looked back at her. Was she telling the truth? Or was this a way to get Rita to trust her? She shrugged.

"Yeah, well. Don't judge a book by its cover."

Sonia turned back to the windscreen. She blipped a foot on the brake as the car ahead slowed and muttered some-thing indecipherable.

"She's gone into hiding," she said.

"Who?"

Sonia turned to Rita. "Layla. My girlfriend. I haven't seen her for more than a year."

Rita caught a red light from the corner of her eye. "Watch out!"

Sonia turned back to the front, but not quickly enough. The brake lights of the car in front, bright and scarlet, were almost in their faces.

"Shit!" Sonia cried. She pulled the steering wheel to one side and slammed on the brakes. The car veered to the right and sent Rita crashing into the passenger door.

"Jesus!" Sonia pounded the horn as the car careered out of control into the next carriageway. The outside lane.

Rita felt something thump into her back and was

thrown forwards. She expected to continue into the windscreen and out the other side but something stopped her. Something that appeared in front of her out of nowhere.

She buried her head in the airbag, breathing heavily. Her heart was pounding and her trousers were damp. Her head hurt, and there was a growing ache at the base of her spine. She groaned and shifted her weight. It got worse.

She turned her head slowly, carefully, to look at Sonia. Her airbag hadn't deployed. Her legs were next to Rita, draped over the steering wheel. Her torso had gone through the windscreen. Rita looked down to see tiny specks of light where the shattered glass had landed.

She pushed herself up, ignoring the pain in her back. She eased her head from side to side and brought her fingers up to inspect her skin. There was no blood. Just a sharp pain in her right eye like the world's worst migraine.

She swallowed, then nearly gagged at the metallic taste. She wiped her lips and drew her hand in front of her eyes to find it smeared with blood. She shifted her head sideways again, clearing the airbag, and spat. A thick puddle of blood landed on the handbrake next to her, and a single tooth. She felt her head lighten and the car seem to dip below her.

Don't faint, she told herself. She pushed at the airbag, struggling to release herself from its grip, and looked at Sonia again. She wasn't moving.

Rita blew out a long slow breath to gather her strength then pushed herself up and through the space where the windscreen had been. She took care to keep her bare wrists away from the fragments of glass and was glad she was wearing a thick prison-issue hoody over her T-shirt.

She made it to the bonnet, kicking against the seats to heave herself up. Sonia was lying across it, facing her. There was a gash on her forehead that looked deep and her blue shirt had a growing bloodstain on the shoulder.

She blinked, making Sonia jump.

"Are you OK?" she asked. Stupid question.

Sonia nodded, then yelped. Rita bent towards her.

"Don't move," she said. "I'll get help."

She turned over and looked up at the sky. It was impossibly white, the glare assaulting her eyes. Movement flashed at the edge of her vision.

She managed to sit up. Sweat was pouring into her eyes. She wiped them and focused on the scene around her.

Behind the van was a black car. It looked grotesquely small, its front completely caved in right up to the place where the back seats would be. Beyond that, the traffic had stopped and people were getting out of their cars, approaching her. A man hovered beyond Sonia, shouting into a mobile phone.

She felt a hand on her wrist and pulled it away, startled.

"Are you alright, miss?"

She turned to see an elderly man looking at her. His eyes were wide and his skin damp; he looked as if he was hyperventilating.

She nodded. "Yes. Thanks."

She looked back at Sonia. She was muttering something. Rita looked down toward her legs. One of them was mangled, twisted between the front of the car and the steering wheel. The other flopped down into the interior of the car in a way that made Rita gag.

Sonia whispered again. Rita bent towards her. The silence that had been enveloping her suddenly broke, the air rent with sirens, and cries, and shouts.

She got as close to Sonia's face as she could.

"There's an ambulance coming," she said. "Everything's going to be OK."

Sonia shook her head and whispered again. Rita twisted to bring her ear closer to the policewoman's mouth.

"Go," she croaked. "Run."

CHAPTER THIRTEEN

İt felt odd to be sitting here in St Stephen's lobby, waiting for a Member to come and greet her, instead of being the MP doing the greeting. The space felt larger now, colder. This must be what it felt like for constituents who'd come here to visit her.

Jennifer looked at her watch. Ten thirty. She was late. Jennifer wasn't surprised; she was a busy woman after all.

At last a door opened and her old friend stepped out. She was dressed as flamboyantly as ever, in a green trouser suit and large yellow earrings that looked as if they might be made from seashells. She had a few grey hairs showing in between the red but otherwise was unchanged from the woman Jennifer had sat next to on the backbenches over two years ago. The woman who had helped her defeat their own Prime Minister, Michael Stuart, in a confidence vote. The woman who had celebrated despite this meaning the demise of their own government.

Jennifer stood up and held out her hand. "Maggie. Thanks for agreeing to this."

Maggie Reilly, fourth term MP for Hull, had a familiar

glint in her eyes, like a fox about to take down a henhouse. Jennifer had worried that she'd refuse to meet – their friendship had waned when Jennifer had joined John Hunter's shadow cabinet. But now she realised that Maggie could smell a fight brewing.

Jennifer had spent the last two weeks trying to get hold of Catherine Moore. But her mobile phone had been disconnected, replaced no doubt by a more secure one carried by an aide instead of its owner. Staff in her constituency office had been cold and evasive. And trying to contact her via the Number Ten switchboard – that was a futile exercise from the outset.

So now she was here, in the House of Commons, putting Plan B into place.

Maggie started walking. Her shoes were lower and better fitting than Jennifer's and it was a struggle to keep up. They hurried along corridors, their footsteps echoing.

Jennifer felt a pang of homesickness tinged by the discomfort of not belonging. They passed a group of Conservative MPs who turned to stare. Jennifer kept her eyes down.

She wondered if John was in the building, if she might bump into him. Two party leaders was too much to hope for in one day. She needed to focus on her quarry.

They stopped at the bottom of a flight of stone stairs, Jennifer nearly crashing into Maggie in her distraction.

"She won't be in place yet," said Maggie. "Come to my office and wait. We should lie low."

She flashed Jennifer a grin and hurried up the stairs. Trust Maggie to treat this like a military operation. Jennifer smiled, glad she'd taken the decision to call her. Yusuf had thought it a waste of time, having no idea how she could get to the Conservative Prime Minister via a Labour backbencher, and a rebellious one at that. But what Yusuf had failed to take into account was that Maggie could get her access to the House of Commons. And today was a Wednesday.

They arrived on the second floor and Maggie's office. It was a mid-sized one; Maggie may not be a minister or shadow, but that meant nothing when it came to allocating offices. Maggie was a senior MP, with nearly four terms under her belt. She'd earned this.

Maggie slumped into a chair and gestured to another for Jennifer. She grinned.

Jennifer smiled back. "How are you?"

"Oh, I'm great. Never better."

"Seriously?"

"Yup. For a loony leftie like me, Opposition is meat and drink. Even in Government, I was against everything. So why not do it properly, eh?"

She winked. Jennifer let herself relax, taking her mind off the reason she was here. Maggie's ebullience felt like fresh air flowing through this old building, after the British Values Centre and its secrecy and double standards.

"So where have you been?" asked Maggie. "You disappeared off the radar."

Jennifer considered. If she'd found out about the British Values Centre as a minister, she'd have been subject to the Official Secrets Act. Maybe even as a shadow minister. But there were no such restrictions for inmates. Which was one of the reasons so few were released.

"They had me in something called a British Values Centre."

"I've heard about those. There was a Muslim woman who got out of one a few months ago, sold her story to the press." Maggie's face clouded. "No one took her seriously."

"They should have. It's all true. All of it, and more."

"Go on then."

Jennifer started to tell Maggie her story. How she'd been given the choice of leaving prison and being sent to a low security unit in the Oxfordshire countryside. Her one-to-ones with Mark Clarke, the counsellor. The group sessions, with a small band of women who had grown to become her friends. Rita – poor, missing Rita – and her failed Celebration, her humiliation in group. Jennifer's own Celebration, her second, and the way she'd found a form of words to convince them she'd repented despite being under the influence of a truth drug. She still didn't know why Mark hadn't been there, whether he'd been caught for planning to help her cheat.

Maggie sat back and listened, making appropriate sounds and facial gestures as the story progressed. When Jennifer finished, she looked like she'd been hit with a baseball bat.

"Shit," she breathed. "It's all true. The bastards."

Jennifer gripped the arm of her chair. She felt dizzy from the relief of telling her story.

A bead of sweat ran into her collar. She needed to focus.

"You're not wrong there," she said.

"I'm going to stop this," said Maggie.

Jennifer felt tired. She knew she had to do something about the centres, to work for Rita's release. But she had Samir to think about. She should work on the two problems together.

"Who's her MP?" asked Maggie, pulling open a desk drawer.

"Whose?"

"Rita's. Your friend, the one who's missing. Her MP can follow it up."

Why hadn't Jennifer thought of that? "I don't know."

"Don't know what?"

"Where she lived. Lives. Who her MP is. We didn't have a chance to—"

Maggie held up a nicotine-stained finger. "We can find out. What's her full name?"

"Rita Gurumurthy."

"And she was a teacher?"

"Yes."

"Well there you go then. There can't be too many Rita Gurumurthys teaching primary school."

"But you don't have access to official records."

"I don't bloody need access to official records. I've got Google, haven't I? I'll find her. I'll speak to her MP. Hopefully it's one of ours." She drummed her lips with a purple fingernail. "On the other hand, sometimes it's easier if it's one of theirs. Anyway, leave it with me. You worry about your son."

Jennifer smiled. "Thanks, Maggie. I appreciate it. I really do."

Maggie waved a dismissive hand. "Least I could do. Now, let's get you to that bitch of a Prime Minister."

CHAPTER FOURTEEN

Rita stared at Sonia, not sure if she heard her correctly.

"What?" she breathed.

Sonia lifted her head then groaned and let it fall back.

"Go. Now."

Rita swallowed. Her throat was dry and tight. She looked up, past Sonia. People were advancing on her, witnesses. They looked wary. Was it her they were wary of? Did she look like a prisoner?

She looked down at herself. She was dressed in a hoodie and jeans, and the handcuffs were back in the van. They had slid off her lap when she climbed up to check on Sonia. The van itself was unmarked, anonymous.

No one could know what she was. They were afraid of a fire, she realised.

She looked back at Sonia. She looked up at Rita, her eyes dull and steady. This woman had been good to her. She'd treated her like a human being. She'd released the handcuffs, offered her chocolate.

Could Rita leave her, to die maybe? To face punishment for letting her run?

She pushed herself upright, sitting on the van's bonnet. The motorway was quiet except for the advancing wail of sirens. The traffic had stopped on both carriageways. On this side, people were getting out of their cars, leaning on open doors, staring. On the other side, the southbound side, they stayed put, rubbernecking through the windows of their vehicles.

The sirens were getting louder now. A car engine started up, then another. People were moving out of the way.

There would be ambulance. Maybe a fire engine. Definitely police. All advancing towards her from the south.

She looked across at the other carriageway again. It was close to her; the van had swerved into the fast lane and only the central barrier stood between her and a man who watched from inside the cocoon of his car, his eyes dull.

She had to run. Now.

She muttered a thank you to Sonia then jumped off the bonnet onto the tarmac. It felt rough through her flimsy shoes.

"It'll be OK," she said. "There's an ambulance coming."

A woman was advancing towards her from the central lane. She looked puzzled, and concerned. So many kind strangers today.

Rita turned away from her. She put a hand on the barrier and leaped over it. She heard a gasp behind her, and a shout of *Stop!* She didn't turn to see where it had come from, but carried on running for the other edge of the tarmac.

She slammed into the side of a car and put her hand on it. It was hot. She edged around it, slipping through the gap between it and the car in front. She carried on, oblivious to the shouts behind her.

Beside her, a car door opened and someone got out: a black man in a Nike T-shirt, bulky and slow. She glanced at him and carried on running.

At last she was in the hard shoulder. She took a quick look back to see that the ambulance had arrived and was parked behind the van. Two paramedics got out. The woman who had asked if she was OK approached them, pointing towards Rita.

She felt her stomach loosen.

Run, she told herself. The police would be right behind the ambulance.

She skidded to a halt as she hit grass, adapting to the new surface, picking up speed again. There was a steep bank down, bordered by a tangled hedge. She took a deep breath and threw herself into it. The barbs scratched her skin through the hoody. Something hit her face and she raised a hand to find her cheek wet: blood.

Beyond the hedge, the noise receded. Sirens and voices were replaced by the thrum of the countryside; birds singing, the distant sound of farm machinery.

Ahead was a field, recently ploughed and rutted. Beyond that – yes! – a road. A proper, surfaced road with two carriageways. Could she hitch a lift looking like this?

She stumbled across the field, tripping twice on the rough earth. The ground was soft and threatened to swallow her up in places. She didn't risk a look backwards, but she knew she had to get away. The police would send a car to the road, as soon as they saw the van.

She stopped by the road and felt a gust of air as a car sped past. She raised her arm and waved wildly but the driver hadn't spotted her. She had to make a decision, fast.

Hitching a lift might take time. If someone did pick her up, then they'd take her to the police or at least a hospital as soon as they saw her injuries. But if she stayed out in the open, they would soon catch up with her.

She had to keep going. She had a head start.

She ran across the road, not pausing to check for oncoming vehicles, and threw herself through a hedge on the other side. It was tall but not as heavy as the last one.

On the other side she stopped to catch her breath. She bent over and balled her fists on her thighs, panting. She coughed twice and stooped to spit more blood onto the ground.

Her heart was going like a racehorse. Her legs ached. She'd been beaten no more than a week ago; every part of her hurt. But her desperation and her will to get away from those beatings, from the humiliation of Celebration, spurred her on.

She looked ahead. She had landed in a wood, deciduous trees tangled with rhododendron bushes and ferns. She allowed herself to breathe; she had cover.

But she had to get as far away from the motorway as she could. She took a deep breath, retched, spat again, then started to run.

CHAPTER FIFTEEN

"Jennifer."

Surprise flicked over Catherine's face for the briefest instant. Her expression was polite but not friendly.

Jennifer stepped forward. Catherine glanced at the aide next to her. Jennifer recognised him from Catherine's time as a junior minister. Jennifer wondered how much he knew about his boss.

"Congratulations," Jennifer said. "Quite an achievement."

Catherine blushed faintly and nodded. "Thank you. What are you doing here?"

Catherine looked at Maggie, who was hanging back. Spectating.

"You didn't answer my calls."

"I'm Prime Minister now. I can't reply to every random phone call that comes into the Number 10 switchboard."

"So you know I called."

"Yes.

"And you know I tried your mobile too, then?"

Uncertainty passed over Catherine's face. She'd developed crow's feet around her eyes, and there was a blemish on her chin that the make-up failed to hide. Jennifer thought of her own grey hairs and the bags under her eyes so deep at times she could have taken them to the supermarket. She hadn't bothered to dye her hair after being released; a lack of artifice felt appropriate now, somehow.

"I don't have that anymore," Catherine replied. "It's in secure storage."

Jennifer knew what she would be thinking: had Jennifer left an incriminating message on it?

Jennifer hadn't, but she didn't need to tell Catherine that.

"I need to talk to you," she said.

Catherine gave the aide a look that said *get me out of here*. She stepped backwards, then realised they were at the end of a corridor. Maggie had prepared well.

She sniffed. "What about?"

Jennifer stepped forward. "Samir. My son."

"I'm not sure that's appropriate. Anyway, I thought you were still in prison."

"You know where I was. I got out. Passed. Surely you knew that too?"

"I need to get to a meeting. Please let me pass."

"I'm not stopping you. But please, Catherine. I really need to talk to you. You're the only person who can help me."

"Prime Minister!"

Jennifer turned to see a young woman heading their way. A lobby correspondent from The Times. The journalist spotted Jennifer and stopped in her tracks. She smiled.

"Ms Sinclair."

"That's me."

The journalist swallowed. "Does this mean you're coming back to Parliament?" She looked between Jennifer and Catherine. "In the Lords, maybe?"

Catherine laughed. "Don't be preposterous. Jennifer has come for a visit, haven't you Jennifer?"

"Um, yes."

Catherine took another step towards Jennifer. She was wearing the same perfume Jennifer had detected in Yonda Hughes's office, back at the centre. Elegant, floral. Expensive.

"Come to Downing Street," she said, her eyes stony and her voice low. "Four o'clock. I'll give you five minutes."

"Five minutes."

"You're lucky to get anything. And keep it low key, will you? The police on the gates will be expecting you. The press won't. They won't be there if they don't expect anything."

Jennifer looked back at the journalist, who was pulling a phone out of her bag.

"Four o'clock," she said. "See you then."

CHAPTER SIXTEEN

DOWNING STREET WAS QUIET. THERE WAS NO PRESS
gathered and only a few officials passing along the road as
Jennifer walked towards the famous black door.

Her job as prisons minister hadn't been Cabinet level so
she hadn't been a frequent visitor, back when Michael
Stuart lived behind that front door. But there had been
meetings here; with advisors, with colleagues, and sometimes with Michael. They'd never been close; John had
always been the filter between them, passing information
and instructions back and forth. When she'd resigned to
rebel against the ban on Muslim immigration, Michael had
broken all contact with her. And it was only after the vote
had been won – or lost, depending on your perspective –
that she'd learned that John had been filtering more than
she thought. Including his own opinions.

She approached the door, raising her hand to knock. It
opened before she reached it, her presence being recorded
by the cameras high above her. Once inside she stood in
the lobby, waiting. Who would Catherine send to
greet her?

After a few moments the aide from earlier appeared. He nodded at her and turned on his heel. He looked irritated.

Jennifer followed, pushing down her unease at being in a Tory Downing Street. It all looked the same; tasteful wallpaper, thick, hard-wearing carpets, antique furniture. Some of the pictures were different from Michael's choices, less modern. Jennifer leaned in to one she recognised, a Vermeer. She wondered how much the art collection in government buildings, particularly this one, was worth. Did it impress people?

They came to a door and the aide knocked.

"Come in." Catherine's voice.

The room was less grand than Jennifer had been expecting. The pictures on the walls weren't old masters, but simple sketches of rural scenes. They looked almost like they'd been done by a child.

The desk was large, placed in front of a tall window, a modern swivel chair behind it and two smaller in front. Catherine sat typing on a laptop.

Jennifer took one of the chairs. Catherine continued to type. Jennifer watched her, smiling. She had all day; she wasn't going to be ruffled by this display of superiority.

After a few moments Catherine closed the laptop and looked at Jennifer. She gave her a smile that didn't reach her eyes. There were dark circles beneath them and in the poor light she looked older.

She looked past Jennifer at the aide. "Turn on the light please, Sam."

An ornate chandelier above them lit up. Now it felt cosy in here instead of dull.

"Do you want me to stay?" the aide asked.

"No. I'll call you when I'm done. Five minutes, tops."

Jennifer heard the door behind her close.

Catherine leaned back in her chair, looking not at Jennifer but at the paperwork on her desk. She leaned forwards and gathered it into a neat pile, tucking it out of sight under the laptop. Jennifer watched all this, listening to the hush of the room. A mahogany clock ticked on the wall to one side. Voices could be heard through the window. Jennifer tried to remember her route here; were they at the front of the building, or the back? The back, surely. For security reasons.

Catherine took a deep breath and stood up. She smoothed her hands on her skirt – she'd put on weight – and rounded the desk, perching in front of Jennifer. Jennifer looked up at her.

"I don't know what you think I can do," she said.

Jennifer stood up and stepped behind her chair, gripping its back with her hands.

"It's just you and me here," she said. "Can we cut the dance?"

"I don't know what you mean."

"Samir is still in detention somewhere. He may even have been deported for all I know."

"No. You'd have had a letter. Or your husband would, while you were away." Catherine narrowed her eyes. "Just how did you get out, anyway?"

"I'm sure you don't need me to tell you that."

"Try me."

"I had a second Celebration. I passed."

"How? You were planning on lying your way out, if I remember right. You wouldn't have got away with it."

"I didn't lie. I told the truth. I told them what they wanted to hear."

"I don't imagine it's the same thing."

Jennifer shrugged. "Must have been. I'm here, aren't I?"

Catherine would know everything about her release. She'd have seen a transcript of her Celebration. She'd know that it had been led by Meena Ashgar, not her own counsellor. She wondered what had happened to him. She wondered if Meena had been telling her the truth, when they'd spoken before her release.

"Anyway," Jennifer said. "I need your help on two counts. Firstly Samir. He did nothing wrong. I met—"

She stopped herself. She wasn't about to tell Catherine that Meena had been Samir's girlfriend. That she was the reason he'd been arrested.

Or should she? Who should she trust, Meena or Catherine?

She looked down. Her grip on the chair was tight and her knuckles pale. She took a deep breath.

"Samir needs to be released. He at least needs to be granted the right to appeal."

"That's not part of the process with terrorist crimes, and you know it."

"Samir isn't a terrorist. And you know that. Otherwise you wouldn't have warned me that he was under suspicion. You wouldn't have given me the chance to hide him."

"You didn't do a very good job of that, did you? He fled your flat as soon as he got the chance."

Jennifer's chest tightened. *Stay calm*, she told herself.

"Can we not go over old ground, please? I just want your assurance that he'll get an appeal hearing. A fair, open one."

"I can't do that."

Jennifer ignored her; of course she could.

"And I want to know where Rita Gurumurthy is."

"Who?"

"I met her in the centre. They beat her and took her

away somewhere. She disappeared. I want to know she's safe."

Catherine shook her head. "Any other ugly ducklings you've taken under your wing? That you want me to help out?"

"What's happened to you, Catherine?"

"I don't know what you mean."

"You used to be one of the good ones. You weren't like Trask. But now here you are, sitting at his old desk and carrying on with all his policies. Worse."

Catherine shrugged. "It's the reality of government. Surely you know all about that. You did when you used Hayley Price's death to advance your own career."

Hayley Price had been a prisoner at Bronzefield when Jennifer was prisons minister. She'd killed herself in custody, almost causing Jennifer to lose her job. Jennifer had rescued the situation with a heartfelt speech in the Commons.

"I learned from Hayley's death. I made changes to the way prisons were run. Made sure it didn't happen again."

"Did you no harm, though."

Catherine looked at her watch. She walked back round the desk, sitting in her chair and opening the laptop again.

"Your five minutes are up, I'm afraid. I wish you and your family all the best, but I'm sure you understand how inappropriate it would be for me to—"

"Do you have any decency left?"

A frown. "I have no idea what you're—"

"We're friends, Catherine. Were, maybe. I could damage you, but I won't. Because I respect you and I don't want to ruin you. Afford me the same respect at least."

"You have no idea."

"I do."

Catherine neared Jennifer, her eyes hard. "You're nothing now. No power, nothing. You can't touch me."

Jennifer could feel her chest rising and falling. Did she dare mention the note? Could she bluff?

"Now, if you don't mind," Catherine said. A door opened and a woman walked in, someone Jennifer hadn't seen before. She watched Catherine, waiting for instructions.

Jennifer swallowed. She couldn't do it. "I'll call you. You'll change your mind."

Catherine gave her a condescending smile. "Good to see you again. Please, give my regards to your husband."

Jennifer let herself be guided out, not sure if she was more angry at Catherine or herself.

CHAPTER SEVENTEEN

STEVE STARTED SITTING IN ON MARK'S ONE-TO-ONES. He didn't want the other inmates to know Mark was spying on them for him. He didn't want him telling his counsellor.

It clearly rattled Mark's counsellor, Dr Higgs. He would lick his lips and scratch his protruding chin while he talked Mark through the six steps. As if Mark needed reminding. He'd been one of the very first doctors recruited to a centre, and knew this better than anyone.

It didn't help him get through the program though. No one was telling him precisely what it was he was here for, which made even Step One a challenge. Maybe they wanted him to incriminate someone else. Jennifer, most likely. He didn't want to do that.

He wondered if her Celebration had gone ahead without him. Was she back in prison now?

Dr Higgs was late today. Mark sat outside his office, waiting. He had a story ready for Steve, something one of the men on his group had said. Something that would send Steve down a blind alley but ultimately come to nothing.

He wondered if he was in there already, with the counsellor.

Instead of in the basement like Burcot Park, the offices here were on the first floor, at the back. They were smaller than his office had been, but had proper windows, looking out over the fenced yard behind the centre where inmates were allowed to exercise for forty minutes each morning. Sometimes he heard activity down there, unfamiliar voices. He longed to walk to the window and check – just to have the freedom to get up and investigate something that intrigued him. But his counsellor would pin him to his chair with his eyes and continue with the one-to-one.

He heard a door close and looked up. He sighed. It was Steve. Coming out of his own office, at the far end of the corridor. He turned back to the door and spoke to someone inside. Mark watched, glad of the distraction.

Steve turned towards him. He smiled, a wide grin that stank of insincerity. He waved.

Mark shrugged and didn't wave back.

Steve beckoned.

Mark looked at his counsellor's door again; maybe it was him inside Steve's office. He thought of the rare occasions that he'd escorted patients to Yonda's office, or rather the occasions when he'd got the orderlies to do it for him.

It normally meant Celebration. And if he was being put forward, then he was being set up to fail.

He stood and rubbed his hands on the legs of his jeans. It was cold here at the back of the building, where the sun never seemed to penetrate.

He started walking. Steve beckoned again, more emphatically. Mark picked up his pace, just a little.

When he reached the door, Steve put an arm on his

shoulder and gave him the sort of smile you'd reserve for an old friend. Mark shuddered.

"I've got someone to see you," he said.

Mark looked from Steve to the door, which was closed now. Prisoners didn't get visitors.

"Who?"

The smiled widened. "You'll see."

Mark waited for Steve to open the door. He didn't.

"Now," Steve said. He pinched his nose then inspected his finger. He frowned and flicked something to the floor. "This may come as a surprise to you. I need you to be on best behaviour. You're representing Linchbourne now."

Linchbourne. It had originally been set up as a prison, when Jennifer was prisons minister. It would have had a different name then.

"Who to?" he asked.

"Someone you know."

For a brief moment he thought it might be Jennifer, somehow reinstated to her old role. But even if she was back in politics, her party were in Opposition.

Catherine Moore, Home Secretary? They'd met in Burcot Park, when she'd come to visit Jennifer. Would she want to speak to him, find out about the circumstances of Jennifer's release, if she'd been released?

The door opened and a waft of heavy perfume leaked out.

Of course. He flexed his fingers and pulled on a smile. He passed Steve, who was holding the door for him.

"Yonda."

She stood up. She was wearing a fuchsia dress with a matching jacket and purple heels. Next to her, on a low table, was a red handbag. Small, shiny. Expensive-looking.

"Mark. Good to see you."

"Why are you here?"

She smiled and let her hand, which she'd been holding out in anticipation, drop.

"I need your help, Mark. With Jennifer Sinclair."

CHAPTER EIGHTEEN

"She said what?"

It was late. Jennifer's train hadn't got in till after ten. By the time she was home, Yusuf was preparing for bed and Hassan was fast asleep. She'd taken Yusuf to their room and recounted her conversation with Catherine.

"She told me I was nothing. She was so cold."

"I'm sorry." He stroked her cheek.

"I was wrong. You were right. As always."

He cupped her face in his hand. She looked back into his eyes, thinking about how much she'd missed him in the centre.

"If you had the note..." he said.

"That's not the point. I'm not doing it."

"But she broke the Official Secrets Act."

"To help us."

He looked away, his hand falling to the duvet. "She's not that person anymore."

"She was my friend. We went through a lot together. The Milan bomb. Our plan to discredit Trask."

"Which she reneged on."

94

"Things changed. She had to do what she did."

Yusuf scraped his fingers through his beard. "I can't believe you're still saying that after everything she's done."

"Well, I've been proved wrong. That should make you happy."

He moved his hand down to her shoulder, gripping it. "None of this makes me happy, love."

She sank back. "Me neither. But maybe she'll be scared I'll expose her after all." A pause. "Maybe she'll help us."

"Did she say she would?"

"No."

"Right. Typical."

Jennifer felt like a balloon about to deflate. She thought of the note Catherine had sent her, before Samir had disappeared. Before she'd been arrested. She couldn't remember destroying it, despite Catherine's instructions to do so. But she couldn't find it.

"So what now?" asked Yusuf.

"I don't know. We wait, I guess. Maybe she'll at least tell me what's happened to Rita."

"Rita?"

"You know. From the centre. The one they beat up, and put in solitary confinement."

"Why would Catherine Moore tell you where she is?"

"I asked her to."

"What?"

"I asked her to. After I said I needed her to get Samir an appeal."

Yusuf took his hand off her shoulder and put it on his own. He started rubbing the flesh. He was wearing a vest that Jennifer remembered from before. It was even more threadbare than she remembered.

"We need to focus on Samir," he said, his voice tight.

"I know." She put a hand on his knee. His thigh was warm through his pyjama bottoms. She felt the muscle tense.

"I want to help my friend too, though. I want to help all of them."

Yusuf looked up at the ceiling. His eyes were red. "Please, love. I just want our boy back."

"This isn't like you. Think of all those constituents you've helped over the years. People who've managed to go into hiding or leave the country, thanks to you."

"Maybe I got my priorities wrong."

Jennifer stared at him. If Yusuf was this ground down that he only cared about his own family, then what help was there for anyone? People were becoming more insular. Her neighbours didn't want to know her. The local party had made it clear they didn't want her near them. People looked at her in the street like she was a threat. Even those who couldn't possibly know who she'd been.

Now even Yusuf was affected.

"No, Yusuf," she said. "You didn't. You really didn't. People needed you. They still do. Yes, we have to help Samir. We have to get him out. But that doesn't come at the expense of who we are."

He gave her a sad smile. "Since when did you get so wise?"

"Since I spent four months locked up trying to convince a psychiatrist that I loved a government that I really hate. Since I saw what they're doing to anyone who doesn't comply."

"OK. But I still don't think she'll do anything. We have to find another way to get Samir out."

"Just wait. For a few days. I'll go back down there. Maggie said she'd help."

"Good old Maggie."

Yusuf leaned in and kissed her. She let the warmth of his touch flow over her. She brought her hands up to his arms and gripped his flesh.

Yusuf pulled back.

"What?" Jennifer asked, frowning. "What's wrong?"

He sprang up from the bed and darted to the door. He grabbed his dressing gown.

"What is it?" she asked. Her lips felt tender from the depth of their kiss. "What? What have I done?"

He looked past her at the alarm clock. It was almost midnight.

"Did you hear that?" he said.

"Hear what?"

He opened the door, peering out into the dark hallway.

"There's someone knocking on our door."

CHAPTER NINETEEN

It was getting dark. Rita had managed to avoid detection near the motorway and had stumbled across fields for an hour or two, trying to get her bearings.

Now she was at the edge of a village. Did she dare to knock on a door and ask for shelter? She was a criminal on the run. Her face would be all over the news.

She sat next to the sign announcing the village boundary, staring at the dark houses. There was no sign of life; no cars passing, no one walking to the village pub. The place could have been abandoned for all she could tell.

There was a bus shelter, a few houses along. She crept to it. She tried to make herself comfortable, attempting to lie between the seats and failing. Two cars swept past, bathing her in light. She wondered if their occupants could see her, if they might recognise her.

She had to move.

She heaved her sore muscles off the bench and clambered down a grassy bank behind the bus stop, her arms flailing to keep her balance as she picked up speed. She hadn't realised how steep it was.

At the bottom she paused to catch her breath, her breath foggy in the cold air. The stars were bright above her, casting the field in a pale glow.

She squinted to see what shelter she might find.

There was a barn at one side of the field below her, little more than a dull grey shape nestled among trees. It had no doors. If it was a house, it wouldn't be occupied.

She hurried towards it, anxious to be somewhere sheltered. The sky was clouding over now and she felt a spot of rain hit the back of her neck.

At the barn she stopped. If there were animals in there, they might not be pleased to see her.

She squinted into the dark space, feeling more rain hit her head and shoulders. It was too dark inside for her to see anything, but she couldn't make out any movement.

She stepped forwards. A bright light flashed in her eyes.

She threw her arms above her head, feeling foolish and scared in equal measure.

"Who are you?" came a voice. It sounded like a man, tired, maybe sick. He had an accent. Pakistani?

"I'm sorry," she said. "I'll go."

She turned and headed back for the field, trying to see the road. But the echo of that light was in her eyes still, and the world was black.

"Who are you?'

The voice sounded different now. Higher pitched, and less close. He'd followed her outside.

"Daddy?"

Rita froze. A farmer guarding his barn was one thing. A Pakistani farmer was another. But a Pakistani farmer with a young child, out here in the dark?

She turned back to the light, breathing heavily.

"I was just looking for shelter," she said.

The man had flicked out the light now, and she could see his shape in the darkness. He was medium height and skinny. Half starved, by the look of it. A little girl huddled next to him, clinging to his waist like it was a lifebelt.

"You won't find any here," he said.

She nodded. Were they like her? Fugitives? She thought of all the anti-Islamic laws that had been introduced, the deportations. Her heart sank.

"I'll leave you alone," she said. "I won't tell anyone I saw you."

"No. Go."

She heard another voice, a woman, then the piercing shriek of a baby's cry. She took a step forward, instinct overcoming fear.

"I said go," the man said. Rita's eyes had adjusted to the low light now. She could see his face. Deep lines ran down his cheeks. His eyes looked hollowed out, like they might sink into his skull. The little girl was wearing a pink dress, heavily stained and torn at the collar.

How long had they been here?

The man stepped forward and Rita retreated.

"Sorry," she said. "I'll go."

She turned and ran, trying not to imagine that poor woman trying to keep a baby alive in a cold barn.

CHAPTER TWENTY

JENNIFER STUMBLED DOWN THE STAIRS BEHIND Yusuf. She was still dressed for Westminster, and almost fell as her tights slipped on the worn carpet.

When she reached the front door Yusuf was already standing on the driveway.

"Who is it? What's happened?" She wrapped her arms around his waist from behind. He felt stiff.

Blue lights reflected off the houses. A policewoman in uniform stood in front of Yusuf, a clipboard in hand.

Jennifer stepped forward to face her. "What's happening?"

The policewoman looked from Yusuf to Jennifer, recognition crossing her face.

"I'm sorry to disturb you, madam. We're looking for a fugitive. A young woman."

"Who?"

The woman looked at her clipboard. "Her name is Lavonia Taylor. She lives at number sixteen."

Jennifer looked past her. Two police cars were parked at

angles outside number sixteen, ten doors down. A crowd had gathered in the front garden: two police detectives, two uniformed officers, and a middle-aged couple, huddled together. Lavonia's parents. Jennifer had met the mother, Celeste, back when she'd been an MP. She'd needed help with a council tax error. The father was quiet and despite living in the same street for over five years had never acknowledged her. After the first year, she'd given up trying.

"A fugitive, you say? You mean she's gone missing?"

"No. An officer arrived at the house at—" she checked her watch, "—eleven thirty-eight. She answered the door and ran straight past him. We're searching neighbouring gardens and outbuildings. Houses, too. We need permission to—"

"Hang on. So you came to arrest her?"

Jennifer tried to remember the girl. She was a bright, cheerful kid with plump cheeks and hair that had been arranged differently every time Jennifer saw her. Her mother was proud of her, said she was a hard worker. Why would they be arresting her?

"What did she do?"

"I'm sorry, I can't tell you that."

Yusuf put his hand on Jennifer's arm. He looked nervous. "It's alright, love."

Jennifer brushed past the woman, heading for the parents.

"I still need your—"

She heard Yusuf's tone grow weary. "We'll give our permission. But I'll need to find the key to the side gate."

He was stalling, Jennifer realised. If they wanted to arrest this girl under the security laws, he wasn't about to make it easier. She smiled.

She heard the policewoman thank Yusuf. She looked back to see him duck into the house. The policewoman moved on to the next house.

Jennifer was level with one of the police cars now, the red and blue lights bright in the dark of the cloudy night. Beyond then, Spaghetti Junction continued to glow orange above the roofline.

Three more uniformed officers were knocking on doors, calling between each other, issuing instructions. If raps on knockers didn't wake the street, their voices would.

She thought of the girl, hiding in a garden somewhere. Hers, maybe. She was only twenty, twenty-one, in her first year of college when the Spaghetti Junction bomb hit, lauded as a heroine after she'd helped an injured woman and her child off a bus on the ruined motorway. What could she possibly have done in the meantime, to be under suspicion?

Then she thought of Samir. The neighbours would have wondered the same about him. Everyone had their secrets.

She reached the driveway where Lavonia's parents stood, clutching at each other. The mother was blinking against the harsh police lights.

"Hello, Celeste," she said, her voice low. "Is everything OK?"

Celeste's husband turned to her, his nostrils flaring. "What do you think?"

"Can I help at all?"

Celeste sniffed. "I don't know."

Jennifer approached her, keeping away from her husband. "What's happened?"

The father eyed her. "None of your business. Not anymore."

Celeste turned to her husband. "Please Robert, she wants to help us. She helped us once before, remember?"

He shook his head. "This is between us. Her being here will only make things worse. People are watching."

His eyes swept the street. Sure enough, people were gathering to watch. Standing at their front doors in their dressing gowns, their faces glowing blue. They all looked so small and frail.

"They're worried," said Jennifer. "We all are."

He snorted. "What if they think we're connected to your son?"

Jennifer opened her mouth. Celeste blushed. Robert continued to stare.

"Mum?"

A boy had appeared at the door in his underpants. He looked a little older than Samir. Celeste hurried to him.

"Get inside, Clyde! You're practically naked."

The boy dragged the back of his hand across his face. "What's going on? Where's Von?"

The woman looked back at her husband, her eyes bright with suppressed tears. "Robert, take him in, please. He listens to you."

Her husband went to the boy, putting a hand on his shoulder, muttering into his ear. The boy's eyes widened. His dad guided him inside the house and closed the door.

"Please," said Jennifer. "I want to help. Did they say what they suspect her of?"

"They said she's been looking at subversive websites."

"Is that all?"

"It's enough, these days. You of all people should know that."

Jennifer blushed. "Yes."

"I'm sorry," said Celeste. "About your son. Robert shouldn't have said that."

"Thank you."

The front door opened again. Robert strode out, his face hard. A police woman approached them from the pavement.

"Go," he said. "This is all your fault. All of you. Bloody politicians."

Jennifer resisted the urge to protest. Maybe he was right. Then she thought of Maggie this morning, the fire in her belly contrasting so sharply with Catherine's cool aloofness.

"You can't help anyway," he said. "You're not our MP anymore, unless you forgot."

She gripped her thumb inside her fist. He wasn't the first to feel this way about her, and he wouldn't be the last.

"My husband can help. Yusuf Hussain. I may not be your MP, but he's your local councillor."

"As if that means anything."

"Robert," Celeste hissed, eyeing her husband. She turned to Jennifer. "That would be good, thanks. When Lavonia comes home, she'll need all the help she can get."

Jennifer looked back at Yusuf. He'd been joined by Hassan, who was huddled into his side. He was getting taller; his head was level with Yusuf's shoulder now.

"I'll talk to him," she said. "If your daughter comes back, or if she's arrested, let us know."

Celeste nodded, her lips tight. She was trembling.

Jennifer put a hand on her arm. "I know how this feels," she said, remembering Samir, the way he looked when he'd appeared in her flat. "We'll sort this. I promise."

She squeezed Celeste's arm and turned back to her own house. Hassan was leaning into Yusuf, crying.

"He thought Samir was back," Yusuf whispered.

Jennifer felt herself crumple. She reached out to Hassan and folded her arms around his head. He shuffled forwards, twisted between her and Yusuf. The three of them stood there in silence, staring at the flashing lights all around them.

CHAPTER TWENTY-ONE

Rita spent the night walking to Worcester. Trudging rough fields, fighting her way through hedges in the rain. The sky began to lighten, grey mist blanketing the fields and a weak sun rising over her shoulder. At last the rain stopped. The crash had been south of Worcester so she needed to keep the sunrise on her right. She thought back to the Duke of Edinburgh award she'd done as a teenager, yomping through marshes and over moors to find their way back to the campsite. She'd been good at it. Lads from another group had teased her for being the only Asian girl there. But when she arrived back first with her friend Amanda, they were quietly admiring. Instead of finding her odd, they were suddenly offering her cheap cans of cider.

Ash's flat was south of the city centre. It didn't take her long to get there. She had to pause a few times, hide as an early riser passed in the morning chill. But she knew this district. The alleyways between the buildings, the alcoves where she could hide.

She settled herself in the shadows opposite the block where Ash lived, resisting the pull of sleep. His tiny one bedroom flat was at the back, overlooking a yard of wheelie bins and discarded shopping trolleys. The only way into the yard was through the flats or along a walkway between two of the shops. There'd be people opening up at this time of day.

Did she dare cross the street, press his button on the intercom? Would he be there? Might someone else have moved in? Someone who might recognise her and call the police.

She slumped back, deciding to wait. Ash was a late riser; he had a stubby Yorkshire terrier who woke him at nine am, wanting to be walked. It would be light by then but nobody would be around. Could she stay awake that long?

She stood and started marching on the spot. She blew on her hands and shook her head from side to side. She had to stay awake.

There was a noise from along the street. She turned to see a car approach. It was modern and black, with dark windows. Not the sort of car you often saw around here. It was clean too, right down to the hub caps. She retreated into the shadows, waiting for it to pass.

The car slowed then parked opposite her. Right on the double yellow lines. She felt panic grip her stomach. Was this car for her?

The driver's door opened. A woman got out and glanced up and down the street. She was tall and wore a brown suit. She reminded Rita of Jennifer. Blonde hair, willowy figure, clothes that were a size too large.

The woman rounded the car and was joined by a short black man in a leather jacket. He was clean shaven. His jeans looked like they'd been ironed.

She put her hand to her chest. They could only be one thing.

They strode up the path towards the flats, looking up at the darkened windows as they did so. Only one was illuminated, the obscured glass of a bathroom on the third floor.

Rita watched, frozen, as the woman bent to the intercom. The door opened and the pair disappeared inside.

Another car appeared and parked behind the first. It was similar, but dark blue. A man got out of the passenger door and hurried to the front door of the flats. Rita waited for him to follow the other pair in. He stopped instead, and turned to face the street. A sentry.

Should she run? She looked up and down the street, terrified that the whites of her eyes would be glowing in the shadows. If she moved out of her hiding place, he would spot her. A bedraggled woman, wearing a torn hoody and grubby jeans with dried blood on her face.

She drew back, feeling the brickwork behind her back. She kept her eyes on the door to the flats, occasionally glancing at the second car to see if someone else would get out. There was a shape in the driver's seat but no movement.

After what felt like hours, the door opened. The man walked out, the black man with the leather jacket. He looked around then said something to the sentry. He turned back to the doorway and was followed out by the woman.

She wasn't alone. In front of her, his head bowed under her palm, and his hands cuffed in front of him, was Ash.

Rita suppressed a cry.

They led him to the pavement and pushed him into the first car, a hand between his head and the doorframe. He didn't look in her direction. His face was red and his eyes were heavy. He looked like he was trying to keep control of himself, to suppress his anger.

The man got in the car and the woman walked round to the driver's door. She flashed a look across the street before getting in the car, making Rita's heart skip a beat.

Rita slid to the floor, her breath ragged as they drove away in silence.

CHAPTER TWENTY-TWO

"Morning love."

Jennifer looked up from her spot at the kitchen table and smiled as Yusuf kissed the top of her head.

"Am I a small child?" she asked, smiling up at him.

"What?"

He dragged a hand across his chin and yawned. He was still in his dressing gown.

"Kiss me properly," she replied.

"Of course."

He came back to stand over her. He leaned over and puckered his lips exaggeratedly.

She lifted herself up from the chair and kissed him. He slipped his arm around her shoulders, holding her in for a few seconds.

Eventually she fell back onto the chair and he continued to the kettle.

"You're in a good mood today," he said, looking out of the window.

"I feel determined. Justified."

He turned. "What about?"

"Seeing Catherine again. Telling her what happened last night. That was Trask's policy. She can't know it's still happening."

He sighed. "Jen, love."

"Don't."

He shook his head. "How do I tell you this?"

"You don't."

"You don't know what it is I need to tell you."

"I do."

"What then?"

"You're going to say that I shouldn't trust Catherine. That she's just as bad as Trask. That it doesn't matter that she's my friend."

"Hasn't it occurred to you that she might have been using you all along?"

She stood up and took a deep breath. The morning air was chilly.

"I'm not that bad a judge of character, Yusuf."

"That's not what I—"

"Look. I'm going to call Maggie at eight. She'll be up and about then. She's the only person who'll help me right now."

"Jen, we need to find that note. It's the only way you'll get her to listen."

"I know. But it has to be our last resort. What if that doesn't work? Then where will we be?"

They both turned. Their front doorbell was ringing, long and insistent.

"Who's that?" asked Jennifer.

"I was going to ask you."

"I thought it would be one of your constituents."

He frowned. "Could be, I suppose. Hell."

He pulled his dressing gown tight around him. He knotted the belt twice and started towards the door.

"No," said Jennifer. "Let me go. I'm dressed."

He nodded assent. She expected him to dash upstairs and throw some clothes on but instead he stayed in the kitchen where he could eavesdrop.

She turned the door handle, expecting to see maybe a lone man or woman, maybe a family. Probably Muslim, more than probably scared.

She took a deep breath. "What are you doing here?"

"I'm sorry. I know this is a bit irregular."

"Irregular? You'll bet it's irregular. Last time I saw you, you were filling me with sedatives and asking me questions."

"Not quite the last time."

Jennifer remembered her last moments in the centre, sitting in Yonda's office, being told she was allowed to go home.

"No," she said. "Not quite."

The woman looked up and down the street. A car pulled out of a driveway. A man walked past with a screaming toddler pulling at a set of reins. Further down, the Taylors' house was in darkness.

"Can I come in?"

"Sorry."

Jennifer pulled back to let her pass. They headed towards the kitchen. Their visitor glanced at the stairs, as if wondering who might be up there. She was pulling at her fingernails.

Yusuf was trying to look casual, as if he hadn't been listening in. When he saw their visitor, he looked puzzled. He didn't recognise her.

Jennifer looked between the two of them. How much

had Yusuf been told about her? Might Samir have confided in him?

She cleared her throat.

"Yusuf, meet Meena Ashgar. Samir's girlfriend."

CHAPTER TWENTY-THREE

Mark hated this. He'd had his job ripped away from him, been sent to another centre as an inmate, and still Yonda had him under her spell.

She'd given him a hundred pounds in cash and the address of a flat in Birmingham. He had no idea if it belonged to the government or it had been rented especially. When he'd arrived, the fridge was bare and the place smelt of feet and stale food. It looked clean enough though; the cupboards bare, wardrobes empty.

He looked out of the window towards the canal. This was no luxury canal-side apartment. A mile or so out of the city centre, it backed onto a stretch of water whose banks were littered with discarded cigarette packets and used syringes. A path two storeys below his window led into the city. He sure as hell wasn't using that.

Spaghetti Junction was half a mile in the opposite direction, the constant roar of traffic pounding in his ears when he tried to sleep. He'd been here two nights. He hadn't done what Yonda had told him to. Not yet.

"She trusts you," Yonda had said to him, in Steve's

office. Steve had watched, his ankle crossed on his knee and a quizzical expression on his face. Mark wondered how Yonda had inveigled her way into his office, even more how she'd found the authority to get Mark released.

He slumped onto the scuffed grey sofa bed that had afforded him so little sleep. It was stained, dim grey stains and smaller, rusty stains that he preferred not to investigate. Or to lie on.

Yonda was expecting a call. He should have called her last night, but had managed to get away with a garbled voicemail message when she hadn't answered her phone. He pictured her sitting at her vast desk in the centre, watching her phone. Waiting. Would Meena be there with her, waiting too?

He stood up. If this took longer than three days, she'd warned him, with a sidelong glance at Steve, he'd be back in the centre. The men's centre, not Burcot Park.

The front door had five locks. He unbolted each of them then slipped into the dark corridor, looking left and right for signs of other occupants. Behind a door he heard a woman shouting. *Eat your effing breakfast, Ollie, or I'll chuck it in the bin*. Ollie. He had a moment of panic as he imagined his own five-year-old son in there, refusing to eat his eggs again.

He crept past the woman's door and headed for the bare concrete stairs. It was raining.

Mark pulled up the collar of his suit jacket, the suit he'd been wearing when Yonda had brought two police officers to his office, and had him taken away. He wished he'd thought to grab a coat as he passed the hook on the back of his door. He wished he'd thought to ask Yonda what was going on, why they were taking him. He wished a lot of things.

At the bottom of the stairs, two teenagers huddled close

together, both clad in hoodies and low-slung jeans that exposed their backs. They must be freezing. One of them nodded at him and the other one leaned back, inhaling deeply as he looked up at the sky. He exhaled a cloud of sweet-smelling smoke. He looked down and passed a spliff to his mate.

"Want some?"

Mark realised the boy was talking to him.

"Er—no. No, thanks."

Maybe Vee had been right, taking their son Olivier abroad. Maybe this wasn't a place to raise a child. He'd be old enough to start school now, somewhere in Canada. Exactly where, he had no idea.

Would helping Yonda bring him any closer to finding his son? Could he make a bargain with her?

He took a deep breath. If he didn't do this, someone else would. He could see the logic behind it. It wasn't just paranoia on Yonda's part.

He turned north, towards the motorway, and started walking.

CHAPTER TWENTY-FOUR

"Samir doesn't have a girlfriend."

"That's what I said," replied Jennifer. "When Edward told me."

"Edward?" said Yusuf. "Hang on minute. It's *her*?"

Meena stood quietly by the kitchen door, watching this exchange. She shrank back as Yusuf raised his voice. He turned towards her, his eyes blazing.

"You're the reason our son was taken away!"

She blushed. "I'm sorry. I never intended—"

He advanced on her. "I don't care what you intended. If Samir hadn't met you, he'd still be here with us today."

"I know." She lowered her head, not making eye contact. "I never meant for him to become involved."

"But he didn't. He wasn't involved. All they had on him was this relationship with you. That photo."

Jennifer spotted Meena frowning. She didn't know about the photo.

She raised her head. "I know you don't want to hear this. But he did get involved." She sniffed. "I'm so sorry."

118

Yusuf raised his hand and held it still, glaring at her. His cheeks were inflamed and he was shaking. Then he loosened and let his arm drop.

"I'm sorry," he said. "You're just a girl."

She nodded.

Jennifer stepped forwards. "How did you get here?"

"I've got a week's leave. I thought I owed it to you to—"

"Too right you do," muttered Yusuf. Jennifer put a hand on his arm. He turned to her, his lips tight.

"How did she find us?"

Jennifer looked at Meena.

"Your file, at the centre," the younger woman replied.

Jennifer felt hollow, thinking about the centre. She'd been trying to put it behind her, even as she was working to get it closed down.

"Have you come to take me back?" she asked.

"What? No."

"Then why are you here?" asked Yusuf.

He backed towards the table, not taking his eyes off Meena. When he stumbled into a chair he let it take his weight, almost falling to the floor as he sat.

"Go easy on her love," Jennifer said. "She's as much a victim of all this as Samir."

"She worked at the centre. She's part of the system."

"We've all been part of the system in one way or another."

He said nothing, but eyed Meena, who shrank under his gaze.

"I didn't believe her at first, either," Jennifer said. "But I think she loved Samir." She looked at Meena. "Maybe still does."

Meena nodded, her cheeks darkening.

"Damn odd way she's got of showing it," said Yusuf. "Getting him involved with a terrorist group."

"It wasn't as simple as that," said Meena. "No one forced him. And it wasn't a terrorist group. It wasn't even an Islamist group. We just wanted to stop the attacks on Muslims. We wanted to stand up for ourselves, since the state wasn't doing it for us. And the mosques—well, the moderate ones were just too weak. Too compliant."

"You're talking about my mosque," Yusuf snapped.

"Sorry. Nothing personal. Like I said, I'm really sorry that Samir got caught up in it all. Really I am."

He shook his head and turned away from her, wiping his eye. Jennifer squeezed his arm but he shook her off.

She turned to Meena. "Tell me how you got here again."

A shrug. "The train. Probably the same one as you."

"They let you have a week off? Did they know you were coming here?" She hesitated. "Did they put you up to it?"

Meena took a step forward. Yusuf's eyes narrowed and she stepped back again. "No one from the centre knows I'm here."

"Not even the women?"

"I couldn't risk telling them."

"No."

Jennifer looked past Meena towards the stairs. Hassan never woke until he was forcibly dragged out of bed, but she didn't want him suddenly appearing.

"Yusuf, do you mind checking on Hassan?" she said.

He looked at her. "Why me?"

"I don't want him to find Meena here. Not like this. Please."

He stood and put a weary hand on her arm. Meena shuffled to one side to let him pass, lowering her head again.

"Sit with me," said Jennifer. "Tell me how they are."

Meena looked towards Yusuf, who was dragging his feet up the stairs. When he was out of sight, she sat next to Jennifer.

"They're not good," she said.

"How d'you mean?"

"Things have got stricter. The orderlies are sitting in on group sessions."

"What's that got to do with anything?"

"If the women don't cooperate, if they get out of line, the counsellors are expected to let the orderlies intervene."

"Intervene?"

"Physically."

"Shit."

Jennifer thought of Maryam, Paula and Bel, left behind. Bel would never survive a regime like Meena was describing. She'd been barely aware of her surroundings most of the time, and could hardly string a sentence together, let alone recite the oath or go through the six steps. Maryam and Paula would do their best, but they were only human. Even Sally, angry, scapegoating Sally, didn't deserve a beating.

"What about Mark?" she asked. "Dr Clarke? Is he going along with it?" She thought of the way Mark had treated her, the promises he had made to help her get out. It contrasted so harshly with the way he'd treated Rita, humiliating her in group and leaving her to the mercy of the orderlies.

"Didn't you know?"

"Know what?"

"Mark's gone. He was arrested."

"Arrested?"

"Just before you left."

"Why?"

A shrug. "No idea."

Did Meena know what Mark had done? He'd attempted to game the system, to load the syringe with something benign and not the truth drug. To help Jennifer lie her way through Celebration. Maybe he'd done it for other women too.

"Who's Mark?'

She jumped. Yusuf was standing in the doorway. Hassan was next to him. He shrank back when he saw Meena.

Meena gasped. Her face softened. "Is this Hassan?"

Yusuf put a hand on Hassan's shoulder. "How do you know his name?"

"Samir told me." She stood up. "And there was me thinking you were just a little brother. You're a young man."

Yusuf fronted and Hassan smiled. "I'm twelve," he said.

"Pleased to meet you, Hassan," said Meena. "I'm Meena. I'm—"

"I said, who's Mark?" interrupted Yusuf.

"Dr Clarke. My counsellor," said Jennifer. "The one who tried to help me." She thought of the way Mark had panicked at Rita's outburst in group, his weary face bent to the intercom. He'd let the orderlies drag her away.

She turned to Meena.

"It's good to see you," she said. "But I don't think you should stay here. The cameras..."

Meena nodded. Her eyes were an orangey-brown colour, with long lashes. Jennifer could understand what Samir had seen in her.

"But I haven't told you what I came here for," she said.

Yusuf sighed and muttered in Hassan's ear. He frowned then left the room.

122

"What's that?" Yusuf asked, his voice weary.

Meena looked at him then at Jennifer. She let her tongue poke out for a moment, her upper teeth resting on it.

"I've found Samir," she said.

CHAPTER TWENTY-FIVE

Rita's entire body hurt. Her feet were covered in weeping blisters, her legs threatened to give way at any moment, and her head felt like it was full of angry wasps.

But still she kept walking. The prospect of stopping terrified her. Fear of the people she might meet. Of being picked up by the police. She hadn't seen a newspaper or TV since her escape, but was sure her photo would be everywhere, telling the world there was a dangerous, subversive woman on the run.

She wondered what had happened to Sonia. Had she survived the crash? Would she be under suspicion herself? Could she end up in a British Values Centre because she'd helped Rita?

What had happened to this country, that people were called dissidents because they showed some human decency?

She'd followed a sign to Birmingham that she'd found when roaming Worcester in despair. It took her along twenty miles of trunk road. Just one village to get through and a small town with its bypass. She kept to the bypass, relying on the fact that it would avoid built-up areas and the possibility of discovery. But the village was more challenging. She to skirted it as well as she could, finding a quiet lane with just a few houses at the edge. The lane continued for a mile or so, veering away from the main road and making her worry that she'd lose her way.

At last she reached a junction with a road heading back the right way, and collapsed with exhaustion and relief. After what could have been minutes or hours, she found herself lying on the grass verge, there for anyone to see.

Two days ago she'd started at a steady walk. Now it was a desperate stumbling ahead, focused only on the next step and then the next until she reached the outskirts of Birmingham.

She got to her house late afternoon, scuttling along familiar pathways and keeping out of sight of the roads. She knew these streets well, the benefit of walking everywhere, and now it kept her safe.

As dusk fell she took shelter in an unused alleyway opposite her house and watched it. There was a spare key under a plant pot at the end of the back garden, which she could access via an alleyway that ran behind the houses. But the authorities would be looking for her.

She looked up and down the street, glad of the hoody to cover her head. It was a warm evening for February. The occasional couple walked past on their way to the pub on the next street. A small group of teenagers loitered on the corner at the far end. But there was something new; a camera, high on the lamp post opposite her house. It was pointed towards her bedroom window.

She told herself it had been put there to watch the street as a whole, maybe focusing on the pub. But there was no doubting what it was watching now.

She yawned and dragged herself up to standing. She couldn't face another night walking, but had nowhere nearby to go. All her friends were teachers at the school. She didn't want to risk their safety.

It was getting dark now. She was tired. She looked like a vagrant, someone the police might pay attention to.

She'd cried as she walked the first night, the tears starting after Ash had been taken away, not stopping for almost six hours. She'd made the wrong decision by escaping, she knew that now. She'd die out here. If not attacked by one of the shadowy figures she'd seen slipping past on the late-night streets, then she'd starve. Prison at least meant food, and the chance of eventual release.

She coughed and bent over to spit out some phlegm. Her chest had been hurting for the last few hours. Her breath had become heavy. She hoped it was just a cold.

She trudged towards the main road, wondering if she should just lie down under a hedge and let the fates take her. It would be easier.

Then she saw the road sign. She bit her lip. An idea. That was it. She knew where she would get help. If she could reach it.

Determination giving her renewed energy, she started walking again, ignoring the light rain that darkened the shoulders of her hoody.

CHAPTER TWENTY-SIX

Yusuf stepped forward and put out a hand, as if he wanted to shake Meena's shoulder, drag the words out of her. Jennifer could hear his breathing; shallow, like hers.

"You found him? You've seen him?" he said, his voice strangled. Jennifer felt something shift inside her, like a tin full of ball bearings turning over in her stomach.

Meena shook her head. "I haven't seen him. But I know where he is."

Jennifer looked up at Yusuf to see her own anxiety mirrored in his face.

"Where?" she breathed.

Meena took a breath. "A detention centre. New one, called Woodhurst. It's the other side of Banbury."

Blood whooshed in Jennifer's ears. Banbury was between here and Burcot Park. She'd passed through it on her way home. Could the train have passed it?

"But that's just an hour away," said Yusuf. "All this time, and he's been so close."

There was a moment's silence. Hassan appeared in the doorway again. "What's that about Samir?"

"I told you to go upstairs," said Yusuf.

"I did."

"I didn't tell you to listen in."

"Sorry. But what is it about Samir? Has she found him?"

Jennifer sighed. "Come here."

Hassan looked at Yusuf, who moved to the table and sat at one end. He looked worried, as if expecting to be in trouble. He said nothing.

Jennifer smiled at him. "Did Samir tell you he had a girlfriend?"

Hassan's eyes widened but he didn't answer.

"You're not in trouble, sweetie."

He gave her a look.

"Promise," she said.

Yusuf was staring at Meena, his brow creased. Had Samir confided in him at all?

Jennifer looked back at Hassan. "This is Meena. She was Samir's girlfriend. They arrested her too, and I met her while I was in the centre."

"What's she doing here?"

"She says she knows where Samir is."

Hassan looked at Meena. "Bring him back, then."

Meena put her hand on the table and held it a few inches from Hassan's. "That's what I want to do. But it isn't all that easy."

"Why not? If you're here, why isn't he?"

"I know it seems odd that I—"

Hassan stood up. "I don't believe you."

"Hassan—" said Jennifer.

"No. If they were both arrested, and she's here and he isn't, then why? It makes no sense, Mum."

"Please. Hear me out," said Meena.

Jennifer looked at her. Hassan was right; her story didn't make sense. "How do we know you weren't sent here by the authorities?"

Meena paled. "I thought you believed me."

Yusuf sat down. "Just tell us how this helps, Meena. Can you help us get him back, or not?"

"I want to, I really do." She looked between them. "I loved your son. Still do. He was worried you'd be angry that he was going out with an older girl. He didn't want to tell you."

"I can't blame him," said Yusuf.

"Please. I'm a Muslim, like you. I'm not one of them. I want to help." She stood up. "But if you want me to leave, I understand."

Jennifer thought of the Muslim women she'd encountered since her arrest: Maryam, robbed of her headscarf, Bel, hardly aware of where she was. Meena, fast-tracked to passing the program and rewarded with a counsellor's job. Then the woman at New Street Station, spat at for nothing more than wearing a hijab.

No one would have spat on that woman, before. How could she possibly hope for mercy for her son, in these conditions?

She motioned for Meena to sit and the younger woman slid into her chair, looking uncomfortable.

"I'm sorry," she whispered.

"Don't be."

Meena shrugged and ran her finger around the edge of her hijab, a tic that Jennifer remembered from the centre.

Yusuf looked at Hassan. "I want her to tell us what she knows. We'll tell you later, once we've gone through it here. Can you wait upstairs please?"

"I want to stay."

"I know, but this isn't suitable for you. I think it's best if you—"

Hassan looked up. "No. Don't leave me out of things. Not anymore."

"Alright," said Jennifer. "You can stay. Meena, tell us what you know about Samir. Be careful of what you say, please."

Meena ran her finger around her hijab again. "He's been there since January. He was in a normal prison for a few weeks and then he was transferred there."

"What kind of place is it?" asked Jennifer. "What's the regime like?"

"If you mean how do they treat the people there, I think it's not too bad, generally. But Samir is being held in a separate wing."

"Separate? Why?" Yusuf placed a fist on the table.

"The main building is for illegal immigrants, and refugees. His wing is for people arrested under the anti-terror laws."

Jennifer had visited those places when she'd been a minister. They were similar to open prisons; detainees were allowed to move around freely and weren't locked into their rooms. The decor was more homely than in the prison where she'd been held, even than in the British Values Centre. People were allowed to personalise their space, to create a vestige of home. But open prisons allowed low-risk prisoners to go out on day release, to take jobs in preparation for life after release. These detention centres didn't. Men, women and children were incarcerated in them twenty-four hours a day, sometimes for years. All they'd done wrong was travel without papers, or trust people-smugglers who'd taken everything from them.

She hadn't seen any separate wings, back then.

"The separate wing," she said, watching Hassan's face. She hated him having to listen to this, but understood his need to be included. "What kind of people will he be with?"

Meena gave her a concerned smile. "I don't know. I'm sorry. But I imagine it's low-level offenders, like Samir. The higher risk ones are deported straight after arrest now."

Jennifer already knew that; she'd challenged the Trask government on it, in the House. But the specifics hadn't been in the legislation, so it had been difficult to scrutinise what was going on, to check that the rules were being applied fairly.

"How do you know all this?" she asked. "Did Samir make contact with you?"

"He can't. I—" she glanced at Hassan. "I broke into Yonda's computer. Her laptop. She had access to prisoner records, and not just for the centre."

Jennifer grinned. "You hacked into her laptop? Why?"

"I wasn't looking for Samir. I had no idea she'd have access to that. I wanted to know what had happened to Mark. Dr Clarke. And Rita."

Yusuf's head shot up. "Jennifer's talked about her. Who is she? What did she do?"

"She was a teacher. Didn't do the oath with her class. But that's not the point."

"What is?"

"She disappeared. She had two Celebrations then I never saw her again. I was worried. And Mark suddenly left, the day of Jennifer's Celebration. No announcement, nothing. Yonda wouldn't tell me where he was."

"Hang on," said Yusuf. "Who's this Yonda person?"

Meena nodded. "Sorry. Yonda Hughes. Governor of the centre."

Jennifer allowed herself a smile. "The Canary."

"Why? Did she sing?"

Jennifer snorted. She noticed Meena smiling. "No. She dressed like one. Plumage. You couldn't miss her. And she had these dogs—"

"Dogs? In a prison? Guard dogs?"

"No. Sorry. This isn't relevant."

She turned to Meena. Hassan was upright now, and listening intently. Yusuf looked preoccupied.

"So where are they?" she asked. "Rita and Mark?"

"Rita was transferred to a prison, as far as I can tell. Mark's in another centre."

"Why?"

A shrug. "No idea. There was a hint that he'd had a relationship with one of the patients."

Jennifer blushed. "A relationship?"

"A while ago. Maybe he did it again."

"What has all this got to do with Samir?" asked Yusuf.

"Sorry," Jennifer said. "You're right."

She hoped that Yonda hadn't jumped to the wrong conclusions. She and Mark had hidden amongst the trees, away from the house. And he'd pulled her into that storage room, the day before her Celebration. He'd said he could help her cheat. It might have looked different to an observer.

She leaned back and sighed. She imagined Samir in the high-risk wing of a detention centre. At sixteen he would be treated as an adult by the system.

"What else did you find out about Samir?"

Meena looked from her to Hassan. "It's not good."

Yusuf's face darkened. "Tell us."

"He's going to be deported. On April the eighteenth."

"What? That's just – what – five weeks, six weeks away!" Yusuf leaned forward, his eyes drilling into Meena's face. She shrank back. *Leave her alone*, thought Jennifer. *It's not her fault.*

Hassan wiped his face. Jennifer wanted to wrap her arms around him. "You OK, sweetie?"

He nodded. His lip was trembling. "Are they going to take him?"

"No," said Jennifer. "We won't let them." She put a hand over his. It stiffened but he didn't pull it away. "Do you trust me?"

He looked up at her. "S'pose."

"Good. You should. We're going to stop this, me and your dad. They won't take him anywhere."

She looked at Meena. "D'you think you can get into her laptop again?"

"No."

"Why not?"

Meena sniffed in a breath. "Because I was caught. If I go back there, it'll be as a patient again."

"What?"

Meena looked back at Jennifer. She looked like she might cry. "I'm sorry. I couldn't think of anywhere else to go. They'd never think of looking for me here."

"Don't be so sure," said Yusuf.

"Go easy on her, love," said Jennifer.

"Why? If Samir hadn't met her, we'd never be in this mess. You only have her word that she didn't deliberately recruit him. Didn't use him." He turned to Meena. "How old are you?"

"Nineteen."

"Three years older than our son."

"Closer to two."

"Semantics. He was sixteen. What were you thinking?"

"I loved him. I still do."

"You're going to tell me next that he loved you back."

Meena nodded.

Yusuf barked out a laugh. "How can a sixteen-year-old fall in love? You intrigued him. The older woman. Bolstered his ego. That's not love."

"You were twenty-nine and I was twenty when we met," said Jennifer. "That was love."

"Twenty isn't sixteen."

"I'm sorry," said Meena. "I really am."

Jennifer moved towards Meena. She felt protective, a feeling at odds with the relationship they'd had at the centre. But Meena had made it easier for her during Celebration. If she'd had another counsellor, she might not be here now.

"Meena's the reason I'm here."

"I don't get you."

"The Celebration ceremony. The truth drug."

"You told me. You worked it out. Found words that would convince them, without lying."

"Yes. But it was Meena who was taking me through it. She said she'd go easy on me. Yonda spotted it. I don't think I'd have managed it without her."

"That doesn't make up for—"

"She's trying to do the right thing, love. She's told us she's sorry about Samir." She paused to look at Meena, her eyes questioning. "I think she wants to get him out as much as we do."

Meena nodded. Yusuf's eyes narrowed.

"If you think they're going to just pick things up again—"

"I don't expect anything, Mr Hussain," said Meena. "I

just want Samir to be released. I want to stop him being deported."

"And how do you intend to do that? You can't hack into any more computers now."

Meena deflated. "You're right. I have no idea. But I hoped you might be able to help."

Jennifer nodded. "We can. There are processes. Things we can do. When I was an MP I got lots of deportations delayed. Sometimes the extra time gave us a chance to track down the documentation, stop it altogether."

"This is different," said Yusuf.

"I know that. But I'm going to talk to my successor. And if that doesn't work I'll go back to Catherine."

Yusuf snorted. "Fat lot of good that'll do."

"She didn't want him to be deported. That's why she helped me. Maybe she will again."

"You haven't learned anything from your meeting with her?"

"Wait," interrupted Meena. "Are we talking about Catherine Moore? The Prime Minister?"

"Yes," replied Jennifer.

"You can get to her?"

"She's a friend of mine."

"Used to be," said Yusuf. Jennifer gave him a look.

"And you think she'll help you?" said Meena.

"No," said Yusuf.

"Yes," corrected Jennifer. "We have leverage."

"Which we can't find," said Yusuf.

Jennifer was sick of going over this conversation. Her friendship with Catherine had been separate from her family life. Yusuf had never even met her. But now they had to collide, if she was to bring her family back together.

A tear landed on the table in front of Hassan. Yusuf

went to stand behind him. He put his hands on Hassan's shoulders; they were shaking.

"I think it's time you left," he said to Meena.

"No," said Jennifer.

Yusuf stood up and pulled Hassan with him. They crossed to the door. Jennifer saw that Hassan's pyjamas were too small, the legs flapping around his ankles.

"Yes," said Yusuf. "Time for Meena to leave. Hassan, go in the living room. I'll be right with you."

Hassan shuffled away.

"I've already said no," Jennifer replied.

"They'll be looking for her. They'll link her to you. Samir, the centre. They're not stupid."

"It doesn't matter."

Meena stood up. "It's alright. I can—"

Jennifer held out a hand. "No. She's got nowhere else to go. If she leaves here, if she uses public transport, she'll be caught on camera. She'll be arrested. And who knows what they'll do to her? I don't imagine you get two tries at the programme."

"What d'you mean?"

"She went through the program. Just like me. Passed. They gave her a job."

"You passed?" said Yusuf, looking at Meena. "How? You were a terrorist."

"No. I was a member of an organisation that sympathised with the terrorists. I was naive. I realise I was wrong now."

"So that hasn't changed."

"No."

"What made you snoop around your boss's computer then?"

"Just because I'm not an extremist, doesn't mean I think the system is perfect."

"You're not wrong there." Yusuf's face softened. "OK. You can stay here for today. But I want you to tell us everything you know. Samir, the detention centre, the values centre. Everything. I want to understand."

"Of course," said Meena, throwing Jennifer a shy smile.

CHAPTER TWENTY-SEVEN

WORRIED WHAT MIGHT HAPPEN TO MEENA IF SHE tried to go home or to the centre, Jennifer persuaded Yusuf to let her stay longer. If they were going to get Samir back, they'd need her help. She knew things about him they didn't. And she knew about the system.

As well as all that, she was young, and scared, and Samir loved her. If she was to be believed. Jennifer could only hope that he'd be pleased to see her.

Samir's was a deportation case now, and Jennifer knew what that meant. She'd helped plenty of families with sons or fathers at risk of deportation. Each time, she'd contact the immigration minister and request a delay while the lawyers did their work. But cases like this had been getting less straightforward. She had to hope it was still possible to delay deportation for long enough to find grounds for appeal.

She knew that Samir had slim grounds. He'd been arrested under the new anti-terror laws and had been in a detention centre for four months. But she had to try.

Four days had passed and it was Friday. The local MP, her replacement, would be in the constituency, holding advice surgeries or attending meetings. She'd checked his website and knew he had a surgery at ten. Chances were he'd go to the office first. She had no intention of seeking his help in such a public place as the advice surgery, but the office was her territory. Her old team might even be working there still.

Yusuf was downstairs arguing with Hassan about homework. She stood in front of the full-length mirror in their bedroom, assessing herself in one of her old suits. It was loose but tailored and it made her look professional. Rational. A former MP, and not the desperate mother of a boy about to be separated from his family for ever.

Meena was still in Samir's room; she'd taken to hiding in there, feeling unsure of her place in this family. Jennifer imagined her coming home with Samir, being introduced properly. What would they have made of her? Would they have suspected she was an extremist? Or would they have seen the same desperation and youthful zeal that Samir had had?

Jennifer went downstairs, picking up her feet in an effort to energise herself. She didn't like going grovelling to her successor. He was only twenty-nine and had won the by-election with a majority of just 225 votes, compared to the quadruple figures she'd enjoyed in her three terms. She couldn't be sure if the drop in the Labour vote had been because people preferred to vote for her, or because they were angry with her.

Yusuf was waving a piece of paper at Hassan. "You can't just roll up to school and tell them you didn't have time to do it."

"I've been busy."

"With what? Playing video games? Watching YouTube?"

Hassan shrugged.

Jennifer stepped into the room. "What's up?"

Yusuf was breathing heavily, working hard to keep control of his exasperation. "Hassan's got English homework due this morning. He only just realised, or so he told me."

"Have you looked at the website?"

"Of course I have."

"Does that say when it was set?"

Yusuf was still glaring at Hassan. "Two weeks ago."

Hassan's eyes were on the floor. "Sorry. Can you write me a note?"

"What for?"

"Dunno. Tell them we've been busy. Mum coming back. Samir."

"Hassan, this homework was set before Mum came back."

"I've been stressed."

Yusuf dragged his fingernails through his beard. "You've had two weeks to do this. That's plenty of time."

There was a pause as Yusuf considered what to say next. He'd been dealing with all this in her absence. She couldn't butt in now.

He turned to her. "You look smart."

"Going to see Tom Hamilton. Remember?"

"Oh. That."

"Who's Tom Hamilton?" asked Hassan.

"Don't change the subject," Yusuf snapped. "Get ready for school."

"But my letter—"

"Uh-uh. You can get a detention again."

"But Dad—"

"No. You have to learn that your actions have consequences."

"Like Samir?"

"Don't you dare compare yourself to Samir."

Hassan bowed his head. "Sorry."

Jennifer stared at Hassan, her mind jumbled. He'd been such a cheerful little boy. And she'd never seen Yusuf this angry with him.

Hassan brushed past her, muttering under his breath.

"Hassan," she warned. "No swearing."

"I didn't."

"I heard you."

"I said—"

"Just don't do it again, alright?"

He shrugged. "Alright. Sorry."

She smiled and gave his hair a tousle. He pulled back with a grimace. "Good," she said.

He ran towards the stairs. She went to join Yusuf.

"Sorry about that."

"Oh, don't worry. Nothing I'm not used to. He's nearly a teenager now, and he's making sure I know it."

"We."

"Huh? Oh yeah, sorry. We. Come here."

She stepped into his arms. He was wearing a t-shirt she'd first seen on him maybe thirteen years ago, and a pair of faded jeans. He smelt of washing powder mixed with aftershave. She'd missed that smell.

She hugged him tighter for a moment then pulled back, anxious not to crumple her suit.

"So," he asked. "What's the plan?"

"I'm going to go to his office. Try and get him alone. He'll help me, I'm sure he will."

"I hope you're right."

"You don't sound convinced."

"Things have changed, Jen. They hate us. Muslims. After the New Street bomb it was impossible to go out in public without being shouted at, or worse."

She leaned into him. "Was it really that bad?"

He nodded, his chin jabbing into the top of her head. "Worse. Hassan was spat on at the bus stop. The school's become split along racial lines; white kids hanging out with each other, and Muslim kids the same. Black and other Asian kids stuck in the middle."

"I didn't realise it was that bad."

"You saw that woman at the station, didn't you?"

She sighed.

"Well, that's just the tip of the iceberg," Yusuf said.

She'd been hiding herself away in the days since she'd got back. Partly it was the need to reconnect with her family, to work her way back into their lives. But she knew she was scared, too. She didn't want to be recognised.

Today that would change. She couldn't help Samir, hiding away like this.

She pulled back. "It's going to get better, I know it is."

"Why? What makes you think that?"

"We'll make it better. Somehow."

She gave him a dry kiss on the cheek and turned for the front door. She looked up the stairs. As an MP, she'd frequently snuck out early to catch the London train, creeping around while everyone else slept and not being able to wish them goodbye. That had to change.

She took the stairs two at a time and pushed Hassan's door open. His room was a mess; dirty school uniform mixed with clean on the floor, sheets of paper scattered on his desk, dirty plates littering the surfaces.

She resisted the urge to tell him to tidy up. "Bye, love. See you later."

He was rooting through his schoolbag. "Bye." He didn't look up.

She took a shaky breath and headed downstairs. This was going to take time. Her family was messed up enough as it was. Would bringing Samir back help them, or throw yet more chaos into the mix?

CHAPTER TWENTY-EIGHT

Rita spent the night tucked into the hollow beneath a railway bridge. It was littered with discarded beer cans, used syringes and small mounds of human waste. She arranged her body so as not to touch any of it, but the tension kept her awake for most of the night.

Waking up was an unsettling experience. At first she thought she was back in prison, then at the centre, in that bathroom. She imagined Tim the orderly waiting outside, ready to come in and give her a beating.

After patting her body down and rubbing her sore eyes, she realised she wasn't in either of those places. She was outdoors. For a cool moment she felt relief, a nanosecond of hope. Followed by realisation, dread and despair.

It was still dark. She could hear animals scuttling in the bushes behind her, and the low sound of men's voices.

She didn't hang around to find out whose voices; instead, she darted into the trees ahead of her, running in zigzags until the park spat her out onto a busy street.

She looped round to pick a route through wasteland;

industrial estates and scrubby grassland. In front of her was water, and a canal towpath.

The path ran below the motorway, the lights of Spaghetti Junction beckoning. Jennifer had mentioned Spaghetti Junction, the fact that she could see it from her house.

Could she find that house?

She came to a junction between two canals. There was an area of concrete, a barren place speckled with graffiti. The motorway roared above her head. She called out, her voice echoing in the empty space.

It was getting dark. She spotted a structure at the far end of the space, an abandoned Portacabin. Could she get in? Did she dare sleep there? It would be a local gathering place, somewhere the homeless knew about.

But she was exhausted. If she didn't stop soon, she would collapse where she stood.

She edged towards the Portacabin. For now, the area was deserted. Could she barricade herself inside, stay safe until dark?

She caught movement from the corner of her eye. She stopped walking, her heart thumping.

She looked sideways, slowly, her senses stretched. There was a depression in the metal fence fifty yards away, a shape wedged in it. She squinted, trying to distinguish the shape from its surroundings. It was a sleeping bag, or rather a pile of them, draped over a human form. The shape shifted again, the owner of the sleeping bags getting comfortable maybe. Or maybe moving to get a better view of her.

She looked at the Portacabin, closer now. Could she run?

Then she heard barking. A dog emerged from under the

sleeping bags, yapping at her. Small and grubby, a terrier of some sort. In normal circumstances, the kind of dog she'd stop to pet.

The dog advanced, baring its teeth, then came to an abrupt stop. It was on a lead. She let herself breathe again, ignoring her desperate need to find a toilet.

The person under the sleeping bags sat up, rubbing their eyes. They wore a purple woolly hat and their face was streaked with dirt, impossible to tell the age or gender.

"Who's that?" a voice snapped. Female, thought Rita. Not young.

"Sorry. Just passing."

"Yeah. Bugger off. This is my patch."

Rita swallowed and said nothing. She eyed the Porta-cabin, wishing she had the nerve to head for it and shut herself in. But even if she got inside she'd be unable to rest.

She scanned the area beyond the structure; it was littered with rubble, concrete blocks and twisted metal. It was like a manmade boulder field.

"Fuck off!" The woman shifted again, shrugging off the sleeping bag. She didn't look as if she could move fast. But she might not be alone.

Rita sped towards the concrete boulders, blood pulsing in her head. She felt her trousers go wet. She started to cry, hot tears flowing into her mouth. Her nose was running and she could barely see.

Crying with pain and frustration, she threw herself behind the largest of the blocks. It loomed above her, its presence at once reassuring and forbidding. Above its bulk, the motorway roared on.

She closed her eyes, wondering if she'd ever get up.

CHAPTER TWENTY-NINE

Tom Hamilton had continued using Jennifer's old office. Situated at one end of a row of shops, it was typical of Labour Party offices; shabby, in need of a few coats of paint and a spring clean. Piles of leaflets spilled off tables and into every spare corner.

She sat in the front office, watching his team at work. Penny, her old agent, was still working for him, but was nowhere to be seen. Two other women sat at desks, answering calls, drafting letters and trying their best to fit everything an MP was required to do into his diary.

She knew one of them: Paula, a Polish woman in her late twenties, who'd been working here for just over a year now. Her companion was new. Jennifer wondered what had happened to Dan, the middle-aged party stalwart who'd spent most of the last thirty years working out of this office and had seen at least four MPs come and go. She hoped he wasn't unwell; he was close to seventy, well past the age at which any sensible person should have retired. But political offices had never been staffed by people who were entirely sensible.

She perched on the edge of a flimsy chair near the door, watching them work. Wondering if she could interrupt. They'd both looked up as she'd entered. Paula had smiled in recognition and stood up immediately, approaching Jennifer and welcoming her with a firm handshake followed by a hug. Her colleague had paled and returned to her keyboard.

Paula was in the kitchen at the back of the building, making her a cup of tea. She pictured the cramped kitchen overlooking a dingy yard that had used to house Dan's bike every day. The kettle was old and unreliable and the tea and coffee were kept in tins that had probably been there since the 1980s. The same rust marks would be there on the sink, impossible to scrub off, part of the fabric of the building now.

Paula reappeared with the cup of tea, in a mug that Jennifer remembered from her own tenure. *If the Tories had a soul, they'd sell it*, it said.

"He won't be long," Paula said. "He's got a packed morning – you know how it is – but he said he'd squeeze you in before his surgery."

"Thanks." Jennifer blew on the tea then sipped it. It was strong, made with UHT milk. So they still didn't have a working fridge.

Paula hovered for a moment, glancing between Jennifer and her desk. Jennifer put her hand to her chest, wishing she'd waited before swallowing the scalding tea. "How have you been?" she asked. "Where's Dan?"

A smile. "He retired."

"No."

"Yes." Paula's blue eyes danced. She had two small boys at home, both at the nursery Jennifer's sons had attended. Their father had left when she was pregnant with the youngest, fed up with life in England. But Paula had never been the sort of person to let an anti-immigrant government thwart her ambition. She wanted her boys to go to good schools, to get degrees one day. And in the current system, they had the advantage of being white. Their lack of an accent helped, too; unlike their mother, they were easily taken for English.

"So what's he doing with himself? Volunteering, I bet. Pounding the pavements."

"That's the thing. He's not. He's gone off round Europe on a long-distance bike tour."

Jennifer laughed. She relaxed in her seat and sipped the tea again. It felt good to see a familiar face, to indulge in gossip. Discussing other women's Celebrations didn't count.

"Good for him," she said.

"You've got a new colleague," she said, glancing at the woman who was peering intently into her computer screen as if it held the answer to life itself.

Paula followed Jennifer's gaze and nodded. "Kelly. Nice girl, good worker."

"I don't remember her."

"No. She wasn't a party member. Not until Tom recruited her."

"OK."

"Don't judge. She's joined now."

Jennifer threw her hands up. "Hey, I'm not saying anything. The Labour Party can't be the only source of talent, after all."

"Far from it."

Jennifer looked at Paula, who had adopted a wistful look. "How is the local party? How's Penny?"

Paula's face clouded. "Not brilliant. She took what happened with you hard. Felt responsible."

"It wasn't her fault—"

"Not like that. She helped you get elected. There were people who said she shouldn't have. Should have known what you were like."

"What I was *like*?"

Paula blushed. "Sorry. But there was a lot of anger. It wasn't nice. I stood up for you, but it lost me a few friends."

"That's ridiculous."

A shrug. "I agree. But people want someone to blame. And it was easy to blame you, after—"

"After what?"

"Nothing."

"Please. After what?'

Paula drew breath. "John Hunter said some things that weren't good. Distanced himself from you."

Jennifer felt her chest grow heavy. "John? Are you sure?"

Paula turned to her. "Hasn't Yusuf talked to you about it?"

Jennifer shook her head.

They felt the air stir as a door slammed behind Paula. She turned. Tom Hamilton strode towards them, a bulging leather messenger bag slung over his shoulder, a plastic bag full of paperwork clutched to his chest as if it were a baby.

Paula squeezed Jennifer's arm then stood up, heading back to her desk.

Tom surveyed the room. "Hi everyone."

Paula and her colleague both looked up and smiled at their boss. Paula's smile didn't stray to her eyes. "Morning," they replied.

"Lovely day," said Tom. Jennifer looked out of the window; it was cloudy, a dark sky heading their way, promising rain. The women said nothing.

"Jennifer," said Tom, stopping at her chair. "I see the girls have made you a brew."

From the corner of her eye, Jennifer spotted Paula wrinkling her nose. She tried to remember if she'd met Tom before. He wasn't local; the party had wanted a fresh start and chosen a candidate from Leeds. He was young with ruddy cheeks that made her think of hockey and boarding schools. His blonde hair flopped over his forehead and he was making jerking movements to try and throw it back into place, unable to use his hands. He was tall and slim, dressed in a nondescript grey suit and the regulation red tie. His shirt was ever so slightly frayed at the collar.

"Yes," said Jennifer, standing. She put out her hand then withdrew it when she remembered his arms were full. "Thanks, Paula."

"Pleasure," Paula called over. Tom nodded at her, grinning.

"So," he said, making the word sound like an explosion. "Drive with me."

"Drive with you?"

"You don't mind, do you? Only I've got surgery in ten minutes and haven't got time to stop."

Jennifer frowned; according to his website, the surgery didn't start for another hour.

"OK," she replied. "How will I get back?"

"Ah." He stopped moving, twisting his lip in thought. "Good question. I can get Paula to come out and give you a lift back. Alright Paula?"

"Fine."

Jennifer pulled the front door open. Tom shuffled past, struggling to keep the papers inside the plastic bag. She wondered what it was that he had to carry around, and why he couldn't work electronically. MPs' constituency offices always housed plenty of paperwork, but more and more of it had been digitised in recent years.

They stepped out into the street, Tom halting to let an elderly woman pass with her shopping trolley.

"Good morning!" he breezed. She ignored him and carried on walking. He looked after her, his expression falling.

Needy, thought Jennifer. *Wants to be loved*. He was in the wrong job for that.

They crossed the road to the parking spaces. Tom strode over to a red Mini. He plonked the bag on the roof and fumbled in his pockets for keys. After searching through his suit pockets, emptying scraps of paper and bits of fluff onto the roof of his car, he slapped his forehead.

"Bugger," he muttered, and opened the messenger bag. He grinned at Jennifer and pulled out a set of keys.

He pulled the door open and tossed his bags into the back seat, making papers spill onto the floor. He muttered under his breath then stood back for Jennifer to get in. He closed the door after her and rounded the car to open the driver's door and ease himself in.

She watched him fold himself into the car, his seat pushed back almost as far as it would go. Why he drove such a small car was beyond her. Still, they would only be crammed in here together for five minutes.

He started the ignition and pulled out into the traffic.

"You're here about your son," he said, not looking at her.

"Er, yes." So there were to be no pleasantries. She wasn't surprised Dan had retired; he was a man who could spend a whole morning asking how you were. "How much do you know?"

He tapped his nose. "He's at Woodhurst detention

centre. He's under threat of deportation. You want me to stop it."

Jennifer breathed in and out slowly. She'd been expecting time to make her case, to work up towards what she was asking him to do. Still, directness meant no wasted time.

"Can you?" she asked.

"Shit, should have gone then. Sorry. Can I what?"

"Can you help? I want to get his deportation delayed, give us time to appeal."

"Hasn't he already had an appeal?"

"I don't know. We haven't been told anything." She flinched as he narrowly avoided hitting a bus as he squeezed past it. "I thought you might know more. Seeing as he's your constituent."

He laughed. "It's not as simple as that."

"Why not?"

He glanced at her, then looked back at the road, swerving to avoid a man who'd stepped in front of the Mini. "Crikey, old man! Look where you're going. Idiot. I don't know anything more than what I've just told you. And even if I did, I couldn't help you."

"I'm sorry?"

"Oh, don't be."

"That's not what I mean. I mean, I beg your pardon? You can't help me?"

"No. Sorry. More than my life's worth."

Jennifer put her hand on the dashboard, her pulse rising; they'd just taken a corner at speed and two mums with pushchairs were running out of the road to avoid them.

"Slow down, please," she said. "You'll hit someone."

"Oh don't be daft. Never hit anything yet."

She frowned at him. *Ignore the driving*, she told herself. *Think about Samir.*

"Why can't you help me? Why is it more than your life's worth?"

He drummed his fingers on the steering wheel. "Don't you know?"

"Know what?"

"You're *persona non grata*. Not just round here, but nationally too. We've all been told to steer clear of you."

"What?"

"You're very lucky I agreed to see you today. But you're my constituent. I think there's rules saying I have to see you. Can't help, though."

"Why? Why have you been told not to help me?"

He slammed on the brakes, coming to an abrupt halt outside the community hall where Jennifer remembered holding her own advice surgeries. He turned to her, twisting in the cramped space.

"Because of your friendship with the Prime Minister. No one's sure which side you're on these days."

"But that's ridiculous."

He shrugged. "Don't ask me. Ask John."

"John Hunter?"

"Of course. He says you're toxic."

"He *what?*"

Another shrug. "Leader of the Opposition. Changes things."

She blew out a long, hot breath. One of her old friends was Prime Minister, the other Leader of the Opposition. Neither wanted anything to do with her.

She looked back at Tim. He was twisting to grab his messenger bag from the back seat.

"Tom, I need you to act for yourself. Don't just do everything the leadership tells you to."

"What, like you did?"

"That's got nothing to do with it."

"You knifed Michael Stuart in the back. Put us out of power for fuck knows how long. And you think I'm going to piss off the party leader to help you?"

She stared at him. What had he been doing when she'd been prisons minister? When she'd resigned? Had he even been involved in politics? He had no idea what it had been like.

"It's not as simple as that."

"Nothing ever is. But I'm a first term MP with a tiny majority. I need to watch my back. Now, I'll need to let you out here."

She looked out of the window. They were a couple of miles away from the constituency office, maybe three miles from her home. She took a deep breath.

"Will Paula pick me up?"

"Paula?"

"You said she'd come and give me a lift."

"Oh, that. No, sorry, can't spare her. Too much going on back at base." He licked his lips, avoiding eye contact. "Got to get your priorities right."

He leaned across to open her door.

She climbed out of the car, her chest feeling hot and her stomach knotted. He pulled the door shut and waved as he turned into the community centre's car park, nearly hitting a woman on his way in.

CHAPTER THIRTY

It was still cold when Rita woke. She'd found an alcove another mile along the canal, tucked between a thicket of brambles and a discarded wheelie bin. The thorns hadn't made for a comfortable nap, but at least no one disturbed her. She'd finally slept as the sky was becoming fully light; she couldn't have been asleep for more than an hour.

She groaned and stretched her arms, longing for the comfort of a bed. Once again she wondered if she'd done the right thing. In prison she would at least have a mattress and blanket. Then she remembered Tim, the sound of his footsteps, the sudden light attacking her eyes. Followed by the feel of his hand on her face, or her arms. He'd told her that she'd be attractive if she didn't smell so vile, making her determined not to attempt to wash in the sink with its dripping tap.

She couldn't go back there.

She heaved herself upright and got her bearings. She was surrounded by brick buildings, warehouses and factories. In front of her, the canal was dull and grey. A single beer can bobbed past, glinting in the silvery light. The dull roar of the motorway was above and ahead of her, interspersed with birdsong, loud and incongruous.

The hedge rustled and she pulled back, startled. A fox emerged, fixing her with its glassy stare. It sniffed the air then trotted off along the towpath as if out for a morning stroll. She watched it recede, occasionally looking back to check she wasn't following.

She had to find Jennifer. She knew that her constituency had included Spaghetti Junction and that she lived nearby. Should she roam the streets, circling the area, watching for her? Or could she risk asking directions from someone?

No. And touring the area blindly was madness; what if she passed right outside Jennifer's house but she wasn't in, or wasn't visible from the street? She couldn't walk the streets peering into everyone's front window. She'd be back in a police cell by nightfall that way.

Her mind felt fuzzy, like she had a hangover. She tried to remember when she'd last eaten. She'd found a half-eaten doughnut in a bin last night. She'd picked it out gingerly, wondering if this was what she'd come to. She'd swallowed it in two bites, relishing the sugary, fatty heft of it as it went down. Other than that, there'd been nothing since the finger of Twix Sonia had given her before the crash.

She had to eat. More importantly, she had to drink. She was in a rundown area, populated by the down-at-heel. There would be a shelter somewhere, a place she hoped wouldn't ask questions. Maybe a soup kitchen.

She brushed her jeans down and smoothed her hair. No harm in looking as presentable as she could, even if she did smell like a cross between a hay bale and a men's lavatory.

She looked up and down the canal, sniffing the air like the fox before her. Which direction?

She blew out a long breath, resisting the temptation to whistle. It made sense to head out of the city centre, towards Spaghetti Junction. Jennifer was that way.

By the time she reached the road heading north into Jennifer's constituency, it was warming up a little. The rush hour was ending but traffic was still heading into the city. A bus passed her. She looked up to see a man looking down at her from the top deck. She bowed her head and hurried on.

She walked a mile or so, scanning for signs of a shelter or soup kitchen. Maybe there would be a church where they fed the homeless. She passed a sign for a Catholic church but it was hidden behind greenery and high gates. She trudged on, her stomach growling.

"Morning."

She spun round to see a man watching her, tucked in next to a car wash. He was in an even worse state than her. His hair was long and tangled, his beard thick. He wore a grey overcoat with no buttons, which he clutched around himself.

She looked around to check if he'd been talking to someone else.

"I said morning." He grinned at her through blackened teeth. "You look like you need some help."

She frowned. Compared to him, she looked like she was living the life of luxury. But then she remembered the urine stains on her trousers, and imagined the blotches on her face. He was right.

"Maybe."

He nodded. "Proud. Good for you."

She turned away to continue walking.

"Looking for food?"

She stopped. Was he going to offer her food? She didn't know which was more horrifying; the prospect of starving, or the idea of taking food from those filthy hands. But she was hungry.

"There's a soup kitchen. They'll give you something."

She turned to face him. "Where?"

He laughed then coughed. The cough became a full-throated rasp which lasted more than a minute.

"'Scuse me. Too many fags. It's at the Baptist church."

"How do I find it?"

He raised his hand to point in the direction she was heading. The sleeve of his coat was torn and hung from his arm, revealing a worn shirt with pink buttons.

"Straight on, by the big roundabout."

"Thanks."

"Pleasure. Good luck."

She offered him a smile and carried on, picking up her pace. The traffic was growing heavier now and the occasional pedestrian would pass her, nose wrinkled. She kept her head down, but none of them made eye contact.

At last she reached the church. It was a modern building, with large windows at the front.

Two young women passed her, both wearing hijabs. They looked bulky, as if they were dressed in every item of clothing they owned all at the same time. They glanced at her then continued their conversation. Were they volunteers, or customers?

She followed them round the back of the church. They went through a door, probably to the church hall. She shuffled in after them and almost lost her balance at the rich tang of coffee and tobacco smoke which accosted her.

Along one wall was a row of formica-topped tables, with people behind wearing aprons and thin rubber gloves. The two Muslim women who'd passed her outside shuffled along the tables, their backs to her. They each held a plastic bag which they would hold out for a volunteer to put something in it. Rita watched. There were tins of soup and baked beans, cereal bars, bread rolls, apples and a pile of sponge cake that looked like it had been thrown around. At the far end was a tea urn and a pot of coffee.

She gasped and bit her lip. She hung back, unsure if she could just barge in and expect to be served.

A young woman appeared next to her. She wore a plastic apron and had her blonde hair shoved into a net.

"Your first time?" she asked. She had a brummie accent.

Rita nodded.

"Have you got a voucher?"

"Sorry?"

"A food bank voucher?"

"Er, no."

The woman looked her up and down. "Don't worry. I'll have a word with Sheila, it'll be fine. Start on the left and work your way along. The team will give you everything you need."

"Do I— do I have to show ID?"

The woman smiled. "Of course not." Her voice was soft, reminding Rita of how Jennifer had become once they'd got to know each other.

"Thanks."

Rita stepped forwards, picking up a bag. She moved along the table, nodding at the volunteers who greeted her, pointing at what she wanted. She would have asked for everything but it felt rude.

At last she picked up a steaming mug of coffee and turned to find a table.

All the tables were occupied. Most of the groups were

men, some old enough to be her father. She scanned for the two Muslim women she'd seen. They were at one end of a long table near the door. She picked her way past the other groups, relieved that she was being ignored, and took a seat at their table.

One of them turned to her. "Hello. Are you new?"

She tried to smile. This felt like a club she hadn't been invited to; did everyone know each other? Was she really welcome?

"Yes. I'm— I'm Ruth."

"Ruth. That's not an Asian name."

She shrugged. "My parents were anglophiles."

"That's a Jewish name, isn't it?" the other woman asked.

The first woman glared at her friend. "Aaisha, don't."

The woman put her hands up. "Sorry. I wasn't being antisemitic. Honest. Just first time I've heard of an Indian woman with a Jewish name."

Rita blushed, wishing she'd picked a different name. She thought about correcting herself then decided better of it.

The first woman brought up a paper serviette and wiped her mouth. "I'm Jamila."

Rita nodded. "Pleased to meet you."

"Where are you from?" her friend – Aaisha – asked. Jamila gave her another look.

"Sorry for Aish. She's so nosey."

Aaisha laughed. "Sorry. Can't help it. Get it from my dad."

"It's alright," said Rita. She searched her memory for somewhere local, close enough to be credible but far enough away that they wouldn't know people from it. "I'm from Tamworth."

Aaisha shuddered. "Horrible place. Sorry, no offence."

"None taken."

Rita picked up her mug and started to drink. She pulled a cereal bar from her bag and wiped it open. The feel of it moving around her mouth and going down her throat felt like heaven.

"You OK?"

She looked back at Jamila, who was staring at her. "Er, yeah."

"Only you made an odd noise."

"Sorry. I haven't eaten for a while."

"You look like it. Glad you found us?"

"Very." She carried on drinking her coffee, wishing she could slurp it all down at once, wishing she wasn't being watched.

"So what brings you to Brum?"

Rita finished her cereal bar and started tearing chunks off her bread roll. She swallowed one; its starchy fullness was even better.

She hesitated, chewing slowly. How much could she tell them?. Could she ask for directions? She eyed them. Jamila, who had spoken, was looking at her while Aaisha was blowing on her coffee and humming to herself.

These women were probably the least likely in the world to alert the authorities. They could even be here for the same reason as her.

"I'm looking for someone."

"A friend?"

"Well..." Could she describe Jennifer as a friend? "No. Not really. Someone who helped me once."

"OK. Try me."

"Sorry?"

"I've lived round here all my life. My son goes to the local primary. I know a lot of people."

Rita looked at the woman again, shocked that she had a son in school. Was she sleeping rough like her, or was she just poor? Her clothes looked clean if shabby and she definitely didn't smell of stale urine.

"OK." She inhaled, almost choking on a piece of bread. She bent her head and leaned in over the table. It reminded her of the dining room at the centre, the hushed conversations with the orderlies overseeing. "She's the local MP. Jennifer Sinclair."

Jamila frowned. "The MP is a man called something Hamilton. I know because his name was at the top of the ballot paper I scrawled all over."

Rita smiled. She liked this woman. In another world, they could have been friends. "The ex-MP in that case." She lowered her voice to a whisper. "Jennifer Sinclair."

"The one that's in prison?"

Rita nodded, her heart thudding against her ribs. She waited for the woman to stand up and fetch someone.

Aaisha looked up from her coffee. "I know her. Or my brother does. Did. She lived in his road."

Rita felt her chest tighten. "Really?"

She nodded and slurped at her coffee. "Yeah. Hillaries Road. Just by Spaghetti Junction. Not far from here."

Rita closed her eyes, focusing on her breathing. She thought of her walk here, from the canal. Could she have walked past Jennifer's house?

"How do I find it?" she asked.

"Easy. Last but one road on the right before you get to the Aston Expressway."

Rita curled her toes inside her battered shoes. She wanted to spring up and start running, to find Jennifer immediately. But she had to eat. And she didn't want to draw any attention to herself.

She finished her roll, listening as the two women fell back into their own conversation. Something about which grocer's sold the cheapest cauliflowers.

At last she finished her cake and coffee and stood up. There was a table near the door with a bin next to it. She looked back at the women before heading for it.

"Thank you."

"Pleasure."

Rita hurried to the table and deposited her rubbish, following the instructions on a piece of paper attached to the wall. Cups in one basket, plastic spoons in another. Wrappers in a bin. Everything recycled. She tried to remember how long it had taken to get here from the dual carriageway the woman had spoken about.

Then she thought of something. She hurried back to the table.

"Excuse me."

The woman looked up at her.

"Sorry, but I don't suppose you know what number? Her house."

Aaisha shook her head. "Sorry."

Rita nodded. "No problem."

She could find it, she knew that. She only had one street whose windows she needed to look in. How long could it take?

CHAPTER THIRTY-ONE

JENNIFER CRASHED INTO THE HOUSE, TIRED AND frustrated. The forty-minute walk back to the constituency office followed by the five-minute drive home had done nothing to dissolve her anger. She'd been recognised by two separate people on the way, both of whom reacted with surprise. One was pleased to see her, the other suspicious. She'd had to snap out of her black mood and switch into professional mode, something she'd become practised at over the years.

She flung her bag onto the kitchen table. She peeled off her jacket and threw it over a chair. It fell to the floor but she ignored it. Her shirt, crisp and white this morning, was sweaty and creased now.

She took a few deep breaths, listening to the house. It was quiet. Yusuf would be out at the homeless shelter, Hassan at school. She had the house to herself. It felt odd.

Then she heard movement upstairs and remembered Meena. Allowing her to stay had seemed like a good idea at the time but now she wasn't so sure. How long before Yonda reported her missing? It wouldn't take much to imagine her coming to the house of her former patient and her ex-boyfriend's family.

But she owed Meena. She'd been gentle with her during her Celebration, ignoring the fact that she was answering the wrong questions. Jennifer smiled. At least her media training had been some use.

She bent to pick up her jacket and headed for the stairs. She needed a shower and a change of clothes.

Meena was coming down, looking embarrassed. She wore the same black trousers and shirt and green hijab she'd been wearing the day she arrived. Jennifer kept offering to wash them but it seemed she preferred to do it herself in the bathroom sink. At least she'd accepted Jennifer's spare pyjamas. They were too long for her, the legs trailing behind her ankles, but it was better than having the poor girl sleep in her clothes.

"Hello," Jennifer said. "How are you?"

"Fine thanks. You?"

"Oh." She hesitated. "I'm fine."

"You don't look it."

Jennifer put a hand to her face. "Don't I?"

"I heard you come in."

Jennifer had slammed the door and stomped her way into the house. It hadn't occurred to her that Meena would hear.

"Oh. No." She sighed. "I went to see Tom Hamilton. The MP."

Meena's eyes lit up. "Oh? And?"

"Not good. Come downstairs."

She turned for the kitchen; the shower would have to wait. Meena followed behind her, almost silent. Jennifer wondered if she'd been washing her black socks every night too. Was that why she got up so late? Was she waiting for it all to dry?

There was a still-warm pot of coffee in the machine. Jennifer grabbed two mugs and poured. She placed them on the table.

"Milk?"

"No thanks."

She opened the fridge, grabbed the milk then sat opposite Meena.

"What did he say?" Meena asked.

"He said he couldn't help."

"But Samir's his constituent."

"It's not about Samir. It's me. I'm toxic, it seems."

"Toxic?"

Jennifer sat back and folded her fingers around her coffee. "An embarrassment. John Hunter – the leader of the party – has—"

"I know who John Hunter is."

"Sorry. Of course you do. Anyway, he's told them not to go near me."

"Why on earth would he do that?"

Jennifer looked up. Meena's eyes were on her, her face calm.

"Can you believe it's because I'm a friend of the Prime Minister?"

"Catherine Moore?"

"The one and only."

Jennifer nodded and drank her coffee. She felt tired. Samir had never felt so far away, even with this girl who claimed to love him sitting opposite her. Especially with her there.

"Doesn't that help?" asked Meena.

"That's what I thought. But she won't help me either."

"How do you know?"

"I went to see her."

"At Downing Street?"

"Yeah."

Meena let out a whistling breath. "You don't mess around, do you?"

Jennifer shrugged.

"So why won't she help you, if she's your friend?" asked Meena.

"As far as she's concerned, that relationship is over. She wants nothing to do with me."

"Oh."

Meena slumped in her chair and picked up her coffee. She winced; it was hot, without milk.

"Can I tell you something?" asked Jennifer.

Meena looked up. "Of course."

"You can't tell anyone. Not Samir, not Yonda."

"I'm not really in a position to tell either of them right now."

"No. Sorry. OK. Well, it's like this." She paused. Could she trust Meena with this? Did it even matter if she did tell anyone? Yusuf wanted her to go public with it, after all. "Catherine Moore helped me. She told me about Samir."

"What about him?"

"That he was under suspicion. She warned me."

"How? How did she know?"

"She was a Home Office minister. She had access to files."

"But wouldn't that be breaking the law?"

"Yes. She broke the Official Secrets Act."

Meena leaned back. "That's your answer then."

"What is?"

"Tell her you'll expose her. She's the Prime Minister. She'll do anything to avoid being arrested."

Jennifer shook her head. "It's not as easy as that."

"Why not?"

"I've got no evidence, for starters. And she's my friend. She may not care about that, but I do. She put her neck on the line for me."

"Isn't Samir more important?"

Jennifer looked across the table at Meena. She seemed so mature, compared to Samir. What had she seen in him?

"Yes. He is. But that doesn't change the fact I have no evidence."

Meena slumped back again, gazing at the table. "How did she tell you? Was it by phone? Email?"

"No. It was—"

"No. She wouldn't have been as stupid as that. Face to face, I'll bet."

"She sent me a note."

"A note?"

"A handwritten note. She put it under the door to my office."

"Do you have it?"

Jennifer shook her head. "I can't find it."

Meena straightened. "Hang on a minute."

"What?"

"A handwritten note?" Meena was rising from her chair. She looked flustered.

"Yes."

"Oh. Oh I think, I mean I could have..." Meena looked up at Jennifer, her expression wary.

"What?"

Meena drew in a breath. "I think I've found it."

CHAPTER THIRTY-TWO

Rita hated this. Standing outside like some idiot, watching people's houses. Looking through their windows like some kind of stalker.

The street was a long one, with over a hundred houses. Despite being close to the motorway, it was quiet, with little traffic. Which made her conspicuous.

She decided to start at the far end and work her way back. But there were no alleyways, no catering bins she could hide behind. This was a neat suburban street with tidy front gardens and cars parked on driveways.

She found a house that looked unoccupied and decided to find shelter in its front garden. It was overgrown with weeds and tall grass and offered the perfect hiding place. But everyone who passed would throw a glance at this house; it seemed they were all aware of it and interested by it.

A middle-aged man came out of the next-door house with a bin bag. She crouched down and watched him, trying not to breathe.

He turned.

"Oi!"

She slid down into the bushes, her heart thumping.

"I can see you, you know. Who are you? That's private property."

"Sorry." She stood, keeping her body low to avoid being seen from the houses opposite, and retreated to the street. He was standing on the pavement outside his house, hands on hips.

"That damned house," he said. "Always attracts trouble. You're not doing drugs, are you?"

"No," Rita replied.

"Well bugger off. Some of us have got teenagers. We don't want your sort hanging around."

She crossed the street so she could get to the top of the road without passing him. She felt his eyes on her back as she hurried away, breathing heavily. Could he have recognised her?

CHAPTER THIRTY-THREE

"You've what?"

Meena shifted in her seat. "I'm sorry. I shouldn't have been going through his things. But it gives me a connection to him, being in there. With his stuff."

"Don't worry," said Jennifer. "Tell me about the note."

"Well, I saw something tucked under his mattress. It must have shifted with me sleeping on it." She tugged at her hijab.

"Go on. Where is it?"

"Wait a minute."

Meena pushed her chair back and left the room. Jennifer stared at the ceiling, listening to the sound of Meena's footsteps upstairs.

Jennifer's hands were shaking, her breathing rough. Why was she taking so long?

She stood and went to follow her. When she reached the stairs, Meena was coming down, a piece of paper in her hand.

Jennifer reached out for it. It was folded tightly. She opened it.

Your son's on a list. Suspected of associating with members of a proscribed organisation. Don't know any more.

Destroy this.

Jennifer put a hand to her chest, staring at the words. They danced in front of her eyes. She was back in her office, before Samir had run away, before they were both arrested. Before she'd known Meena existed. Catherine had summoned her to a pub outside Westminster, then not turned up. On the phone, she'd told Jennifer to go back to her office.

"Is it enough?" asked Meena. She was hovering, peering around her at the note. Jennifer realised again how short she was, or maybe it was just her own height.

"I don't know. Her name isn't on it."

"Nor Samir's."

"But the handwriting. It could be matched."

Meena nodded. Jennifer heard a car pass outside. She glanced at the door.

"Come back into the kitchen."

They took their places again, the note lying flat on the table between them.

"What are you going to do?" asked Meena.

Now that she had it, her evidence, Jennifer was more confused than ever. She needed to get to Catherine. If she told her, if she warned her...

"Are you going to the press?"

Jennifer looked up at Meena. "Why would I do that?"

"You've got evidence that the Prime Minister broke the law. It changes everything."

"No."

"It does."

"Not that. No, I'm not going to the press. I'm going to Catherine."

"Catherine Moore?"

"Of course."

"Why?"

Jennifer felt her shoulders slump. She was tired. She'd dreamed about Samir last night. He'd appeared in his room, been there when she'd opened the door to check on Meena. The whole thing had been a mistake. He'd never been arrested, never been under suspicion. He was still here, where he should be.

Except he wasn't.

"You already told me she won't listen to you," Meena said.

"She might now."

"You know her better than me, I suppose."

Jennifer eyed Meena, wondering how well she really did know Catherine. Had everything she'd said to Jennifer been a lie, a front to use her, find out what the Opposition was doing?

No. It had been more than that.

She stood up. "I'll talk to her. She's a politician. I know what they're like. She'll do anything we ask, if it means holding onto power."

"I hope you're right."

"I am. We're going to get Samir back. Trust me."

CHAPTER THIRTY-FOUR

Rita walked slowly up and down the street at irregular intervals. In between, she took shelter in a bus stop on the main road. She received uneasy looks from the people waiting.

She stank. Her hair was a thicket of tangles. But the buses were frequent and no one had time to call the police.

She walked along the road maybe seven times that first day, each time going slowly, scanning the houses as surreptitiously as she could. She picked times when she thought Jennifer might come out, or at least there would be enough traffic for her not to be noticed: rush hour, the school run. She felt more comfortable at night, knowing the shadows acted as a disguise. And those houses that left their front curtains open were easy to peer inside, but Jennifer wasn't among the occupants she saw.

The night grew darker. It was getting cold. She decided to head back to the church and see if she could find shelter. No one was there but she found a spot tucked into the side of the building and managed to get snatches of sleep. In the morning a woman woke her.

"Hello."

Rita sprang up, panicking. Sleep still tugged at her and made her mind foggy. She said nothing, unable to find the right words.

The woman smiled. "I'll give you the name of a hostel. You shouldn't be out here in the cold."

The woman approached her. Rita shrank back and the woman stopped. She was short and chubby, with curly red hair and a green coat with a pocket hanging off. She looked kind, if a little down-at-heel herself.

The woman continued towards the door Rita had entered by the previous day. "Come on in. You need some breakfast."

Rita followed, her stomach growling in response.

CHAPTER THIRTY-FIVE

Catherine didn't return Jennifer's calls. She tried the Downing Street switchboard, her constituency office, even the Palace of Westminster. No call came back.

She called Maggie.

"I appreciate this. I know you've helped me get to her before."

"No worries. If it means a bit of fun at the Prime Minister's expense, I'm game. So what do you need me to do?"

"Get close to her. In the lobby, on the way into a vote or something."

"That's easier said than done."

"There has to be a vote coming up where you're supporting the government."

Maggie laughed, her voice deep and cigarette-scarred down the phone. "There's a vote on Thursday. John's supporting her. But not me."

"You're breaking the Whip?"

"Come on. That hasn't stopped me before."

"Alright. So can you find another opportunity to get

close to her? I want you to tell her something. I don't want her aides to hear."

"I'll manage something, don't worry. So what's the message?"

Jennifer licked her lips. She'd gone over this many times. She needed something that would be clear to Catherine, but to no one else. It had to sound innocuous, while being anything but.

She'd written it down.

"Right. I need you to say exactly these words. Exactly as I tell you."

"Hang on."

The line went quiet. Jennifer listened to movement in the background, wondering if Maggie had changed her mind.

"Maggie?"

"Sorry. Needed to find a pencil. Fire away."

Jennifer cleared her throat. "OK. Here it is. Tell her: *Jennifer says thanks for the letter you sent her. She's so glad she's found it.*"

"What letter?"

"I can't tell you. Sorry."

Maggie snorted. "Oh, this is fun. Cloak and dagger. Don't worry, love. I'll be discreet."

Jennifer swallowed. Maggie was normally about as discreet as a cockerel at dawn. But she was the only person who Jennifer could trust to help her. She'd considered John, but after what Tom had said, he was out of the question.

"Leave it with me," said Maggie. "D'you want me to call you when it's done?"

"You don't need to. I'm sure I'll be getting a call."

"Right-o. Take care, Jennifer."

"I will. Thanks."

The call came that evening; a mobile phone number Jennifer didn't recognise. She answered it, hesitant.

"Hello?"

"It's Catherine."

"Catherine, hello. How are—"

"Let's drop the pleasantries, eh? You're trying to—" She hesitated. Jennifer wondered if anyone would be listening in; Downing Street staff, security services, hackers?

"I'm not trying to do anything. I'm just asking for your help."

"You've got a funny way of going about it."

"This is important to me. My son could be deported."

"Look. Come to my constituency office. Glenda will give you a call, time and date."

The phone went dead. Jennifer stared at it and allowed herself a smile.

Yusuf made a copy of the letter for her and hid the original in a safe he'd bought especially.

"It's a bit much isn't it, for a letter?" she asked.

"Not this letter. You have no idea who could be after it. We need to get our burglar alarm checked properly, too."

She frowned at him, worried at what she'd started. Had she made her family targets again? Was Hassan safe?

On Sunday, she headed out for their meeting, her briefcase perched on the passenger seat next to her, empty save for a notepad and the photocopy. She patted it each time she stopped at traffic lights, making sure the passenger door was locked.

She arrived at 8am. A dark car was parked outside with one occupant in the passenger seat. A uniformed policeman stood at the front entrance. Jennifer looked ahead, hoping they hadn't spotted her.

She went to the rear entrance, as instructed. Catherine's constituency office was very different from Tom's. Housed in a Regency building in the town centre, it was tastefully decorated. No piles of leaflets or smell of ink. It felt more like a doctor's surgery, or the offices of a small consulting firm.

She waited in silence, clutching the briefcase on her lap. A clock ticked loudly on the wall and church bells peeled beyond the tall bay window. The walls were freshly painted in a pale shade of yellow and flowers sat on the desk in the centre of the room, clear except for the *Telegraph* and *Financial Times*.

After fifteen minutes there was a knock on the door. She sat up to attention.

It was the same woman who had unlocked the back door and let her in.

The woman didn't make eye contact. "Follow me, please."

Jennifer followed her up a narrow staircase that ran along the back wall of the house; the old servants' stairs. At the top the woman turned briefly to check Jennifer was still with her, then knocked on a bright blue door.

"Come in."

The woman stood aside to let Jennifer pass. Jennifer nodded her thanks but the woman didn't return her gaze. The door closed behind her.

Catherine was perched on a large wooden desk in the

centre of the room. There was a framed photograph of her shaking hands with Leonard Trask on the wall, along with a couple of Impressionist prints. Shelves lined one wall but they were half full, not stuffed with books, leaflets and various junk like in Jennifer's old office.

"Thanks for coming. Take a seat."

Jennifer stepped forwards and put her hand on the back of a chair. Catherine showed no sign of sitting herself, so Jennifer decided to stay standing too. She licked her lips.

Close-up, Catherine looked tired. There were blue rings under her eyes. Her skin seemed sallow. This wasn't the Catherine that Jennifer had seen at Downing Street. Had Jennifer got to her, or was she just not wearing as much makeup?

"I didn't want it to be like this, Catherine."

"Of course you didn't. But here you are."

"Yes."

"Go on then."

"Go on what?"

"Show me what you've got."

Jennifer opened her briefcase and pulled out the slim brown envelope containing the photocopy. She had a heart-sinking dread that she'd left it on her desk at home, that she'd open the envelope and find it empty.

She plunged her hand inside and let out a breath.

She held the sheet out. Catherine made brief eye contact then took it.

She surveyed it for a moment.

"This is a photocopy."

"I didn't want to bring the original."

"You thought I'd snatch it off you, tear it up?"

"No."

"Hmm." Catherine looked at the paper again, muttering

under her breath. "So are you going to give me the original back, then?"

"Of course. But not yet."

"No. You want your son's release."

"Yes. And my friend. Rita Gurumurthy. I want to know where she's being held."

"That one's easy."

"Is it?"

Catherine shook her head, leaning back on the desk. Her finger brushed a half-drunk mug of coffee; she frowned at it and pushed it to one side.

"Surely you've been watching the news."

"Yes."

"And you haven't seen what Rita's been up to?"

"They say she escaped. I think she's being held somewhere."

"Believe what you want. She escaped. The van transporting her was in a crash. She took advantage of it."

"I don't believe you."

Catherine sighed. "Watch this."

She rounded her desk and opened up a sleek laptop. She peered at it for a few moments then turned it towards Jennifer. Rita was onscreen, a grainy image of her on the bonnet of a white van. She was leaning over a woman who appeared to be bleeding. Around her were parked cars.

"It's a bad photo. Might not be her."

"Press play."

Jennifer reached out and clicked Play. The image broke into life, Rita moving across the bonnet. The camera was high up, at a diagonal from her. She turned to the woman lying on the bonnet then looked up. Jennifer bit her lip. It was Rita.

She watched as Rita slid from the bonnet of the van and stopped to look round her. People were getting out of the cars, walking across the motorway. A woman seemed to speak to Rita. Rita turned away from her and ran for the central barrier. She climbed over it and ran across the other carriageway, disappearing from view as she got halfway across.

"Satisfied?" Catherine had her arms folded across her chest.

Jennifer felt winded. She could only hope that Rita had found her way to safety. She nodded.

"There's still Samir," she said.

Catherine shook her head. "He's a terrorist sympathiser. I can't make exceptions. Sorry."

"He's no such thing. He's just a kid who got in with the wrong people."

"People like Meena Ashgar?"

Jennifer felt her cheeks turn hot. "Yes."

"The girl at your house?"

Jennifer almost fell backwards. "If you know she's there, why hasn't she been—"

"Arrested? The DPP is still making a case. It won't be long. Meanwhile, we're keeping an eye on her. And on you."

Jennifer thought of the camera mounted to a lamp post in her road.

"If you don't arrange an appeal for him, I'll go public with this note."

"Will you?"

"Yes. I've still got contacts."

Catherine shook her head. "Think about it. You're a former MP who was arrested for hiding a terrorist."

"He's not—"

"Semantics. You've just got out of prison. I'm the Prime Minister. Who d'you think they'll believe?"

"They'll believe the evidence. The note."

"It doesn't have my name on. Or yours. Or Samir's. It's nothing."

"I'm sure the handwriting could be matched to yours."

"Even if it was, it's vague. I wasn't stupid, Jennifer. Even back then. I thought about what I'd write."

"So why did you tell me to destroy it?"

A shrug. "It appealed to something in me, I guess."

There was silence while the two women stared at each other across the desk. Jennifer didn't know what to say; she couldn't back down, but Catherine had taken her victory from her.

"You said I just got out of prison. You know that's not true."

"Semantics, again."

"I don't think so."

"It doesn't matter."

"I think it does."

Another sigh. "I'm sorry it's come to this, Jennifer. I tried to help you. I cared about you, and your family. I wanted to help. But things have changed. I suggest you take care. Think about who you talk to, who might be watching."

She rounded the desk, holding out her hand. Jennifer ignored it. Instead, she drilled her thumbnail into her palm, resisting an urge to scream. She needed to get home, to regroup. Was she prepared to go public with what she knew about Catherine? And if she did, would it work? She still didn't know.

CHAPTER THIRTY-SIX

IT WAS THE THIRD DAY OF RITA'S VIGIL. SHE'D BEEN TOO scared to seek out the hostel; they'd want to know who she was. She'd headed back for the canal and underpass instead, finding an alcove in the struts supporting the motorway. It was noisy and smelt of urine, but at least she had been undisturbed.

It was mid-morning. She heaved herself off the bench in the bus stop, about to make what she reckoned was her twenty-fifth walk down Jennifer's road. Her search was beginning to feel hopeless. What if Jennifer hadn't gone home? What if she had, but had then left for somewhere more discreet? Or what if she was hiding in one of these houses, never to emerge?

Rita didn't know how long she could wait. She could feel her ribs through the flesh of her stomach. She had developed a heavy cough. This morning she'd spat up blood, frightening herself when she drew her hand from her mouth and looked at her red-splattered palm. If she needed medical attention, she'd be forced to reveal her identity.

Maybe that would be for the best. Maybe she needed a warm cell, three meals a day.

And electric shocks.

No. She had to find Jennifer.

She rounded the corner into Jennifer's road, almost stepping into the road in her fatigue and hunger. A car sped past, swerving to avoid her. A small red smart car, a driver but no passenger.

She gazed at the car, too worn down to react. In another life she'd have raised a fist, shouted at the driver. She'd have taken a photo, capturing the registration number. But she'd have done nothing with the photo, eventually deleting it from her phone in resignation. And besides, she'd stepped into the road. This was her fault.

The car drew to a halt. Rita stood, unable to move. A lump formed in her throat. The driver would ask questions. They'd want to know who she was, what she was doing here. She looked back towards the bus stop. Should she run?

Could she?

The driver's door opened and a woman got out. She was tall with mousy blonde hair, wearing a suit that hung loosely on her.

She turned to face Rita. "I'm so sorry. Are you OK?"

Rita opened her mouth, then laughed.

"Rita?"

She tried to speak but nothing came out. Her head felt light, her legs loose beneath her. She began to sway. She threw a hand out for balance.

"Oh!" The woman ran to her and took her weight just as her legs gave in. Rita let herself fall into the woman's arms.

"How did you get here?'

Rita shook her head; she wasn't ready to speak. Above, silhouetted by the pale sky, Jennifer looked down at her, puzzled.

CHAPTER THIRTY-SEVEN

JENNIFER LOOKED AROUND HER. A CAR PASSED, A SMALL girl with pigtails in the back seat peering out at her. Rita was heavy in her arms, despite having lost weight. She looked dreadful. Her hair was a tangled mass of black curls, her face was blotched with dirt and blood, her clothes dingy and torn. She smelt bitter, like someone who hadn't washed for days, and there was a faint tang of stale urine.

She heaved Rita up, dragged her to the car. She opened the passenger door and pushed Rita in. Rita slumped onto the seat, not regaining consciousness. Jennifer hauled her feet inside, recoiling at the thick mud on her flimsy trainers.

Jennifer rushed round to the driver's door then drove the short distance to their house. Yusuf's car was in the drive.

She left Rita and hurried to the front door, dropping her keys in her haste. As she straightened to put them to the lock, the door opened.

"I'm so glad you're home, love," she gasped.

"What's up?" His face fell. "It's Catherine, isn't it? What did she—"

"No. It's not Catherine. It's Rita."

"Rita?"

"My friend from the centre."

He glanced past her and frowned. Jennifer turned to see Susan coming out of her house. She waved. Jennifer waved back, trying to smile.

"Come inside," Yusuf said.

"No. I need your help."

"I can help you inside."

"No." She grabbed his hand. "It's Rita. She's in my car. Unconscious. I can't get her into the house on my own."

She pulled him out of the house, ignoring his protests, and to the car. Inside, Rita was regaining consciousness.

Jennifer looked towards Susan again. "We have to get her inside, but without drawing attention to her."

"That's not going to be easy."

She opened the passenger door. "Hey, it's me. Jennifer. I'm back. Me and Yusuf are going to take you inside. Can you walk?"

Rita grunted. Jennifer turned back to Yusuf. "We have to try."

"OK. Here."

He slipped past her and bent to Rita. "Hi Rita. I'm Yusuf, Jennifer's husband. Are you OK?"

Rita gave him a weak smile. "Fine. Thanks."

"You don't look so fine. Let me help you."

He reached an arm around her and pulled her up and out of the car. She leaned into him, muttering.

Jennifer heard a car engine behind her; Susan was leaving. She moved behind Rita, hiding her friend as best she could.

When Susan was safely gone, she moved back to Rita's other side.

"It's alright," said Yusuf. "If we both support her it'll look more suspicious. She's taking her weight. I can just steady her."

Rita muttered something, then coughed. Jennifer bit her lip. She should have stayed in the centre, should have helped her. She'd told herself she'd be more help to her friends on the outside. Was that a convenient lie?

They guided Rita into the house. Jennifer kicked the front door closed.

They took Rita into the living room and eased her onto the sofa. She slumped back, her eyelids fluttering.

"I'm going to get you something to eat, and a drink," Jennifer said.

Yusuf put a hand on her arm. "I'll do it. You stay with her."

She nodded and sat down next to Rita. She took her friend's hand. It was pale, the veins prominent. How long had she been sleeping rough? Had she come here from that accident, or had Catherine lied?

She wiped a tear from her cheek and looked for a tissue.

Rita doubled over, coughing. She groaned and hawked up some blood. It landed on the coffee table. Jennifer stared at it then back at Rita. This was bad.

She eased Rita back to a comfortable position and waited a few moments. Rita's eyes rolled in her head but she showed no sign of coughing again. Jennifer followed Yusuf into the kitchen.

"She's really ill. Maybe we should call an ambulance."

He scratched his cheek. "I don't know."

"We can't take care of her here."

The microwave bleeped and Yusuf took out a mug of soup. A pile of buttered bread stood on a tray, waiting.

Yusuf placed the mug next to the plate and picked the tray up. He looked at Jennifer.

"Do you know how she got here? How she got out."

"Catherine showed me a video. She escaped, from a car crash."

"You thought that was a lie."

She shrugged. "I don't know what to believe anymore."

He moved towards the door.

"I'm worried about her," Jennifer said. "That cough. But you're right, we can't call 999."

"I know someone. A doctor. Muslim, he's helped some of the families that have gone into hiding. I'll call him."

"Bringing more people here is a bigger risk, surely."

Yusuf put the tray down. "It's up to you. She's your friend."

Jennifer heard more coughing from the living room. She felt her heart skip. "Call him."

Yusuf scratched his chin. He'd shaved; his beard was the neatest Jennifer had seen it for years. "Let's see how she does with some food inside her first."

"She just coughed up blood."

His face darkened. "Oh, I don't know. Let's just give her this food, then decide. I don't want you getting into any more trouble. If they find out you harboured someone who escaped, they'll send you back there."

She closed her eyes. A headache was brewing above her eyebrows.

"OK. Let me take it to her."

She took the tray and padded into the living room. Yusuf followed.

Rita was where she had left her on the sofa, her eyes open. She was blinking and looking around. When she saw Jennifer her face broke into a smile.

"Jennifer! Am I glad to see you." She lifted herself up but quickly slipped down again.

Jennifer sat next to her. She placed the tray on the table in front of them. She avoided the blood. Yusuf spotted it and left the room, looking for a cloth.

"Me too," she said, reaching round to give Rita the gentlest hug she could.

She picked up the soup and handed it to Rita. Rita closed her eyes and inhaled its smell, then took a noisy slurp.

"That's good. Thanks."

"There's bread too."

Rita nodded, drinking again. Jennifer waited for her to finish the soup and then the bread. Yusuf reappeared and cleaned the coffee table. He looked at Jennifer, raising his eyebrows in a question. She shook her head. The panic was over.

Rita sniffed and put the plate down on the tray. "That's better."

Jennifer swallowed. "How did you get here? Did you pass your Celebration?"

"No. I escaped." A smile flickered on Rita's lips. The colour was coming back to her cheeks.

"Escaped?"

"They were transporting me. There was a crash. I ran."

"So it's true."

Rita's eyes widened. "You knew?"

"You've been on the news. I didn't believe it, thought it was a story to mask something worse."

"Like what?"

"I saw you. Before my Celebration. I could tell they'd been hurting you."

Rita's eyes dropped. "Tim. Bastard. They locked me up in the basement."

"We looked for you everywhere. Me and the girls. Maryam saw you."

"I know," said Rita. "I saw her."

"Where were they transporting you?"

"No idea. The guard was nice, though. She gave me a Twix."

Jennifer nodded. "That was almost a week ago."

A shrug. "I've lost track."

"Have you eaten since?"

"I found a place near here. A church. They fed me."

"The food bank."

"Yeah."

Rita sank back into the chair. Her face had paled again. There were dark circles under her eyes.

"Let me make a bed up for you. Hassan can move in with us and you'll have his room."

Rita closed her eyes. Her breathing was shallow and slow. "Thanks."

Jennifer heard movement on the stairs, Yusuf going up to change Hassan's bed. She decided to wait here with Rita until he came down.

The living room door opened. Jennifer turned.

"That was quick," she said.

But it wasn't Yusuf. Instead, Meena rounded the door, her face falling when she saw Rita.

Rita stiffened. "You," she croaked.

Meena frowned. "Rita?"

Rita put her hand to her chest. "Please don't take me back."

CHAPTER THIRTY-EIGHT

RITA WOKE WITH A START. AFRAID, SHE JERKED INTO wakefulness, checking her surroundings.

But she wasn't under the motorway, or tucked into the wall of a church. She was in a living room.

She rubbed her eyes. Her body ached all over. Her left cheek was sore. Her head felt like it had had concrete poured into it.

Then she remembered. Jennifer. This must be her house. How long had she been here? Had she slept the night on this sofa? A duvet with the silhouettes of blue cats had been laid over her and her head was supported by a soft white pillow. Her hair was tangled and dirty. She felt sudden shame at soiling Jennifer's clean bed linen.

She pulled herself into a sitting position, her legs still along the sofa. It was soft and beige, a bit like the rest of the room. The walls were off-white and over the mantelpiece hung a photo of Jennifer with her family. Her husband and two boys. The oldest looked about twelve. That must be Samir. She wondered if he was here, if Jennifer had found him.

She heaved her legs to the floor and sat facing forwards. She felt shaky, as if she might faint. Had she fainted in Jennifer's arms, out there on the street? Had Jennifer carried her in here?

She wanted to stand but wasn't sure her legs would hold her. Instead, she took deep breaths, enjoying the clean air of this house, the distant smell of brewing coffee. As her senses became attuned she heard voices.

"She was walking from the bus stop. Looking for me?"

"How did she get here?"

She tried to call out, not liking to eavesdrop, but her voice was hoarse. It didn't do any harm to listen and find out what was going on.

She leaned back and closed her eyes, trying to ignore the throbbing behind them.

"She escaped. When she was being transported."

"D'you think they'll come here, looking for her?"

"We can't kick her out, just because we're worried—"

"I know. She's your friend. We'll get her better, then work something out."

"I wonder how long she's been like that. Sleeping rough."

"A while, I think. Judging by the state of her clothes." He lowered his voice. "And the smell."

Rita lifted her sleeve to her face and sniffed. She recoiled; he was right. She had to get up, find her way to a bathroom.

"I'm worried they'll be looking for her. They know you just got out. They'll put two and two together, eventually."

Another voice, a woman. Higher pitched than Jennifer's; a young woman. Rita looked at the photo again. Did Jennifer have a daughter?

Then she remembered. Meena. Meena Ashgar. Her old counsellor.

She breathed hard, in and out, trying to hold onto consciousness. She stared at the photo, focusing on the little boy's smile. He was eight or nine, Year Four by the looks of it. He was missing a front tooth.

After a few moments she felt her breathing return to normal. She forced herself to be quiet. Why did Jennifer have one of the counsellors here? Had she come for Rita? Was Jennifer helping her?

Jennifer had been speaking; Rita had missed what she said. Then Meena spoke again.

"What did Catherine Moore say?"

Rita frowned. She didn't remember that name from the centre.

The blood was coming back to her legs now. She stood, pushing up with her hands like a pregnant woman. She teetered in front of the sofa, wishing there wasn't a coffee table in her way. She kept her eyes on the photograph, the boy's gap-toothed smile, using it for balance.

"It wasn't good." Jennifer again.

"How?" Yusuf asked. The voices were becoming sharper now. Rita wasn't sure if it was because she'd stood up or if the fog was clearing from her brain.

"I told her I've got the note. I showed her the copy. She said it meant nothing. It doesn't have her name on, or mine. Or Samir's."

"Even so," said Meena.

Rita was puzzled. Why was Jennifer talking to Meena about her son?

She shuffled sideways between the sofa and the coffee table, her gaze fixed on the photo. It was in a gilt frame, dented in one corner.

At last she reached the end of the sofa. She could see out of the window. Sheer curtains obscured the view but she could still make out the shapes in the street outside. Cars, more houses. It was daylight.

"I say we go public with it," said Yusuf.

"I'm not sure," said Jennifer.

"Why not? You've tried your way. She won't see reason."

A pause. "I already brought one government down, love. I'm not sure I've got the energy to do it again."

"So how are we going to get Samir back?" asked Meena.

Rita frowned. Should she go in there, tell them she was awake? That she'd been listening? She wanted to know what Meena was up to.

Maybe she should get out of here.

She cleared her throat. "Hello," she said to herself, relieved to find her voice coming back.

"I've got another idea though," said Jennifer, in the other room. Rita frowned, feeling guilty at eavesdropping.

Rita caught movement from the corner of her eye, in the street outside. She turned and placed her hands on the windowsill through the curtains. She froze.

Approaching from the end of the street was a car. It was a blur through the window, but she caught a snatch of orange as it turned towards the house.

She drew closer to the window, holding her breath. She reached out for the curtain.

She stopped. If they weren't here for her, she shouldn't reveal herself.

She had to see.

She pulled to one side and eased it open, just a centimetre.

The car drew up outside. It slowed.

It was white, with an orange stripe along its side. They'd found her.

CHAPTER THIRTY-NINE

"Jennifer!" Rita cried. *Not now*, she thought. Not after all she had gone through.

The voices in the other room stopped. Rita heard footsteps. She looked round. Jennifer was standing in the door, Meena beside her.

She jabbed a finger at Meena. "You! You told them!"

"What?" said Jennifer. "What's going on?"

"She told them where I was. She's been waiting for me here. You let her." She bit her lip. "Why?"

Jennifer was next to her now, at the window. She smelled of floral perfume, mixed with coffee. She wore a beige suit that was a size too big for her.

"I don't understand," she said. "What are you talking about?"

Rita didn't take her eyes off Meena. "They sent her here to find me. I walked right into their trap." She looked back out of the window. "Shit."

Jennifer put a hand on her shoulder. She shook it off.

"I had no idea you'd come here," said Meena. "I'm not going to take you back."

Rita looked back at her. "I don't believe you."

"It's going past," said Jennifer.

Rita spun to the window. Sure enough, the police car was passing the house. Maybe it had missed the number. Maybe it would turn round, so it was facing the right way when it had to leave.

"That didn't mean anything," she said.

"Look, it's slowing," said Jennifer. "Oh hell, it's going to the Taylors'. Yusuf!"

Yusuf came in, looking confused. "What's all the shouting?" He was tall, a couple of inches taller than Jennifer, with a figure somewhere between muscle and middle-aged spread. His beard was peppered with grey hairs. He had clear brown eyes that sparkled. He looked nice.

He joined them at the window. Rita drew back, overcome by his masculine smell; aftershave, sweat. It reminded her of Ash. She felt her chest hollow out.

The car had stopped. A policewoman was getting out of the driver's side. Her colleague, a man, was getting out of the passenger door. He opened the back door and reached inside to put his hand on the head of the occupant. A gesture Rita remembered from those two policemen who'd taken her from her classroom to the centre, months ago.

A young black woman climbed out of the back, twitching to throw off the policeman's hand.

"Who's she?"

"Lavonia. Our neighbour's daughter. She was arrested a few nights ago," said Jennifer. "I'd better go out and see—"

"No," said Yusuf. "Let me talk to them."

"No," said Jennifer. "We don't want them coming in here."

Yusuf turned to her. "I've been helping them. If I don't go out, they'll knock on the door."

Rita saw Jennifer deflate, but she nodded agreement. She looked between Jennifer and her husband, wondering who was in charge in this marriage. Had Yusuf been arrested too? Had he spent time at another centre?

Yusuf left the room. Meena joined them at the window. Curtains had been drawn back in the windows opposite and a thin middle-aged woman came out of her front door. A hulking teenage boy lurked in the doorway behind her.

Rita drew back. Jennifer had known about her escape; so would everyone else. She might have been recognised on one of those forays up and down the road.

Meena was right behind her, her breath hot on Rita's neck. She shuddered at the feel of it. She turned to glare at the counsellor then slid past her to sit on the sofa. She was feeling light-headed again.

"Can I have a glass of water?"

Jennifer paled. "Of course, sorry. I'll get you something to eat. A sandwich? And a cup of tea?"

Rita craved some of that coffee she could smell but wasn't sure she could keep it down. She nodded her thanks.

"Where's the toilet?"

Jennifer led her to a toilet under the stairs and went into the kitchen. Rita sat on the toilet, taking stock of her situation. Meena had done nothing so far to indicate that she was about to take her back. And the police car hadn't been for her after all. But it had been dropping someone off. There was nothing to say it might not also pick someone up.

She stared at the walls of the confined space. They were covered in sheets of paper; attendance awards, good behaviour badges, childish drawings. It was like a living history of Jennifer's family. She wondered where they were. She felt sick to think that the younger one might have been taken away too.

She flushed the toilet and washed her hands and arms as thoroughly as she could in the tiny sink. In the kitchen, Jennifer was standing near the kettle, stirring a teabag in a mug. She smiled to see Rita.

"Good to see you on your feet. You were in a bad way."

"Where are your children? I mean, if that's not a difficult question."

A shadow passed over Jennifer's face, then it brightened again in a way that spoke of some effort. "Hassan's at school." Her voice dropped. "Samir's in a detention centre."

"I'm sorry."

"Thanks. We're going to get him out. With Meena's help, I hope."

"I don't understand. Why is she here, if it's not to arrest me?"

Jennifer laughed. "Even if she wanted to arrest you, counsellors don't have the power." She frowned. "At least, they didn't before I was arrested. But she's here because she knew Samir."

"She what?"

"Weird, I know. She was his girlfriend. It was because of that he was arrested."

"And you let her in here?"

Jennifer shook her head. She dropped the teabag in the bin and handed the mug to Rita. "I was angry at first. I didn't want to trust her. But she says she loves him. And she didn't know that he'd be under suspicion too."

"What did she do?"

"She was in a proscribed group." Jennifer's voice darkened. "Like Samir. But she's left the centre. She's on our side."

Rita sat down at the table and sipped her tea. The warmth of it going down her throat felt like silk.

"Am I safe here? Or am I going to get you into trouble?'

"Don't worry. We're not going to kick you out."

Rita nodded and drained her tea. The sandwich was next to it, on a blue and white striped plate. Tuna. She bit into it, the saltiness exploding on her tongue.

"That's good. Thanks."

"When did you last eat? No, I already asked you that. Sorry."

Rita shrugged, her mouth full. She heard the front door slam, followed by voices in the hall. Footsteps went up the stairs.

"They didn't have grounds to keep her in for any longer. Lavonia, I mean. The Taylors' girl." Yusuf had appeared at the door. He looked flustered.

"Good," said Jennifer. "She's too young."

Yusuf sat down. "I don't believe we've been properly introduced. I'm Yusuf. Jennifer's husband."

"I guessed as much," Rita said, swallowing the last of her sandwich. "You don't want me here."

He blushed. "What made you think that?"

"I overheard you talking. After I woke up."

"Oh." He scratched his beard, making a rasping sound that set Rita's teeth on edge. "Well, Jen's talked me into it. Have you got anywhere to go, once you're better?"

"No. I went to my house, but it didn't feel safe. And I saw my boyfriend being arrested."

"Oh. I'm sorry."

She wiped her hands on her jeans and remembered how filthy she was. "Can I use your shower?"

Jennifer stepped in, putting her hand on Rita's chair. "Come, I'll show you where the bathroom is. Find you some clothes."

Rita smiled at her and stood. Jennifer headed for the door.

"Back soon," she told Yusuf. "We still need to talk about Catherine."

Rita followed her upstairs, wondering who this Catherine person was. How many fugitives could one house take in?

CHAPTER FORTY

"Yonda Hughes."

"It's me. Mark."

"Mark. At last. What the fuck are you playing at?"

Mark gritted his teeth. He looked around the coffee shop where he'd found shelter from the cold. In the opposite corner, two young women bent over cups of coffee, toddlers squirming in two pushchairs next to them. An old woman watched them from another table.

"I called you once already."

"You left a voicemail. That's not the same thing."

"I haven't made contact yet."

"What? You've got her address. You've been there four days now at my expense and you still haven't spoken to her?"

"It's not as straightforward as that."

"Tell me, Mark. On what planet is this simple task I gave you not straightforward?"

"She's never alone."

She sighed. He imagined her at her desk, fidgeting with whichever brightly coloured chain of beads she was wearing today. He wondered when she was going to tell him to give up. When he was going to hear the police arrive at his flat, to take him back.

She was right; this job was straightforward. But that didn't make it easy.

"Who's with her?" she asked. "*Why* is she never alone? Her husband's out at that shelter every day and her son's at school."

Mark pulled the phone away from his ear. This wasn't his own phone, it was one Yonda had given him. She was probably using the GPS to track him.

"Her husband's at home in the daytimes. I guess he wants to keep her company."

"Mark."

"Yes, Yonda." He could hear his breathing. He moved the phone away from his mouth.

"I suggest you think carefully before you lie to me."

"Why would I lie to you?"

"Oh, let me think. To protect your favourite patient?"

"She isn't my favourite."

"I'm not talking about Jennifer."

"I don't know what you're talking about."

Calm down, he told himself. His voice had become shrill. He covered the phone with his hand and took a breath.

"I can't do this. I'm a doctor. This isn't in the job description."

"Very well. I'll let management know they need to come and get you."

He swallowed. "You do that."

"You don't mean that. Think very carefully about what you're—"

"Bye, Yonda."

He ended the call and downed his coffee. It was bitter, dragged in his throat. Outside, Erdington high street, just half a mile from Jennifer's house, was full of shoppers. He scanned the crowds, just in case. But he knew she wouldn't be here. None of them would be.

He walked back towards Spaghetti Junction, past the end of Jennifer's road. He wasn't planning on going to her house again. It had been enough seeing Meena going in. Enough to jolt him awake.

At the bus stop near the end of the road, there was a bin. He tossed the phone into it and continued walking into the city centre.

CHAPTER FORTY-ONE

"She looked rough."

Yusuf was leaning on the kitchen counter, staring out of the back window.

"A shower will do her good," said Jennifer. "Thanks for letting her stay."

He turned and gave her a tight smile. "We've got you and Meena here already. One more's not going to make any difference."

"Where *is* Meena?"

"Samir's room."

"Again."

They both looked towards the ceiling. Upstairs was quiet, the only sound that of running water.

"Maybe we should tell Meena and Rita they need to find somewhere else," said Jennifer. "Hassan needs a bit of normality."

"Let's see how he reacts, eh? You never know, it might reduce the impact of you being back."

She swallowed. "He's coming back to me. Slowly."

"That's good."

She joined him at the window. The garden was bathed in low sunshine and the lawn was damp from a shower.

"How were the Taylors?" she asked.

"Not good. Celeste is a state. Her husband's angry."

"I don't blame him."

"She's had a warning. Seditious behaviour. They've got no idea what she's supposed to have done, or who informed on her."

Jennifer closed her eyes.

"They're putting an extra camera up," said Yusuf. "Outside their house."

"Can't the council object, refuse to let them use the lamp posts? It's Home Office, isn't it?"

"We tried that already. They ignored it."

She felt her body sag. "How has it come to this?"

"It's like a lobster in a pot of boiling water. And the bomb attacks gave them ammunition."

She shook her head and felt for his hand. He took a shaky breath.

"So," he said.

"So." She stroked the dark brown hairs on the top of his hand.

"Catherine," he said. "Who are you going to tell?"

She dropped his hand.

"She's not going to get him out."

"It feels so disloyal. She did it to help us."

"She's not helping us now." His voice was hard.

The water stopped running upstairs and the house fell silent. Jennifer took a deep breath.

"I'm going to call Lucy Snape."

"Good."

She pursed her lips. "I'll go to our room. Get some privacy."

She headed upstairs. She could hear Rita moving around in the bathroom, trying on the clothes Jennifer had found for her. Samir's door was closed and no sound came from beyond it. It was as if he'd never gone.

She went into her bedroom and clicked the door shut. She sat on the bed and took a few sharp breaths. She pulled her mobile from her pocket.

She pushed out a breath and dialled.

"Guardian news desk, Lucy Snape speaking."

"Lucy, it's Jennifer Sinclair."

There was silence at the other end.

"Hello?" said Jennifer.

"Shit. Sorry, I thought you were a prank call. Are you calling from prison?"

"No."

"Where are you?"

"I've been released."

"Blimey. They kept that quiet."

Jennifer heard rustling as Lucy put her hand over the receiver. Talking to a colleague, no doubt.

"Are you recording this?"

"No. Only the government can tap calls now. So how long have you been out? You just been released?"

"Not long. Days, just over a week."

"Shit. I can't believe they didn't announce it. At least John Hunter—"

"No. Anyway, can we get to the point?"

"Go on then. What have you got for me?"

Jennifer's phone felt hot next to her ear.

"I want to tell you a few things about my arrest and imprisonment. The circumstances."

"That's a bit woolly. Tell me where they held you. Why they released you."

Jennifer heard footsteps outside the door. She pushed the phone closer to her mouth.

"I was arrested because I hid my son. He was suspected of being a terrorist sympathiser."

"I know that. Have you got anything new for me?"

"Bear with me."

Lucy said nothing. Jennifer could hear her breathing at the other end of the line. She sounded breathy, like she'd taken up smoking.

"So," Jennifer continued. "Do you know where people who are arrested under those laws are taken?"

"Prison, of course. Or a detention centre."

"No."

Jennifer looked at the door, hoping Yusuf wasn't listening.

"Where, then?"

"A facility called a British Values Centre."

"A British Values Centre?"

"That's right."

Jennifer heard muttering. She wondered who else was listening in.

"What's that?" asked Lucy.

"It's like a cross between a prison and an old-fashioned mental asylum. Mine was at Burcot Park, in Oxfordshire. They put us through this program, gave us drugs."

"Hang on, I know about this. There was that woman who sold her story to the *Sun*."

"Yes."

"She made it up. For the cash."

"No. It's all true."

"So how come I haven't had other inmates coming to me after they get out?"

"Hardly anyone gets out. They don't allow visitors."

"How did *you* get out?"

"There's something called Celebration. They gather all the inmates, or patients, and they take one woman and make her go through the six steps of the program, in public. If she passes, she gets out."

"That doesn't make sense. Surely you tell them what they want to hear."

"They give you a drug. Sodium thiopental. It's a truth drug."

"A truth drug?"

"It works. I was given it. It makes it impossible to lie."

"Jennifer, are you OK? This sounds like something out of George Orwell."

"It's real."

"OK. I'm going to have to find another source. To corroborate it."

"I've got someone you can talk to. She went through the program and passed. They gave her a job as a counsellor. She was there at the same at time as me."

"Give me her details."

"Her name's Meena Ashgar. I can get her for you if you call me again later."

Jennifer heard the doorbell ring downstairs.

"I've got to go. But Lucy, look. It happened. There are hundreds of women still there. There are other centres, for men too. My counsellor was taken to one."

"Can you get him to talk to me? That would help."

"I don't know where he is."

A pause. "Is there anyone else who can corroborate this, apart from this Meena?"

Jennifer thought of Rita, next door in Hassan's room. "No."

A sigh. "OK. I'll talk to my boss, see what he thinks. Can I get you on this number?"

"Yes. Text me first. I don't want my kids disturbed."

"Right."

She put her phone down on the bed, relieved to take its heat away from her face. She thought of the cameras at Burcot Park, the only tech she came into contact with. Could Meena get access to them? There couldn't be any better evidence.

She stumbled out of the room. Meena was at the top of the stairs, listening. Her hands gripped the bannister.

"What is it?" whispered Jennifer. She could hear voices downstairs; Yusuf, and a man she didn't recognise.

Meena shrugged.

She squeezed Meena's shoulder. "Be right back. Got something to ask you."

She headed downstairs, feeling a sense of purpose for the first time in days. Exposing the British Values Centres would show Catherine she meant business.

Yusuf looked back at her.

"Hello."

She slipped in next to him and took his hand. There was a man standing on the threshold, dressed in a dark blue suit; CID, she guessed.

"We can't help you, I'm afraid," she said. "We don't know the Taylor family very well."

"It's not about that," muttered Yusuf.

"What, then?" she hissed.

"Ms Sinclair," the man said. "I believe you have Meena Ashgar on the premises. We've come to take her back."

CHAPTER FORTY-TWO

"I DON'T KNOW WHO YOU'RE TALKING ABOUT," SAID
Jennifer.

Yusuf gave her a look.

The man's face was impassive. "She's been captured on
camera entering this house. She hasn't been seen leaving."

"Who are you?" she asked. "Where are you from?"

"I work for the Home Office, British Values division."

"There's no such thing."

"Am I right to believe your name is Jennifer Sinclair,
and that until recently you were a patient at a British Values
Centre?"

She met his gaze. "Prisoner."

"That's not how we think of it." He looked from her to
Yusuf. "And your son is Samir Hussain, currently under
detention under the Prevention of Terrorism Act?"

"Yes," Yusuf replied. "You still haven't told us who
you are."

"I can give you a name, if you'd like."

"Will it be your real one?"

"I can't tell you that."

Yusuf looked at Jennifer. Did he blame her for bringing this to their door?

Jennifer gave him a *sorry* look and glanced up the stairs. All was quiet. She wondered what the two women were doing up there. If they'd spoken to each other.

The man pulled something else from his pocket; a leather wallet. He took out a sheet of paper, folded in four. "I have a warrant to search the house if needs be."

"That won't be necessary." Meena was at the top of the stairs. Her expression was calm and her eyes steady. "I'll come with you."

Jennifer shook her head. "No. They can't just—"

"They can." Meena gave Jennifer and Yusuf a smile, like a guest leaving after a weekend stay. "Thank you. Thank you for letting me stay here."

Jennifer's throat felt dry. Having Meena up there in Samir's room felt like a connection to her son. She'd liked it, the prospect of getting him back which Meena brought.

Meena scanned Jennifer's face. "Don't forget what we talked about. It's important."

Jennifer nodded. Meena would want them to continue the search for Samir. She felt a maternal urge to hug her.

"We will. Don't worry."

Yusuf slipped in beside Jennifer and put his arm around her. "It was good to meet you. I hope we see you again soon."

Meena gave him a tight smile. She turned to the man.

"Where will you be taking me?" Her voice was brusque and her posture straight. She was no longer Samir's girl-friend, but a professional again. A counsellor.

"A British Values Centre."

"Burcot Park?"

"Not Burcot Park, no."

Jennifer squeezed Meena's hand. It was dry and cool.

There was a sound from upstairs; the toilet flushing. Jennifer stiffened.

"Is there anyone else here?" asked the man.

Jennifer gave him her most convincing smile. "My son. Our younger son. He's not very well."

The man shot a look upstairs. Jennifer resisted the urge to turn around. *Stay where you are, Rita,* she thought. Why weren't they asking for her, too?

The man took Meena's arm. He guided her outside.

Jennifer and Yusuf followed.

"They're all watching," muttered Yusuf.

Jennifer looked up. Sure enough, curtains had been pulled aside, the neighbours all spectating. Terry next door had stood up, trowel in hand, openly staring.

"Morning," she said to him.

"Morning." He disappeared behind the hedge, back to his gardening. And eavesdropping.

She sighed. This wasn't just about her own family. Did Catherine watch all this, cocooned in Downing Street? Did she care that neighbour was pitted against neighbour?

The man guided Meena into the back seat of the car. A woman waited in the driver's seat. Meena gave a small wave. She looked small, childlike. Jennifer waved back.

She watched until the car had turned out of the road before going back into the house. The optimism she'd felt after her conversation with Lucy had left her. She wanted to curl up in a corner and give in.

Yusuf was in the living room, staring at the photo over the fireplace. Samir at thirteen. His cheeks rosy as he smiled, the last photo where he hadn't been scowling. Even that had been an effort. Hassan, in contrast, was giggling at a joke Yusuf had told him. That was well before his tenth birthday, the day of the Waterloo bomb when she had feared for their lives. The day that had started all this.

Yusuf lowered himself to the sofa. "What did Lucy Snape say?"

Jennifer joined him, their thighs touching.

"I didn't tell her about the note."

He pulled away. "What? Oh hell, Jen. When are you going to understand that—"

"I told her about the centre instead. The Celebration ceremony. She knew nothing about it."

"No one knows anything about it."

"Well that's about to change. She said she had to corroborate it somehow, and she'd talk to her editor."

"Is she going to call you back?"

"Yes."

"When? We don't have a whole lot of time."

"Soon. She won't want to sit on this."

"I hope so."

He turned to her. He pulled his knee up and grasped it in his hands. "Do you really think this will make any difference?"

"Catherine will know where it came from. She'll see that I'm not bluffing."

"But you are."

It felt like a slap. "That's not fair."

"Jen, you've got a note that proves the Prime Minister broke the Official Secrets Act. The same Prime Minister presiding over prisons where they brainwash you and deporting kids who've done nothing wrong. You have to expose her."

"And who's to say we'll get anyone better, if she goes?"

He sighed. "This isn't Michael Stuart."

"It's impossible to know the consequences if I do it again."

"You're not doing it again. This is different. It's not your own party, for a start."

"I know. But I didn't see what would happen then and I don't trust myself to now. It's too big a risk."

He pursed his lips. "Jen, that was about a principle. This is about our family. Your friends. The risk is worth it."

"You're right. I'm sure you are. But just let me try this, eh? Give it a week. If she doesn't respond, I'll go public with the note."

"That gives us just five weeks."

"If the Prime Minister has broken the law, things will change very quickly."

CHAPTER FORTY-THREE

THERE WERE TWO FAINT TAPS ON RITA'S DOOR, THEN A pause before the third. Yusuf's signature knock, something he wasn't even aware he did.

Rita liked Yusuf. There was a straightforwardness to him, an ease. He was comfortable in his skin. When Jennifer was with him, her rough edges became smoother, and she seemed less panicked. But Rita knew that both of them were feeling anxious right now. Their son was due to be deported in less than six weeks and Jennifer still hadn't heard back from the journalist she'd called. And no one had any idea where Meena was.

"Come in," she replied.

Yusuf pushed his head around the door. "Come downstairs. We think you should see what's on TV."

"Oh hell." She looked at Hassan, who was lying on the floor with his iPad. He didn't react. "Sorry. Am I on *Crimewatch* or something?"

He smiled. "Don't worry. It's the centre."

Her eyes widened. "They've done it?"

He shrugged.

She slid off the bed, threw Hassan a smile and followed Yusuf downstairs. Jennifer was in the living room, hunched forwards on the sofa. Yusuf joined her and Rita took an armchair, feeling awkward.

She looked at the screen, her stomach tightening.

A young reporter was talking to the camera. Behind him was Burcot Park. They were on the front driveway and she could see the spot where her own room was, up in the eaves. No window; just a roof light. The room had been cramped and cold, with the door hitting the bed every time it had opened. But it had been better than that bathroom. She was having nightmares about it, imagining the pipes bursting, being left to drown. There was another dream that ended just as Tim raised his hand to her.

"This is Burcot Park, one of the new British Values Centres which the government has established," the reporter said.

"How do they know?" said Jennifer. "Lucy's at the *Guardian*. She'd never have given this to the BBC."

No one answered her.

The reporter continued. "We've been invited to see behind the facade of this centre, the flagship of a new government programme designed to reduce reoffending among low-risk prisoners detained under the anti-terror laws."

A woman stepped into shot. Rita inhaled. "That bitch."

Jennifer had paled.

"Who's that?" asked Yusuf.

"Yonda Hughes. Prison governor," said Jennifer.

"Why is she dressed like that?"

Rita snorted. "Because she's a bloody canary."

"Sorry love," Jennifer said, putting her hand on Yusuf's knee. "Prisoner joke."

"I can see why. She looks like she's going to make the camera explode."

"I don't get it," said Rita. "Why have they been invited? That's not what you said would happen."

"I know," said Jennifer. "Let's watch it. See what they've been allowed to show."

"Ms Hughes, you're in charge of this facility," the interviewer said.

"That's right," said Yonda. Rita shrank into herself, remembering the governor's bright shape at her own and Jennifer's Celebrations.

"Before we go inside and meet some of the inmates, I'd like to ask you a few questions."

"Of course."

She wasn't correcting him, wasn't calling them *patients*. That wasn't like her.

"What is the purpose of this facility?"

"It's a kind of open prison. But focusing on a specific kind of prisoner. Our main role is education."

"What kind of education?"

"We rehabilitate our women. Make them ready to be part of society again."

"Can you elaborate?"

"They're rebels, these women. Terrorist sympathisers. Subversives. Our education programme is designed to help them understand British values. Democracy, the rule of law, that kind of thing."

"What!" cried Jennifer.

"We help them understand the benefits of being a citizen of this country. Help them see their place in society. We want to help them learn, not just keep them locked up."

"And are they locked up? I don't see any perimeter fences."

"We find we don't need them. Our women don't try to escape."

Jennifer flashed Rita a look. Rita raised her eyebrows.

"Thank you, Ms Hughes." He turned to the camera. "Earlier today, we were given access to the inside of this centre. Here's the footage we captured."

Rita leaned further forwards. Would they have been given access to the one-to-ones, the group sessions? To a Celebration?

On the sofa, Jennifer was holding Yusuf's hand, biting her lip.

The shot switched to the dining room. Paula and Maryam were sitting at a table just behind the reporter. Not their usual spot. Rita locked eyes with Jennifer again.

"This is the dining room, where the inmates take their meals. We have two women here who we've been allowed to talk to."

He approached Paula and Maryam. Rita held her breath.

Jennifer's mouth was open. She was squeezing Yusuf's hand.

Maryam was wearing a hijab. Rita had never seen her in one before. It made her look older, and thinner.

The reporter sat at an empty chair, pulling it in to the table.

"Good morning," he said.

Maryam and Paula muttered in response.

"The governor has said we can talk to you about your experience here."

They nodded.

"Can you tell us what it's like? Maybe if we could start with you, Maryam Jalil."

Text appeared at the bottom of the screen: *Maryam*

Jalil. Terrorist Sympathiser.

"Is that true?" asked Yusuf. "She's a terrorist sympathiser?"

"No," replied Jennifer, her eyes on the screen. "She hid her neighbour's son. He was going to be deported."

Yusuf nodded and glanced towards the door. The interviewer continued.

"Can you describe a normal day here for me?"

Maryam cleared her throat. She looked at the camera then back at the interviewer. "We have sessions with our counsellor. Or group. We eat. We fill the time."

"Can you give me more detail? The sessions with your counsellors? What do you talk about?"

Maryam's face darkened.

"It's educational. They help us to learn to be..." She frowned. "To be more productive members of society."

"Why is she saying that?" asked Rita.

"They've threatened her," replied Jennifer. "Yonda. They must have."

The camera turned to Paula. Maryam had always been nervous, playing with her loose hair during group sessions. Maybe Paula would be bolder.

"Can you tell us about your group, please?"

Paula nodded. "We have groups of six. We help each other."

"In what way?"

There was movement off-screen. Paula glanced to her right, at something or someone Rita couldn't see. Then she stiffened.

"Can you tell us in what way you help each other?" the interviewer asked.

"We support each other, through the program."

Off-screen, someone coughed. The interviewer glanced

towards the camera then back at Paula.

"That's your educational program," he said.

"Yes."

"Thank you. Now we have one of the counsellors to speak to."

The camera panned out to reveal a fourth person sitting at the table. Rita put a hand on her chest. Jennifer sprang up from the sofa. She kneeled in front of the TV, her mouth open.

Text appeared again at the bottom of the screen. *Meena Ashgar. Counsellor.*

Rita's throat felt tight. Was she back there as a prisoner, or had she really been given her job back? She'd listened to Meena being taken away and had spent the two days since terrified of the knock coming for her.

Meena gave the interviewer a tight smile.

"You're a counsellor here?"

She nodded. Her eyes were bloodshot and her head-scarf crooked. Jennifer looked back at Yusuf, who beckoned her onto the sofa.

"I am."

"What is your role with the prisoners?"

"I deliver the education program."

"Which is?"

"It's designed to help them understand what they've done wrong. To see their place in society, so they can integrate when they get out."

"And does it affect recidivism rates? Are the women less likely to offend, because of this program?"

"That's not my area. I don't know."

"She does know," said Jennifer. "She told me that she'd only seen two women get out before me. They've threatened her too."

She looked at Rita who nodded. "Not a surprise, really."
Jennifer's face fell.

"Sorry," said Rita. "It was never going to work. They're in charge. They can make it look how they want."

Yusuf kept giving Jennifer wary glances, as if steeling himself for something.

"I don't get it," said Jennifer. "How did the BBC get hold of it?"

"Maybe it wasn't them," said Yusuf. "Maybe it was the government. If your Lucy Snape went snooping, they'll have set this up in response."

Jennifer nodded. "Yeah."

The TV had switched to a studio. The anchor-man, Matthew Kumar, was talking to camera. Rita remembered watching him before her arrest, having a bit of a crush on him. He stood in front of a wall of graphics.

She looked at Jennifer. Her plan had just made things worse.

She had days, if not hours, before they came for her.

"I'm going to bed," she said. She stood up.

"Hang on." Jennifer had a hand out, and was staring at the TV.

Rita turned back to it.

"We're going live to the Prime Minister, who we're hoping will tell us why this program has been kept secret for so long."

Rita shrugged. "Night."

A dark-haired woman appeared on screen, a green lampshade and a curtained window behind her. Jennifer looked up at Rita.

"That's Catherine," she said. "My old friend Catherine Moore. She's the Prime Minister."

CHAPTER FORTY-FOUR

CATHERINE LOOKED AS SHE HAD THAT SUNDAY. HER hair was dark and bobbed, her suit a different colour – pale blue, this time – but equally immaculate. Her makeup was subtle, her lips giving off the faintest pink sheen under the lights.

"Thank you for speaking to us, Prime Minister."

"Pleasure to be here, Matthew."

"Hang on," said Rita. "Is she the one who came to see you? That visit, at the centre?"

Jennifer nodded. Her heart was fluttering. She'd hoped that the next time she saw Catherine on TV, she'd be under attack, maybe on the verge of resigning.

Yusuf put a hand on her back. She shrugged it off and looked back at him. His skin was sallow and his eyes bloodshot.

Rita sat down.

"Prime Minister, as you know we've just learned about the British Values Centres that the government has established. Tell me, why have they been kept secret for so long?"

Catherine smiled. "It hasn't been a secret, Matthew."

"But the centres have been open for six months now, is that correct?"

"Seven months, in the case of Burcot Park."

"Burcot Park is the site we just visited. So if it's been up and running for seven months, why has there been no government announcement?"

"We don't announce everything we do. If we did, you'd accuse us of media overload."

"But don't you think, Prime Minister, that an initiative like this is something people should be aware of?"

Catherine leaned forward. She glanced off camera then leaned back again. She looked calm and confident. Jennifer mirrored her, leaning forwards, hardly daring to breathe.

"This particular centre is part of a pilot scheme. I'm sure you'll be well aware that the government often pilots new initiatives before rolling them out more widely. If they work, we announce their rollout."

"So if this had failed, it would have remained a secret."

Catherine shook her head, smiling. "Nothing is being kept secret here. Have you, or any of your colleagues, asked me about this before?"

"No, but—"

"Have you taken the trouble to ask me what regime we are pursuing for the prisoners interned under anti-terror laws?"

"No. Prime Minister, with all due respect, please answer the question. Why is it that it's only now that we learn about these centres?"

Another shake of the head. "We've repeatedly released figures showing that the prison population is growing because of the growing number of terror suspects we've successfully tracked down. The prison system is unable to cope. These new centres provide an alternative. I'm sure if you ask any of those women, they'd prefer to be in a low security installation like Burcot Park, rather than a traditional prison."

"Is Burcot Park the only one, the only part of the pilot?"

"There are two. Burcot Park, and a separate facility for male prisoners. That one's larger, as you can imagine. Just as pleasant though."

"Where is that?"

Rita pointed at the screen. "She's lying."

"What?" Jennifer had missed Catherine's answer. Would she have revealed where they'd taken Mark?

"That isn't the only one. For women. They took me to another place. High security, locked down twenty-four hours a day." She slumped into her chair.

"Where was it?" asked Yusuf.

"I don't know." She paused. "Somewhere near Swindon, I think."

"Hedge Hill," said Jennifer. "It's a women's prison. Built when I was prisons minister. It's modern, high security."

Rita nodded and looked back at the screen. Jennifer thought of the note, hiding in her bag.

"Yes," said Catherine. "I can confirm that we'll be instituting four more of these facilities. Three will be converted from existing buildings owned by the state, and one will be a new building project. We've been very pleased with the outcomes of the pilot."

"So do you have data to back that up?" asked the interviewer. "Recidivism rates, prisoner numbers?"

"It's early days, Matthew. I can't share anything just yet. But I'm sure we'll have good news to share with you very soon."

Jennifer stood and crossed to the TV. She switched it off.

"I can't listen to any more of this."

Rita looked at her. None of this made sense.

Jennifer turned to Yusuf. "I'm sorry."

He nodded. "It's alright."

"No. It's not. I trusted her, and all she's done is lie to us. And now on live TV. I'm calling Lucy."

CHAPTER FORTY-FIVE

RITA DIDN'T KNOW WHAT TO THINK ANYMORE. THEY'D exposed the centres, but now the Prime Minister was on TV, showing the world what wonderful places they were. The same Prime Minister who was happy to lock up her own friends.

She watched Jennifer and Yusuf arguing over what to tell the journalist. In the centre, Jennifer had just been one of many women. Maybe she was too pally with Dr Clarke, but she sat with them, plotted with them, and went through the same humiliations as them. Out here, in the real world, she was different. Her friends were journalists, and prime ministers.

Did that make her part of the system? Was she more interested in changing it from the inside than she was in exposing it to the light?

Yusuf was saying something about the BBC, suggesting they might have got the story from Jennifer's contact. Rita didn't really care. She was tired. Her stomach hurt from the days without food.

She stood up. "I'm going to bed."

Jennifer nodded at her. "See you in the morning."

Yusuf threw her a smile. He had a nice smile; she could imagine him with his council constituents, doing everything he could to make their problems go away. She wished he could do it for her.

She left the room, struggling against a seized-up calf muscle. She plodded upstairs.

She fell onto the bed and lay on her back, staring up at the ceiling. She thought of Meena, taken away so suddenly. She was only a staff member who'd gone AWOL. She wasn't an escaped convict.

Yusuf had told her she'd been carried in by him and Jennifer, after passing out at the end of the road. It would have taken time. Plenty of time for the cameras to see her.

She was putting them all at risk. Not just Jennifer – she could look after herself – but her family. Her boy Hassan. She couldn't be responsible for him joining his brother in a detention centre. Being deported along with him.

She'd come here with nothing but the foul clothes she'd been sleeping in. Jennifer had given her clean ones. She'd told her to help herself to food.

She turned to the door. There was a rucksack hanging on its back. Pokémon. Hassan would miss it. She hoped he'd forgive her.

She grabbed it and stuffed what few clothes she had into it.

CHAPTER FORTY-SIX

"Ring her in the morning, Jen. When your head is fresh."

Jennifer sighed. Yusuf was right. But what if she waited, and something happened in the meantime? Another revelation from Catherine, a knock on the door? Had they grounds for taking her back? Would they prove she cheated Celebration, now they had Meena?

And Rita: Rita was vulnerable. She must have been picked up by those cameras. Jennifer had to act fast, before they came for her too. Before any chance she had to save Samir was gone.

"First thing," she said. "I'll call her at six. I don't care if I wake her. She'll be less likely to lie that way."

She gave Yusuf a kiss and slipped upstairs. She paused outside Hassan's room, listening. Rita must be asleep.

She crept into her bedroom. Hassan was asleep on the floor, one hand thrown out. It twitched. She crouched and kissed him lightly on the forehead.

Poor Hassan. What did he make of all this, all these

strangers coming and going? Would he ever trust Jennifer again?

Yusuf appeared and slid into bed. She got in next to him, blinking up at the ceiling. She longed to turn on the light, to talk.

She turned to Yusuf. He turned his head and stared at her in the darkness.

"What are you thinking?" she whispered.

He wiped an eye. "Samir."

She reached out for Yusuf, who pulled her into his arms. They lay there, silently holding each other, until the curtains started to lighten.

At six am, she slid out of bed, tiptoeing past Hassan's mattress. He was curled up in a ball, snoring lightly. He'd need to be up soon, getting ready for school. The ordinariness of it felt wrong.

Yusuf grabbed her hand as she passed his side of the bed.

"You calling her?" he whispered.

She nodded. He gave her hand a squeeze.

She crept downstairs. The house was quiet, the kitchen flooded with sunshine. Her phone was where she'd left it on the kitchen table the night before. She picked it up, her hands shaking.

"Uhh? Who is it?"

"Lucy. It's Jennifer. Jennifer Sinclair."

"What? It's— it's six am."

"I know. Sorry. I wanted to be sure I caught you."

"You've done that alright. What is it?"

"Did you tell the BBC what I told you?"

"What?"

"That piece on *Newsnight* last night. Was it you?"

"No. It bloody wasn't."

"Who then?"

"How should I know?"

Jennifer believed her. Her tone was less guarded than usual; she hadn't put on her journalist's mask for the day.

"I've got something else to give you. Something bigger."

"If it's about these centres, then my editor is—"

"It's not." She took a breath, glancing up the stairs. "It's about Catherine Moore."

There was a knock at the front door. Jennifer frowned and looked at the clock.

She ignored it, waiting for Yusuf to appear.

"Go on then," said Lucy. Jennifer could hear noises at the other end of the line, as if Lucy was moving things around. Then she heard the tone of a laptop starting up.

The knock came again. There was no sign of Yusuf.

"Hang on a second, I've just got to answer the door."

"Come on—"

She put her phone to her chest and ran to the door.

Outside, wearing a coat over what looked like an old-fashioned nightie, was Susan. The neighbour who'd let her use the phone on her first night home.

She pushed the phone further into her chest, to muffle any sound.

"Morning, Susan. Everything OK?"

"Not really." Susan looked down at her slippered feet.

"I'll get Yusuf."

Susan stepped forwards. "No. I have to talk to you."

She could hear Lucy's voice, tinny against her chest. "What about?"

"I'm so sorry. It's Tom."

"Is he OK?" she asked. "Has he been arrested?"

"Arrested? Why on earth would you think that?"

"Sorry. I just, what with the cameras, and Lavonia and everything..."

Susan pulled her dressing gown tighter and drew herself up straight. "My son isn't the type. But he has done something you need to know about."

She could hear Lucy's voice now, rising in pitch. She put the phone to her ear.

"I'll call you back in five minutes. Don't go anywhere. You're going to want to hear this."

"Why can't you tell me now?"

"I've got a neighbour at the door."

"Jeez. OK. Five minutes. If I have to."

"Thanks." She hung up.

"Come in," she said to Susan. "Tell me what's happened."

CHAPTER FORTY-SEVEN

Susan perched on a kitchen chair, pulling her dressing gown tighter. She wouldn't meet Jennifer's eye.

Jennifer sat opposite her. "What is it?" She tried to sound concerned and gentle, but she was impatient to speak to Lucy.

Susan pursed her lips. "I'm really sorry, Jennifer."

"Why? What's up?"

Jennifer glanced up at her then looked down at her hands. Her fingernails had been bitten and there were red blotches on the skin.

"Go on," said Jennifer. "You can tell me. I won't judge."

Susan's eyes shot up. "He hasn't been arrested. I've already told you that."

Jennifer held in an exasperated sigh. "What, then? Tell me, and I'll try to help."

Susan twisted her hands together on the table. "That woman you brought in here a few days ago. The one you dragged in from your car."

Jennifer said nothing but felt her chest tighten.

"He told them. Rang the hotline." She looked up.

Jennifer met her gaze. "Why would he *do* that?"

Susan bit her lip. "Don't be like that. He's only doing as he's told."

"Told by you?"

"No."

There was a moment's silence. Jennifer stared at Susan, remembering the look on her son's face on the night she'd come back home. Hard. Distrustful.

"She's that escaped prisoner, isn't she?" said Susan. "The one in the crash."

"No. You're thinking of Meena. Samir's girlfriend. She was here for a few days, but she's gone now."

"I saw her leave yesterday. That's not her."

Jennifer drilled her fingernail into the ball of her thumb. "When did he make the call?"

"Last night."

She closed her eyes. How long did that give them, before the police arrived? Hours? Minutes?

"Like I say, I'm sorry. I gave him a right bollocking for it."

Jennifer nodded.

"I know they want us to spy on our neighbours, but I think it's wrong. Even if she was an escaped prisoner."

Jennifer heard movement upstairs. Susan followed her gaze.

"It's not as simple as that, is it?" Susan said.

Jennifer nodded.

"What was it she did? Your friend?'

"I don't think that's any of your business."

"Right. Sorry."

Samir had come home more than once accusing Tom of racism. She'd protested; he couldn't assume everyone who didn't like him was racist.

Maybe he'd been right.

She stood up. "OK, well, thanks for letting me know."

"What are you going to do?"

"I don't know."

"You'll need to tell her."

It's not for you to tell me what to do, Jennifer thought.

"Anyway, if you don't mind…"

Susan stood up and headed for the front door.

As Jennifer was about to put her hand to it, there was a loud knock. Three raps in succession. Urgent.

She felt her heart jump. The police, already?

Susan stared back at her, her eyes wide.

Jennifer took a deep breath and pulled the door open. She plastered on her most innocent smile.

"You!" Susan cried. "I told you to stay home."

Susan's son was tall and stockily built, with a mass of curly yellow hair. He glared at Jennifer and muttered something under his breath. She held his gaze.

"Come on, you little bugger," said Susan. "Stop causing trouble."

They hurried across the road. Susan darted a look back at Jennifer as she crossed. Jennifer pulled the door closed and leaned against it, her legs weak.

"What's up? Who was that?"

Yusuf was on the stairs, dressed and ready for work.

"Did you call her?"

She shook her head. "No. Well, yes, but I was interrupted."

"I heard the door close. Who was it?"

"Can I tell you later, after I've called Lucy back?"

"Course."

She went into the dining room, to her corner desk. She'd

lost her advantage now. Lucy would be awake, ready to lie to her.

She realised she'd left her mobile on the kitchen table. She stood and went to fetch it.

As she passed through the hall, she heard cars pull up outside. The blip of a siren.

She turned to the kitchen. "They're here," she whispered to Yusuf.

He nodded.

"Susan's son told them," she said.

"He did *what?*"

"He rang the hotline."

"The little bastard."

"We need to warn Rita. Can you go up?"

Yusuf looked at her pyjamas. "You go. Get dressed. I'll hold them off."

She crept up and paused outside Hassan's door. There was no sound from behind it.

Poor Rita. She'd come here for help and now she'd be going right back where she came from. Would she be in the same place as Meena?

Jennifer doubted it.

Jennifer had failed her. All her experience and access to power counted for nothing.

She pushed Hassan's door open.

"Rita?" she whispered.

No reply. She pushed the door further.

"Wake up."

She crossed to the bed. The curtains were closed and the room was in darkness. There was a lump in the bed. She put a hand on it.

"Wake up, we need to get you out of here."

She looked towards the curtained window. Could she

get Rita out safely? Or would they have officers in the garden, ready for them?

She pushed at the bedclothes again. She flicked on the bedside lamp and leaned on the duvet. It collapsed under her weight.

The bed was empty.

CHAPTER FORTY-EIGHT

THE CANALS WERE QUIET. RITA SPED ALONG THE towpath, dodging discarded litter: beer cans, sweet wrappers, crisp packets. Above her, the motorway had begun its morning roar, louder than the night she'd slept here.

It was cold, an icy chill rising from the grey water. She wished she'd stopped to borrow a coat. Jennifer wouldn't have minded.

Even so, she'd appeared in Jennifer's street, ousted her son from his bedroom and stolen a rucksack full of food. Then she'd left with no word. Jennifer may have been acting too slowly, but she was her friend. She'd promised to help her.

Had she done the right thing?

She felt her stomach gurgle and reached into the rucksack for a chocolate-covered cereal bar. The smooth sweetness coated her mouth, feeling luxurious. She swallowed the rest and pocketed the wrapper. Destitute or not, she wasn't about to add to the piles of litter.

She was only planning to run for a day. But hunger was

clawing at her every minute, making her dream of choco-lates, and doughnuts, and fish and chips.

Fish and chips. She would kill for a bag of that. But she had no money. She'd opened Jennifer's bag on the hall floor and considered taking just a fiver, or maybe a tenner, but decided against it. Food and clothes were one thing; Jennifer had offered those to her. But money was quite another.

Maybe where she was going she'd be able to get some-thing greasy, something satisfying. Yusuf had heated up a curry for her the previous evening and it had been a feast for her senses, spices balanced perfectly, the fluffy naan bread making her mouth water.

She'd have to make do with cereal bars and crisps for today. She'd left a couple behind, assuming they were for Hassan's packed lunch. Maybe there'd be a curry where she was going. She knew the name of the place, and its general location, but would have to ask directions when she got there. She hoped she'd find someone willing to help. At least she didn't smell anymore.

CHAPTER FORTY-NINE

"Do you have a warrant?"

Yusuf was standing in the doorway, barring their way. Jennifer looked at him, worried he'd make them suspicious.

She put a hand on his back and grabbed the door, pulling it open wider. Two men stood in their driveway. The senior was a couple of steps away from Yusuf, facing him down. The other, younger with red marks on his neck where he'd caught himself shaving, stood behind, shifting his weight from foot to foot. Both were in plain clothes.

"Good morning, officers," she said. She glanced across the road to see Susan's house in darkness. A curtain twitched in the neighbouring house. "How can we help you?"

She felt Yusuf stiffen beside her.

"Good morning, Ms Sinclair," the senior detective said. His name was Detective Inspector Tom Gordon; she recognised him. They'd shared a platform at an event raising awareness of domestic violence. Only a year ago, she realised, surprised.

"We have reason to believe that—" he cleared his throat, "—that an escaped prisoner has been to this house. A Rita Gurumurthy."

"I don't know what you're talking about, Tom," she said.

Yusuf put a hand on her arm. DI Gordon stiffened; she'd gone too far, using his first name.

"We have video footage of you carrying her into the house." He glanced at Yusuf. "You and Mr Hussain."

She shook her head. "You've got it wrong. The woman you're talking about is Meena Ashgar. My son's friend. She wasn't well, so we had to help her inside."

Yusuf's grip on her arm tightened.

"Can we come in please?"

"Of course." She stepped back and the two men clattered inside. The younger man at the back nodded at her. She looked into the street to see two cars outside. The first, dark grey and polished, sat across their drive. The second was a marked police car. A woman and a man sat inside it, looking around at the street. The neighbours would be watching them in return.

As they stepped back to let the police in, Yusuf shot her a look. She gave him a tight nod in return. He shrugged, puzzled.

"So," she said, closing the front door. She needed to get this over with, get back on the phone. "There seems to have been a misunderstanding."

The detective inspector smiled at her. "I don't think so."

She frowned.

"She was a fellow inmate of yours, we believe."

She thought of the documentary. Rita hardly breathing while Catherine lied to camera. She looked up the stairs, hoping she was right in assuming that Rita had run. If she came out of the bathroom now...

"Meena? No, she was a counsellor. Still is, I believe. She came for a few days, then returned yesterday."

"I'm talking about Miss Gurumurthy. She escaped while being transferred to another facility."

She took a breath. "Ah. I remember her now. Rita. She was there at the same time as me, but I only met her a couple of times. She was being held in another part of the centre."

"So did she come here?"

"Why would you think she'd do that?"

"Maybe she believed you could help her."

Ice slipped down her back. "I'm not an MP anymore. That wouldn't be something I'd expect anyone to believe."

The DI grunted and turned to Yusuf. "Do you know anything about this, sir?"

"Only what my wife's told you."

The junior detective nudged his boss and muttered in his ear. The DI nodded and looked at Jennifer.

"We're going to need to search your house."

"I already told you that—"

"We have reason to believe that Miss Gurumurthy is here. I'm sure you won't mind us looking for her, if you say you don't know her."

"Dad? Dad, what's going on?"

They all looked up. Hassan was standing at the top of the stairs, rubbing his eyes. Jennifer looked at her watch: seven thirty. She'd forgotten to wake him.

"Nothing, sweetie," she said. "Can you get your school uniform on for us?"

Hassan ignored her. "Dad?"

Yusuf pushed past the two policemen and went up to Hassan. "Don't worry. They just want to talk to me about work. That happens sometimes, doesn't it?'

Hassan shrugged.

"Go and get dressed for me, will you? I'll get you some breakfast."

Hassan looked at the policemen again. DI Gordon smiled up at him while his colleague's neck turned red. Then Hassan sniffed and retreated to his room. Jennifer wondered if she'd missed anything of Rita's.

No. It had been empty. Hassan would probably forget she'd been there.

But he might not.

"Yusuf love, can you help him find his school uniform? I didn't put it away."

Yusuf gave her a puzzled look; they both knew he'd put it away on Monday. She frowned at him, hoping he'd understand her. Then he gave her a brusque nod.

"So," she said, turning back to the policemen. "Sorry about that."

"We need to search your house."

Yusuf appeared again at the top of the stairs. "Do you have a warrant? You can't search the house without a search warrant."

"We don't, but I'm sure we won't have any trouble getting one within the next few hours."

"Then go and get it."

She looked up at him. Was Rita up there, after all? Did Yusuf think she was hiding somewhere else in the house?

"We can do that. But we will leave a car outside, and an officer at the back."

"You can't do that," she said.

"We can. We're looking for someone who has absconded from a sentence handed down under the Prevention of Terrorism Act. You know that we can."

She screwed up her nose. "Alright then."

"Alright what?"

"Search the house. Go ahead. Search it now."

CHAPTER FIFTY

"Why did you do that?"

Jennifer and Yusuf were in the kitchen, whispering. Hassan was tying up his shoelaces.

Jennifer looked towards the hall. One of the uniformed officers was standing there, her back to the front door.

"What if she's hiding somewhere?" Yusuf asked.

"She's not. She's gone."

"We can't know that," he said.

"All her stuff's gone. The clothes I lent her. And she's taken food, too."

She went to the drawer where they kept snacks. "Was this almost empty last night?"

"No. I couldn't get it shut."

"Well, at least we know she won't starve."

"What are you going to do? Did you speak to Lucy?"

She sighed. "Not properly. I was interrupted by Susan."

Bangs came from upstairs; furniture being moved.

"How do we get into the loft?" a voice called down. Jennifer felt her chest tighten. Yusuf looked at her, his face pale.

"If they find her, they'll take you back," he said. "Maybe worse."

"They won't find her. I know Rita."

She stepped into the hall. "There's a pole, behind the curtain!"

She listened to the loft hatch being opened, her heart pounding.

"You've got to make that call," said Yusuf. "You can't let this distract you."

"I can't do it with them here."

"Go out then."

She turned to the policewoman.

"Sorry, but I can't let anyone out until the search is complete."

The loft hatch slammed shut and DI Gordon appeared at the top of the stairs.

"There's no one here."

"That's what we told you," Jennifer said, trying to hide her relief.

He reached the bottom of the stairs and turned to Yusuf. "Is there anywhere else you might have taken her?"

Yusuf shook his head. "No."

"Am I right in thinking you're the manager of the HomePoint homeless shelter?"

"Yes."

"Could you have taken her there, perhaps?"

"I haven't taken anybody anywhere."

"Well. We'll see. I'll expect to see you there this evening."

"You can't just—"

"If we believe an escaped prisoner is hiding out in your shelter, Mr Hussain, we can."

"You'll need a warrant. I'm not subjecting our service users to—"

"We'll get one."

Jennifer could see the tension in Yusuf's body. He stared at the detective.

"Very well then." He held open the door.

"Thank you." DI Gordon turned to Jennifer. "Ms Sinclair, good to have you back."

She said nothing and closed the door after them. Yusuf's face was red.

"*Good to have you back, Ms Sinclair*. She's *your* friend, so why is it me he's treating with suspicion?"

"Don't be like that. It's not my fault."

"It's because I'm Muslim."

"No, it's—"

He tightened his jaw. "Don't defend them, Jen. None of them. Just stop them. Tell them the truth about your precious Catherine and put an end to it."

She grabbed her phone from the hall table. Yusuf stormed into the kitchen, snapping at Hassan to find his bag. She dialled Lucy.

It rang out. She looked at her watch: eight fifteen already. Where had the last two hours gone?

After four rings, it switched to voicemail. She hung up and tried again.

Voicemail again. Lucy would be on the Tube, on her way to the office. Either that, or she'd decided it wasn't worth speaking to her.

"Lucy," she said to the voicemail. This was her third attempt. "It's Jennifer Sinclair. I'm sorry about earlier. But I've got something for you. It's big, I promise. Exclusive. Call me as soon as you can."

She went upstairs, taking her phone with her. She needed to get dressed.

Ten minutes later, she was in the shower when she heard it ring out. She turned off the water and grabbed the phone from where she'd perched it on the side of the bath.

"Lucy?"

"Er, no. Is this Jennifer Sinclair?"

She grabbed a towel and wrapped it round her, tucking the phone under her chin.

"Yes. Who's this?"

"It's Tom Hingle from the BBC. We'd like to bring you in for an interview."

CHAPTER FIFTY-ONE

RITA SPENT MOST OF THE DAY TRYING TO FIND somewhere quiet to hide. She began at the station, managing to sneak an hour on a bench in a quiet corner. She had to move when a woman pointed her out to a member of staff. She sniffed at the woman, with her beige coat and expensive handbag, then sloped away, walking the streets on the shadier side of the station. She walked round in circles, passing the same row of Chinese restaurants three times. The smell of cooking wafted out at her, making the one remaining bag of crisps in her rucksack feel very paltry indeed.

Could she beg for some money, get a takeaway? No, she hadn't stooped that low yet.

She dragged her feet through the station again, watching for the man who'd moved her on. He was nowhere to be seen, probably finished his shift. Could she risk staying here again?

There were cameras everywhere. She'd soon be recognised. She'd spotted her own photo on the cover of a newspaper in the station branch of WHSmith. She'd had to lean against a wall for support before she got her breath back. But it was just a tiny mugshot. It wouldn't draw attention to her, she hoped.

She walked through to the other side of the station and out the double doors. People passed her; some strolling, others rushing for trains. She kept her head down. She needed to find somewhere quiet.

She walked up a hill, past shops and cafes, keeping her eyes ahead. She'd pulled her hair down so it partly covered her face. She needed to work out where she was going. Maybe risk asking for directions.

She stopped in the middle of the pavement. A man glared at her, annoyed that she'd got in his way. He swerved around her, muttering under his breath. As he marched off down the hill she turned and stuck her tongue out at him. She sniggered at herself.

At the top of the hill was a cathedral, surrounded by grass. She found a shady corner and slumped down on the grass. She could pretend to be just another office worker, enjoying the fresh air.

"That's my patch."

She looked up to see a woman standing over her. Her hair was black and matted and her mouth had more gaps than there were teeth. When she opened it, a smell of decay gusted out.

"Sorry?"

"You're in my spot. I live 'ere."

Rita looked down at the grass. How could anyone live here?

She looked at the woman again. She'd dropped three bulging carrier bags on the grass. Her feet were swollen and puffed out of her worn black shoes. Her legs were veined and blotchy.

If this was home to this woman, Rita wasn't about to deprive her of it. She stood up.

"Sorry." She gestured at the spot. "All yours."

The woman grunted thanks and kicked one of the bags towards the hedge.

Rita started to walk away. The thought of spending another few hours walking the streets, hoping she'd strike lucky, was exhausting. Then she had a thought.

She turned back to the woman. "Excuse me?"

"I'm not sharing."

"No. That's not what I mean. Look, do you know where HomePoint is? The shelter?"

"That place. Full of muggers."

Rita sniffed. It wasn't the clientele she was interested in. Yusuf would help her, she knew it. The shelter would be an easier place to hide than the house.

"But do you know where it is?"

"'Course I do. Just over there, on Lionel Street."

She gestured towards the far end of the square surrounding the cathedral. Now Rita had an address. She'd be fine.

She thanked the woman and headed across the grass. The shelter wouldn't be open yet but it didn't hurt to take a look. And there might be a queue. She had no idea how this worked.

She was about to step onto the path when she felt a sharp tug at her back. She spun round.

"Hey! What are you—?"

Two kids were running away from her. Boys – teenagers, by the looks of it. They had her rucksack. Hassan's rucksack.

CHAPTER FIFTY-TWO

MARK DIDN'T DARE GO BACK TO THAT FLAT. THE POLICE were sure to be there, waiting for him.

Instead, he'd wandered the city, glad of the cash Yonda had given him, the decision he'd taken to eke it out. He found a greasy spoon in a back street and bought egg and chips, allowing himself to forget his predicament as he enjoyed the feel of it sinking into his stomach.

Yonda had mentioned a shelter, where Jennifer's husband worked. Would he be able to get a bed there?

But he didn't know where it was. And even if he did find it, it was a link, somewhere Yonda might send them to look for him.

The station was anonymous enough. He found a cafe outside its back entrance, where the streets were grimy and filled with traffic and roadworks, rather than swept and filled with pedestrians and shiny new trams, like on the other side. He ordered a pot of tea with a couple of slices of toast and sat down, trying to figure out his next step.

He still had a flat in Oxford, not far from Burcot Park.

He hadn't used it much lately; it had been easier to live in at the centre, easier than the reality of his lonely flat every night. He hadn't even unpacked half the boxes he'd brought from his family home in Manchester. But they would be watching it.

He sat back in his chair, trying to look like a professional taking a break before work despite the stains on his suit. He'd managed to find a youth hostel for the last two nights. It was cheap, but his money was fast running out. It wouldn't be long before he'd need that shelter where Jennifer's husband worked.

His tea long since finished, he'd done all the people-watching he could stomach. He glanced at the man behind the counter to find him watching him. He was middle aged, with olive skin and a protruding stomach that spoke of eating too much of his own wares. Mark nodded and gave him a curt smile.

"You going to order anything else?"

Mark felt in his pocket. He had just fifteen pounds left. He fished out his money. Fifteen pounds and twenty seven pence.

"Sorry. Mind if I just sit here for a while? I haven't got anywhere to go."

The man frowned and retreated through a swing door. Mark cursed himself.

He'd be calling the police. Getting the vagrant in his cafe moved on.

He stood up. His money was still on the table. If he left a tip, would the man be less likely to call the authorities? Or was it too late?

A few pennies weren't going to make much difference. He picked up the notes – three fivers – and pulled his jacket tight around himself. The top button had come off.

He pushed out of the door to the cafe and looked back to where the man had disappeared. Maybe he was just talking to someone in there, a colleague. Maybe he was taking a break, reading a newspaper or watching TV.

He shouldn't be so paranoid. All he'd done was sit in a cafe for too long. Something he'd done plenty of times as a junior doctor. But then he'd been armed with clean clothes, the money to buy regular cups of coffee, and a laptop.

He dragged his feet up the steps to the station. It was early still, commuters rushing past him, distracted, phones shoved up against ears or held out in front of them.

"Watch it!"

He'd slammed into someone.

"Sorry."

The woman gave him a condescending look then turned to her companion. She wore a beige coat that looked expensive. Her lipstick gave her the air of a pantomime villain. He thought of Yonda then shook the image away.

The station was only narrowly warmer than the street outside. He spotted a row of seats in a corner, away from the platforms and the crowds. He could rest there for a while, maybe work out if his cash would get him back to Oxford. He couldn't wander the streets of Birmingham forever.

He sat down and looked round. There was a woman leaning against a wall a little way away, with her back to him. She had a Pokémon rucksack on her back, and her clothes looked loose. He looked for a child, the owner of the rucksack, but there was none.

The woman raised her head and pushed her dark hair back. He stopped breathing.

She sniffed and walked away from him out of the station. Her face was blotched red and her eyes darted from side to side like an animal nervous of an imagined predator. She looked tired and scared.

What was Rita Gurumurthy doing here?

CHAPTER FIFTY-THREE

RITA RAN AFTER THE BOYS.

"Give that back!"

They darted down an alleyway. One turned to laugh at her. "Pokémon!" he shouted. She gritted her teeth and sped after them.

The alleyway was tall, lined with featureless office blocks. The boys had disappeared round a corner. She picked up pace.

She turned a bend and saw them slowing as they reached the end of the alleyway. Beyond was the main pedestrian route down to the station. It was busy and the boys had to stop to pick their way through.

The alleyway spat her out and she crashed into a man walking past.

"Sorry!"

She put a hand on his arm by way of apology and carried on running. The boys had disappeared into the station. She didn't pause but dove straight in after them.

As she entered the station, she braked to avoid a family

coming towards her. She swerved past them, scanning the crowd for the boys. Then she spotted a flash of a familiar logo. She picked up speed again.

They'd stopped moving now. She slowed and found a vantage point behind a pillar. They were in front of the departures boards. One was leaning over, his hands on his thighs, and the other was laughing. He held the rucksack in his hand, dangling by the hand strap.

They thought they'd got away from her.

She darted to another pillar. She could come at them from behind while their attention was diverted. But she had to be quick.

She ran to another pillar. They had their backs to her now. The laughing one had slung the rucksack over his shoulder.

She darted out and grabbed it. The boy spun round.

"Help!" he cried. "Help me! Thief!"

She pulled back, her heart slowing.

Around them, people turned to stare. She looked at the boys. The one not holding the rucksack had stood up, and was staring at her. He was Asian, with wavy dark hair and a green t-shirt that seemed to glow under the lights of the station. He couldn't have been more than fourteen.

His friend clutched the rucksack and started to cry. He was white; his skin turned red and blotchy.

She glared at him. *I'm a teacher*, she thought. *I can spot a faker*.

But the people surrounding them were taken in. A woman rushed to the boy, putting a hand on his shoulder and asking if he was hurt. And a man – large, wearing a grey suit that was a size too small – advanced on Rita.

"What kind of person steals off a child?"

A woman edged in next to him. "She's probably going to use it to put a bomb in."

Rita stepped back. She backed into someone.

"What's going on?"

She turned, readying herself to dart round this person and run out of the station. Could she make it?

But she'd backed into a policeman.

"Shit," she muttered.

"Pardon?"

"Nothing."

"Do I recognise you?"

"No. Those boys stole—"

"That's not true." The man in the tight suit was behind her. "I saw it all. She ran out from behind that pillar and tried to steal his bag. Lucky I was there to stop her."

The policeman frowned. "Is that true?"

"Yes," replied the man. "Bloody Muslims. All the same."

Rita turned to him. "I'm not a Muslim, you twat! And I didn't steal that rucksack. It's mine."

The policeman put a hand on her shoulder. "Really, a Pokémon bag?"

She looked towards the boys. The one with the bag was sitting on the floor now, letting himself be consoled. Revelling in it. His friend looked anxious.

"Do you have any identification in the rucksack?" asked the policeman.

She felt her shoulders slump. "No." There was nothing in there but a packet of crisps and some trading cards she hadn't spotted when she'd emptied it the previous night.

"What's your name?"

She said nothing.

"Please, tell me your name."

"Maryam."

"Maryam what?"

She couldn't think of anything. "Maryam Gandhi."

"Seriously? OK then, Ms Gandhi, you'll need to come with me."

CHAPTER FIFTY-FOUR

*T*HE CHANCE TO TELL YOUR STORY ABOUT THE *B*RITISH *Values Centre*, they'd told her. They were looking for grit. A chance to pit one former MP, arrested and disgraced, against one current Prime Minister, currently riding high in the polls.

Jennifer had insisted on doing the interview in the Birmingham studio. She wouldn't leave her family to go to London. Not now.

She'd also insisted on being interviewed live. She didn't want anyone editing her words, twisting what she had to say. Or cutting the parts of the interview where she would stray from their intended topic.

The next available live slot was on that evening's *Newsnight*. The short notice reminded her of the times she'd had to think on her feet as a minister. She'd often received a call in the afternoon telling her she would be interviewed that evening, or in the morning scheduling an interview for lunchtime.

It had been months since she'd done it. Months in

which she'd been arrested, appeared in court, been sent to prison and then subjected to the humiliation of the centre.

Now it was time to tell the truth. Not just about the centre, but about the Prime Minister.

She sat in the green room at the TV studios in the city centre, watching the makeup being applied. Her skin was sallow from the months of incarceration. She still hadn't found the time to get her hair cut or her roots dyed. She looked quite different from the confident woman who'd stood on the floor of the House of Commons five months before, waiting for her friend to join her in denouncing the former Prime Minister Leonard Trask. They'd spent weeks planning together, but when Samir was arrested the plan had come to nothing. Catherine had become Prime Minister and Jennifer had been arrested.

At last the cloth protecting her suit was whipped away and the makeup girl smiled at her in the mirror. She smiled back. Her face looked orange now, but would pale under the lights. Her hair had been combed and styled but was too long and messy. She'd have to do.

"Ready?"

She turned to see a production assistant waiting, the same woman who'd welcomed her when she arrived. Rosie Pink, her name was. She looked it too; strawberry blonde hair and freckles peppering pink cheeks. She was also young enough to be Jennifer's daughter. About Meena's age.

She followed Rosie along corridors, thinking about her family. Yusuf had taken Hassan with him to work, unable to find a babysitter. She's asked him if he wanted to come here with her – a TV studio, won't that be fun? But he'd refused, backing into his dad and shaking his head as if Jennifer were a stranger offering him sweets.

Samir, as far as she knew, was still in the detention centre. Did they have access to TV, she wondered. Would it be switched to *Newsnight*? Maybe, if they knew an inmate's mother was due to appear. She only hoped she could do what she needed to, that some of his anger over her friendship with Catherine might dissipate tonight.

At the poky studio, she was ushered into a chair, camera mere inches from her face, and told the drill. *Watch the light – you'll be counted in – eyes on the camera right there.*

She wiped her nose with a tissue and sat back, working on her composure. She could see her face reflected in the camera lens, tiny and pale. S*mile*, she told herself. Or would that be a mistake?

Through an earpiece she could hear the main studio in London. They were introducing her slot, running over what they'd covered the previous night in their film from the centre. There was more footage; more talking heads from Yonda and an interview with Sally, the woman in her group who'd been arrested for spreading right wing hate speech. Jennifer shuddered. Sally would be loving this.

At last the signal came and she pulled on what she hoped was a serious smile.

"So, Ms Sinclair. You spent fourteen weeks in one of these centres. Burcot Park, the one we've just seen."

"That's correct. I accepted a transfer there from prison."

"Was that a voluntary transfer?"

She knew where this was going. "It was. But if I'd known more about the regime in these centres, I might not have taken it."

"No? But it looks like a much easier option than prison."

She allowed herself a laugh. "That's what they want you to think. It's not the reality."

The interviewer's forehead creased. "Go on."

"The regime in the centres consists of a six-step program. It's a bit like Alcoholics Anonymous, but for political prisoners instead of alcoholics."

"Political prisoners? That's quite a loaded term."

"The women I met there had committed political crimes. There was one who hid her neighbour's son when he was suspected of involvement in a terrorist group. One was a lawyer who represented people arrested under the Prevention of Terrorism Act. Another helped people move between hiding places, and one who distributed extremist literature. I also met a teacher who failed to recite the oath of loyalty with the children in her class."

"Would this be Rita Gurumurthy, the escaped convict?"

"Rita was tortured. She was illegally held in solitary confinement."

"Do you have evidence of that?"

She stared at him. A bead of sweat ran into her collar.

"Let's get back to the regime," she said. "To get through the six steps, prisoners have one-to-one sessions with a counsellor. They then have group sessions with other inmates. These are brainwashing sessions, designed to change the way that inmates think."

"The governor of Burcot Park has just told us that the purpose of the centre is counselling. Not brainwashing."

Jennifer swallowed. Yonda Hughes would be watching this, sitting in her vast office maybe, wearing one of her trademark suits. "She's lying."

"Ms Sinclair, with all due respect. Are you simply trying to discredit the government?"

"In this instance, no. But I do have further information that I believe would discredit the government. Would put it to shame, in fact."

The interviewer's voice rose. "Yes?"

Jennifer patted her suit pocket.

"You'll be aware of the circumstances of my arrest," she said. "Of my son's arrest." She blinked, hating to mention Samir.

"You hid him, knowing that there was a warrant for his arrest."

"Of course I did." She frowned. "Any mother would. But I knew he was under suspicion, a few days earlier. That's why he left our house, and came to my flat. This was before any formal notification from the police."

"Are you telling me that you had inside information in your role as Shadow Home Secretary at the time? Did John Hunter tell you?"

Jennifer remembered her meeting with John in his office. The day Catherine had sent her the note. He'd known something, but hadn't told her what it was.

"No," she said. "Absolutely not."

The interview put his hand to his ear and frowned. Jennifer took another breath and opened her mouth to speak. *Ask me where I got the information*, she thought.

The interviewer squared his shoulders. He looked puzzled.

"I apologise Ms Sinclair, but we need to interrupt this interview to go live to Downing Street."

CHAPTER FIFTY-FIVE

"Name?"

Rita looked down at her feet. She was wearing a pair of Jennifer's trainers. Too big, they'd given her blisters.

"I need you to give me your name."

She looked up at the custody sergeant. He swayed in front of her.

"Um. Meena. Meena Gandhi."

"Are you sure about that?"

She nodded. Her head throbbed and her legs felt numb from all the walking. But the pain was nothing to the fear of being recognised and taken back.

"Only my colleague says you gave your name as Maryam Gandhi."

"Meena's my nickname."

"Seriously? Your name is Maryam but your nickname is Meena?"

She flashed him a grin. "Yes."

He shook his head. He was short and fat, with wispy ginger hair that came not just from his head but from his ears and nostrils. Rita wondered if he'd ever thought about buying a pair of tweezers.

He sighed. "Very well." He picked up a cheap biro and used it to tap at the keys of a computer. In between strokes, he chewed its end.

"Address."

"What?"

"I need your address."

"I don't have one."

He looked over the monitor. "You don't look homeless."

"I got some clean clothes. From the shelter. A shower, too."

"Which shelter?"

She closed her eyes. She didn't want to get into trouble. "St Barnaby's."

"No such place."

"Sorry?"

"I said, there's no such place as the St Barnaby's shelter. Not in Birmingham, at least. Are you from Birmingham?"

"No. Er... Derby. I'm from Derby."

"Derby." He turned back to the screen. "And do you have an address there?"

She felt her cheeks grow hot. "No."

"Alright. I'm going to put you down at the nearest shelter, in that case. HomePoint."

"No."

He raised an eyebrow. "Why not?"

"Nothing. It's OK."

He dropped the pen and walked round the desk. "Do you know why you're here?"

"Some kids stole my rucksack. Ha— my rucksack."

"No. You stole it. You've been charged with theft."

"You've got it wrong. They took it from me. I was getting it back."

He put a hand on the desk next to her balled fists. She shivered, not wanting him to touch her.

"So you – a homeless woman, from Derby – are walking around Birmingham with a Pokémon bag, and some kids steal it. Instead of alerting us, you decide to steal it back."

"Not steal."

"Anyway, it's not my job to worry about what you say you did or didn't do. You'll be interviewed in the morning. I suggest you think about your story."

"It isn't a story."

He laughed. "They all say that. Come on, time to go to your cosy cell."

She shuddered, remembering her cell at Burcot Park. She said nothing. How long could she keep up this pretence of being Maryam Gandhi from Derby? How long before someone recognised her?

She followed him to her cell, matching his pace. He stopped at a metal door, picked out a key from the chain on his belt, and opened it.

"In you go."

She shuffled past him, holding her breath. Expecting the stink of urine and sweat. But instead, the cell smelled of bleach.

"Sit tight. See you in the morning."

CHAPTER FIFTY-SIX

JENNIFER STARED AT THE CAMERA. THE LIGHT HAD gone off and she'd been abandoned.

Rosie Pink appeared, rounding the camera to speak to her. Jennifer wondered if she'd been in the room all along or if she'd been watching via a screen somewhere.

"Sorry about the interruption. They'll be back with you soon."

"Did I hear him say they were going to Downing Street?"

"Mm-hmm."

"Was that planned?"

A shrug. Rosie looked down at a clipboard. "Don't think so. D'you want to watch?"

"Yes. Yes I do."

"No problem."

Rosie picked up a remote control and pointed it in the direction of the screen Jennifer had been watching, the one showing her interviewer.

Another screen next to it came to life.

There was Catherine, sitting in a floral armchair. She

wore a green jacket that complemented her dark hair and glowing cheeks. She wouldn't have had time for extra makeup, not unless she'd been planning this.

She was smiling, waiting for the interviewer to stop speaking. He was announcing the switch to Downing Street. He looked perturbed, staring just past the camera from time to time as he listened to his audio feed. So this wasn't planned.

Jennifer gripped her knees and leaned forward. What lies was Catherine going to come up with this time?

"Prime Minister, this is an unexpected surprise."

"Oh I don't think so, Jeremy."

"We weren't expecting to hear from you this evening."

"Well, thank you for giving me the opportunity to speak."

"Am I right in thinking that you want to rebut some of Jennifer Sinclair's claims about the British Values Centres?"

Catherine paused for a moment, her mind seemingly elsewhere.

"Yes. That and to make an announcement."

"An announcement?" The interviewer was struggling to keep the tension out of his voice.

"Yes. But let me deal first with Jennifer's claims."

Behind the camera, Rosie waved to get Jennifer's attention. Jennifer frowned at her, then realised she was telling her she'd be back on air shortly. She looked at the camera. The red light came back on.

She rearranged her features, trying not to show her surprise at Catherine's intervention. Her anger that she'd been hijacked.

The interviewer was still questioning Catherine. "You're refuting them?"

Jennifer opened her mouth to speak, wondering how

this was being shown to viewers. Were she and Catherine being broadcast next to each other, in two simultaneous feeds? Or was she invisible while Catherine spoke? She had to assume she was being watched.

"I am. You've seen from the earlier reports that the British Values Centres are nothing like she describes. We set them up to provide an appropriate environment for giving prisoners the support they need to understand the gravity of their crimes and to reduce recidivism rates."

"But you still haven't provided any hard figures on that."

"Jennifer gave some examples of women she claims to have met, and that she claims did not deserve to be there. While I won't be so crass as to name individuals, I would like to say that as an inmate, she won't have had access to the full facts of each of these women's crimes. All she'll have had is their own story. Their own protestations of innocence."

"Is it true that one of these women was a teacher who simply failed to recite the oath with her class?"

"Well, seeing as you're dealing with specifics, let me do so too. The woman you refer to is Rita Gurumurthy. She recently escaped custody while being transported to another facility. There is a nationwide police hunt going on for her as we speak. We believe she could be dangerous. She threatened a family not long after escaping. A family with a baby."

"So what do you say to Jennifer Sinclair's accusations that the purpose of the British Values Centres is a form of brainwashing?"

Catherine laughed. "I say she needs to read less science fiction. Don't forget this is the woman who hid a suspected terrorist. She was in a position of trust as an MP and member of the shadow cabinet, and she betrayed that trust."

Jennifer put a hand to her chest. She needed to interrupt, to reclaim the debate. But how did she respond to that, without coming across as self-serving?

"The suspected terrorist was her son," the interviewer pointed out. "She claims that—"

"But don't you see," replied Catherine. "That only makes it worse. What kind of mother, what kind of public servant, allows the situation in her own home to get so bad that her son becomes an extremist?"

A flush had blossomed on Catherine's neck, something Jennifer hadn't seen since she was a backbench MP. And her voice was becoming strident, not the smooth tones she'd worked so hard to hone.

Jennifer cleared her throat. "If I may interject?"

The interviewer nodded. "By all means."

"Before the sudden jump to Downing Street, I was talking about the fact that I knew my son was under suspicion. That I knew he would be arrested."

Catherine wrinkled her nose. "Jennifer. Good to speak to you again."

"Likewise."

"Can I just remind you of your position here?"

"Go on."

"You were recently released from Burcot Park. Your son is currently in detention because of his crimes."

"Hang on—"

Catherine raised a hand. "Crimes that I'm sure viewers will agree were shocking for the son of an MP."

Jennifer fished in her pocket.

"I don't want to talk about that this evening. What I do want to do is tell people that you—"

"Wait," interrupted Catherine. "Jeremy?"

"Yes," replied the interviewer. He'd been watching with

pleasure, his eyes dancing in the knowledge that he was presiding over an interview – a spat – that was surely going viral already.

"I mentioned to you that I had an announcement."

"Wait," said Jennifer. "Let me—"

"Go on," said the interviewer. "Your announcement, Prime Minister."

"Thank you." Catherine leaned back and her face regained some of its colour. "I'm sure that viewers will understand when I say how horrified and appalled I am by the lies that have been hurled at this government in recent days."

Jennifer watched, her thumbnail drilling in to her palm. *Damn you Catherine...*

The interviewer said nothing, waiting for Catherine to continue. Jennifer considered interrupting but decided against it.

"I believe that the people of this country have the intelligence to see through the lies and accusations of people such as Jennifer Sinclair. I believe that, like me, people want to keep this country safe, and do what we can not only to prevent terrorist attacks but to deal effectively with the perpetrators of all attacks against our great nation, whether those be through violence or via subversion and lies."

Jennifer blinked. She thought of Michael Stuart, the prime minister she'd betrayed, standing in front of the door of Number Ten, delivering a similar speech. He'd called a confidence vote in his government, and lost.

Was Catherine about to do something equally rash? Was she that scared?

The interviewer opened his mouth but Catherine continued.

"I'm also aware that I became Prime Minister after the

unfortunate illness of my predecessor Leonard Trask, and that the country has not had an opportunity to support my government's policies at the ballot box."

The interviewer perked up. "Prime Minister, are you saying that—"

Jennifer held her breath.

Catherine continued, ignoring him. "I believe that the methods my government has adopted will strike the perfect balance. Instead of looking to punish subversives and potential terrorists, we seek to cure them. To convince them of the error of their ways. The British Values Centres are at the heart of that approach. It's a gentler approach than that of Leonard, or indeed that of Michael Stuart, who preferred to take a hammer to crack a nut, as it were."

"You're wrong," interrupted Jennifer. "The centres are the biggest hammer there is."

Catherine's gaze went over the top of the camera, as if she was looking at Jennifer directly.

"To pursue this radical approach, we need a mandate. Which is why I shall be visiting the Queen tomorrow morning in order to call an election."

The interviewer was nearly leaping out of his seat. He swallowed hard, his eyes bright.

"What will the date of the election be, Prime Minister?"

"Four weeks from now. On April the fourteenth."

CHAPTER FIFTY-SEVEN

Rita spent the night staring at the ceiling, waiting for daylight. She hadn't worn a watch since arriving at the British Values Centre, where she'd developed the ability to guess the time based on the quality of light, something she was priding herself on.

But here, the light was a constant orange glow from a streetlamp outside. All she could hear were regular comings and goings of police cars and the occasional voice.

At last the orange began to lighten and turn to a pale blue whiteness. Daylight.

She stood up and paced her cell – ten, twenty, a hundred times. She needed to keep her muscles awake. If she was going to be taken back to the high security centre, she'd need her wits about her. And who knows, an opportunity to run might present itself.

The grille in the door slid open and a face appeared. Not the custody sergeant from last night but someone new; a woman. Her eyes were large and seemed friendly enough.

"Stay where you are."

Rita had been sitting on the bench where she'd tried to

sleep, bored of her circuits. She shrugged her shoulders and stayed put.

The woman opened the door and came in then.

"Come on then."

Rita frowned.

"We haven't got all day."

"Where are you taking me?" she asked, her voice shaking.

"You're being released."

"What?"

"Come with me. They'll explain it all at the front desk."

She followed the woman, wondering if this was a lie to get her out of her cell where there'd be orderlies from the centre waiting at the front desk, or another officer waiting to transfer her. There would be no Twix bars this time, no offers to sit up front.

She clenched her fists as she walked, trying to stay calm.

"Here you are."

She stopped at the desk. The atmosphere was very different today; instead of the single custody sergeant, there were people coming and going. Uniformed officers, plain clothes detectives. None gave her a second glance.

A man she didn't recognise was standing at the desk. He wore a brown suit that needed cleaning. He smiled at her as she approached, a smile that didn't reach his eyes.

"Maryam Gandhi?"

"Yes."

"It's your lucky day."

"Sorry?"

"Someone saw you with that rucksack, earlier in the day. Turns out you didn't steal it after all."

She forced herself to breathe. "Who?"

He shrugged. "A man who was at the station. Lucky for you he saw you with it earlier, then again with the boys."

She wanted to shriek with relief. "So I can go?"

"Indeed you can. And there's someone here waiting for you."

She frowned. Who would know she was here? Not Jennifer, not with her using a false name.

"Who?"

"We rang the shelter. The one on your record as your temporary address. The manager is here for you. A Mr Yusuf Hussain."

CHAPTER FIFTY-EIGHT

JENNIFER DROPPED HER MOBILE ON THE KITCHEN table, frustrated. This was her third unsuccessful attempt to get through to Catherine.

The surprise election announcement had pushed her story into obscurity. The red light on the camera had pinged off almost immediately. She'd been left in a darkened studio with an apologetic Rosie.

"So sorry," she'd said. "But this is the story now. I'm sure you'll understand."

She did. Of course she did. Catherine had diverted attention away from Jennifer by creating a sensation. There had been no hint of an impending election, no mutterings from the government or the media. Catherine had only been PM for a matter of months. Was she really confident she could win an election?

She thought of Michael Stuart, his misguided attempt to derail her campaign against him by attaching the immigration vote to a vote of confidence in his government. It had almost worked – if just one more rebel had switched sides, he would have won – but ultimately, it had failed. And not just for Michael.

Against her better judgement, she delved into the pile of mail on the kitchen worktop and pulled out the letter about Samir's deportation. Four and a half weeks away. Four days after the election.

The door banged open and she flinched. Hassan had left for school half an hour earlier. She wasn't expecting to be disturbed till the afternoon. With Meena and Rita gone, and Yusuf working long hours at the shelter, the house echoed with emptiness. She wondered if it would ever be full again.

She looked up to see Yusuf coming in, arms full of paperwork and his laptop.

"Working from home?" she asked him.

"You could say that," Yusuf replied. He dumped his work onto the kitchen table. "Guess who I've found."

Jennifer looked up. Shuffling in behind him, her head bowed, was Rita.

She stood up. "Rita! What happened to you? Are you OK?"

Rita shrugged. "Sorry."

She shook her head. "Don't be."

"I took Hassan's bag. Some kids stole it from me." Rita looked at Jennifer. "I'll replace it."

Jennifer put an arm around her friend. "Don't be silly. I'm just glad you're safe. Where have you been?"

"I tried to go to Yusuf's shelter." Rita glanced sideways at Yusuf. "Thought I could hide there."

Jennifer looked at Yusuf. "And you found her there?"

"No. She got herself arrested. They called me."

"Why?"

"I told them the shelter was my address. Couldn't think of anything else," said Rita.

Jennifer pulled back. "But... but why didn't they take you back?"

Rita grinned. "I gave a false name."

Jennifer smiled and pulled Rita to her. She felt damp and her skin was tracked with tears. "Well done."

Yusuf started moving around the kitchen. "Anyway, you must be starving, Rita. How about eggs on toast?"

"Sounds delicious."

He turned to her and smiled. "You go and get changed and I'll cook. Want some, Jen?"

"Er, yes. Please."

Rita left and headed upstairs. Yusuf cracked six eggs into a pan and left them to simmer. He turned to her.

"Have they announced it officially yet?"

She nodded. "She's just come back from the palace. Made another speech outside Downing Street. More thinkspeak. D'you think people will buy it?"

"Does that matter?"

"What d'you mean?"

"Well, once they know what she did, it'll all be over for her. Won't it?"

She dropped into a chair. She felt tired. "I honestly don't know anymore."

"If she gets back in, Samir—"

"You don't have to remind me about Samir. What are were going to do about Rita? Did anyone see you come in?"

"I don't think so. But its impossible to tell. Anyway, she's not going to stay here."

"Oh?"

"I think she had the right idea," he said as he flipped the eggs. "The shelter. I can keep her hidden away there."

"Are you sure? If she's found, they'll shut you down."

He turned to her. "She's your friend, Jen. We need to help her. We need to help everyone we can. I'll sort it."

She stood and leaned into his back. He reached round and grabbed her hand. She held it then let go to wrap her arms around him.

"Watch out. I don't want these eggs to burn."

She pulled back and sat down again.

He swirled oil around the pan. "So what are you going to do about Catherine?" His voice was tense.

"I'm going to make a call."

"She won't listen."

"Not her. Someone else."

CHAPTER FIFTY-NINE

THE CALL WAS A SURPRISE.

"What do you want, Catherine?" Jennifer asked.

"I want to speak to you. In person."

"It's too late for that."

"I don't believe it is."

"You've already made it clear you're not prepared to help me."

"And you've made it clear you won't actually carry out your threats. What was that charade on *Newsnight*, anyway?"

"It wasn't a charade. If you thought that, you wouldn't have called a snap election."

Catherine laughed. "This is nothing to do with you. But then, you always did have an over-inflated sense of your own importance."

"You can say that if you want. I know I scared you. But it doesn't make any difference."

Jennifer took a deep breath.

"You know what I want," she said. "And you know what I'll do if you can't deliver."

"I don't know what you're on about." Catherine's voice sounded haughty, more strident than in her backbench days. Or was it the stress?

"Oh, don't give me that—"

"We need to talk. Let's work this out in person. Soon, before the campaign starts to take over."

"I'll come to your constituency. But this is the last time, Catherine. If you don't—"

"No. Not there."

Jennifer shook her head. Should she just slam the phone down?

"Are you still planning on deporting him?"

"It's not me, Jennifer. I'm not the hand of God, you know. Come to the House. See me there."

"The House of Commons? Not Downing Street?"

"No. Too public. Arrange a meeting with your ridiculous friend Maggie. Tomorrow morning, before Prime Minister's Questions. Before we dissolve Parliament for the election."

"I'm not doing this, Catherine. You've wasted my time before and—"

"Come. I'll find you."

CHAPTER SIXTY

Rita spent the day hiding in a cupboard in Yusuf's office.

She crouched on the floor, listening to the comings and goings of his day. Meetings, visitors, minor crises. Every time someone entered the room she held her breath, terrified they'd open the cupboard and find her.

But Yusuf had locked the door. She was safe.

By the time he let her out, the blue-white light seeping through the gap at the top of the cupboard door had turned yellow. She stumbled out, her legs seizing up with cramp.

Yusuf grabbed her arm. "Steady, now. Take a breath or two. Sorry you had to stay in there."

She gasped in the cold air of his office, relieved at last to inhale something that wasn't her own recycled breath.

"Sit down," said Yusuf. He pulled out his chair. "Here."

She fell into the chair. Her chest was tight. She felt faint. "Don't put me in there again."

"Don't worry. I've found somewhere better. Somewhere with a window."

She nodded. There was a carrier bag on the table: Tesco. "Is there anything to eat?"

"I brought you a sandwich, and some fruit. Chocolate."

Chocolate. The thought of it made her dry mouth water. She raised her eyebrows at Yusuf and he gestured towards the bag. She ripped it open. Inside were two ham sandwiches, a bag of apples and a Twix. She smiled at the Twix, wondering how Sonia was, if she'd recovered from her injuries.

"Ham sandwiches?" she said. "But you're Muslim."

"I am. You're not."

"OK. They look good to me."

She ripped the packets open and swallowed the sandwiches in a few heavy gulps. They were dry and processed but they filled her aching stomach. She ate one of the apples then opened the Twix.

After a moment's hesitation she held it out to him, offering him a stick. He'd pulled up a chair and was sitting on the other side of the desk, watching her eat. His eyes kept creeping towards the door.

"Are we OK here?" she asked.

"Not for long. Safest to move you. Things are quiet up here now. They're doing dinner downstairs, everyone's busy. But there are dorms along from here. We need to move you quickly."

She waggled the Twix at him and he shook his head and pushed it back. "You need it more than me. But thanks."

He smiled. His teeth were white and looked like he had a good dentist. He'd trimmed his beard since she'd run from their house. It made him look younger. She pictured him and Jennifer together, in happier times. Then she thought of Ash. Where was he?

"Can I use your phone?" she asked.

"My phone?"

"I'd like to call my boyfriend. He was arrested before I came to you. He might have been released." She shrugged. "You never know."

He pushed the phone on the desk towards her. She was about to pick it up when it rang.

She jumped back in her seat, almost falling to the floor. Yusuf frowned and picked it up. He licked his lips and rubbed his beard.

"Hello, Yusuf Hussain."

Rita could hear her heart pounding in her ears. She watched him, the Twix melting in her clenched fist.

Yusuf let out a long breath and threw her a smile.

"Jen. Why didn't you use my mobile?"

Rita let her hand relax, dropping the chocolate to the floor. She was shaking.

Yusuf nodded. "OK. Good luck," he said, then replaced the handset.

"Everything OK?" Rita asked.

"Yes. Jen's going to London."

He reached into his pocket for his phone and tutted at it. He pressed a button then handed it to Rita.

"Here. Use this."

She took the mobile from him, pausing to remember Ash's number.

Yusuf busied himself putting files away in a metal filing cabinet. She looked around his office, noting how tidy it was, trying to distract herself from her nerves. Would Ash want to speak to her? Could his number have been diverted to the police, and they'd be waiting for her?

She pulled the phone away from her ear. She should hang up. But then there was a click.

Too late now.

"Hello?" she said, her voice small. Yusuf stopped moving and then started again, rearranging the photos of his family on top of a book case. She looked at them. Samir was handsome. She hoped Jennifer could get him back.

"This is Ash. Leave a message."

She opened her mouth to speak. She closed her eyes, torn between telling him she was thinking of him and staying hidden.

She swallowed and hung up.

"Everything OK?" asked Yusuf.

She wiped a tear from her cheek. "Fine."

"Good. Let's get you moving then."

CHAPTER SIXTY-ONE

MAGGIE PUSHED OPEN THE DOOR TO HER NEW OFFICE in Portcullis House, over the road from the Commons. Jennifer was jealous, but then Maggie had more than served her time in the dingy offices in the main building.

"How did it go?"

Jennifer shrugged and dropped her bag on one of three visitors' chairs. "Good. I think. Thanks for getting me access."

"No problem. I think it was a bit of a surprise, having me turn up with you."

Jennifer laughed. "Nothing would surprise me anymore."

Maggie shrugged her jacket off and hung it over the back of the chair. Jennifer was surprised to see her taking so much care.

Maggie leaned back and pushed her chair towards a chest of drawers. "Coffee?"

"Yeah. I need it, after that."

Maggie poured the contents of a filter jug into two

chipped mugs and pushed one across the desk. "D'you think it'll work?"

Jennifer frowned. Maggie only knew this was something to do with Samir.

She reached into her desk and pulled out a miniature of whisky. She waved it in Jennifer's direction.

"No thanks."

Maggie shrugged and poured a tot into her own coffee. She sealed the lid and slipped the bottle into her desk then took a gulp.

"Better than the fags, at least."

"You've given up?"

"Trying." Maggie rolled up a sleeve to display a nicotine patch. "Three weeks and counting."

"Well done."

"Three weeks, two days and..." she examined her watch, "...five hours. Not bad."

She put the mug down, placed her elbows on the table and gave Jennifer a look that said *I hope you know what you're doing*. "It's time."

"Oh." Jennifer put her mug down and glanced at the door. "I'm not sure what..."

"You going to PMQs?"

A grin. "Wouldn't miss it for the world."

Jennifer nodded. Prime Minister's Questions was due to start in an hour and a half.

"D'you want to watch too?" asked Maggie.

"I can't."

"I'll take you up to the Strangers' Gallery."

"You sure? You don't want to be on the floor? You don't want to ask your own questions?"

"I don't think they'll need me."

There was a knock at the door. Just one short rap. Jennifer stood and smoothed her skirt.

"No," said Maggie, rushing round the desk. "I want to do this."

She hurried past Jennifer and flung the door open. Her shoulders fell at the sight of the man standing in the corridor; young, besuited. An aide.

"Who are you?"

"I've come to fetch Jennifer Sinclair. Is she here?"

"I am." Jennifer approached him. "Who wants to know?"

He frowned, not expecting the question. "The Prime Minister."

Maggie grabbed her hand. "Go get 'em, kid."

CHAPTER SIXTY-TWO

Rita followed Yusuf along a corridor, towards an open doorway at the far end. She could hear voices from below, smell the roasted meat from the kitchen. Those ham sandwiches had staved off the hunger pangs, but the smell of hot food made her mouth water.

"Where are we going?"

"Just up ahead. Not far. Shush." Yusuf looked past her towards the stairwell. He was moving in sharp bursts, like a frightened animal.

"You OK?" she asked.

He nodded. "Yes. It's just, you can't be found here. The shelter is under constant threat of closure as it is."

"Oh. Sorry."

So even here she was unwelcome. At Jennifer's she would put the whole family at risk; at home she would be arrested, and at Ash's – well, Ash's flat was empty.

Would she ever stop running?

They stopped at the doorway and Yusuf stood back for her to pass. She gasped.

It was a bathroom.

Visions of the basement bathroom at the centre flashed through her head. The darkness. The scurrying sounds of rodents. The beatings.

She tried to breathe.

"I can't go in there."

"What?"

"I just can't."

He sighed and shook his head. "Look, this is the only place I can put you. The loo here is always playing up; I'll just say it's out of order and no one will come in. I'll lock it from the outside."

"No!"

"You can lock it from the inside." He held out his hand. "Here's the key."

She reached for it, tentatively as if it was on fire. It was large, made of a dark metal. Old.

"I can get out at any time?"

"Theoretically."

"What do you mean, *theoretically*? You're not holding me prisoner up here."

His eyes crinkled. "Of course I'm not, Rita. You're free to go if you want."

"Good."

"Only, I wouldn't advise leaving unless I come to tell you it's safe."

She drew a deep breath. She could do this. There was a window in there. The tiles were clean. And she couldn't hear any tap dripping.

"Can I have a chair or something?"

"Of course. I'll fetch you one. Get inside while I do it. You can lock yourself in and I'll knock four times." His eyes roamed her face. "OK?"

She nodded. Her chest felt tight and her legs weak. She

pushed herself across the threshold, forcing her feet to move. Focusing on the window, and the obscured light filtering in from the street. The toilet was old, with a high cistern. The sink was large, with a line of yellow stain under the tap. Other than that, it was clean. No smell.

She turned to see him walking away from her. Gulping down shallow breaths, she fumbled the key into the lock and shut herself in.

CHAPTER SIXTY-THREE

THE AIDE LED HER TO THE LIFT. SHE STOOD SIDEWAYS-on in silence as they descended. Should she make small talk? Check where he was taking her?

She opened her mouth to speak then decided against it.

At the ground floor they headed for the escalator, then down the tunnel to the Houses of Parliament. Jennifer expected one of the guards to stop them any moment; she was a visitor, accompanied not by a Member but an anonymous aide.

In the back corridors of the House of Commons, the man didn't break stride or even look back to check that she was keeping up. Jennifer's legs were longer than his and she could easily match his pace. She glanced at her watch, wondering how long this was going to take.

They came to a door. The man knocked then pushed it open. Jennifer walked in after him. She was reminded of Hassan's tenth birthday, the day of the Waterloo bomb. John had brought her to a room very much like this. She half expected to see a bank of security cameras and a disgruntled civil servant. She wondered what John was

doing now. Whether he was ready for what was about
to come.

There was no bank of screens or civil servant. Instead,
Catherine sat alone in the centre of the room. She inhabited
one wing-backed armchair, incongruous in this small space,
while another sat next to her, at diagonals.

The aide muttered something then left, closing the
door, remaining outside, no doubt.

Catherine gestured towards the empty chair. "Please,
take a seat."

"No thanks."

Catherine frowned.

"This won't take long," said Jennifer. "I'd rather stand."

"Do you have it?"

"Yes." She reached into the inside pocket of her jacket
and produced a sheet of paper. She unfolded it and handed
it over.

Catherine held it out as if it was contaminated. "This
isn't it."

"Yes, it is."

"No." Catherine looked from the paper to Jennifer, her
eyes sharp. "It's a copy."

"I'm not giving you the original until I have your assurance that Samir will be freed and you'll close the centres."

"The British Values Centres?"

"Of course."

"But you got out. Why should you care now?"

"I've got friends still in there. What you're doing
there, it's—"

"Ah. I see. Rita Gurumurthy. The runaway. Where
is she?"

"I don't know."

"Was she with you, before they searched your house?"

Jennifer hated that Catherine knew everything about her. "Yes. But she left."

"Where did she go?"

"I've no idea."

"Hmm. Well anyway. The answer's yes."

"Sorry?"

Catherine gave her a smile. "Yes. I'll do as you ask. Once I have the original."

"You'll close the centres? That easily?"

A shrug. Jennifer could smell Catherine's perfume in the confined space, overlaid with the faintest tang of sweat. Had she got to her? If so, Catherine was putting up a good act.

"They aren't working. It's a pilot. Nothing permanent. We'll just put those people into the prison system. Is that what you want?"

Jennifer clenched her fist. "No."

"Look. I want that note. I'm prepared to give you what you want. But I want the original first."

Jennifer shook her head. "It's too late."

"What do you mean, too late?"

"I don't have it anymore. I gave it to someone else."

"Yusuf? He's keeping it safe for you. I can send a car round..." She pulled a phone out of her pocket.

"No. Not Yusuf."

"Who, then?"

Jennifer allowed herself a smile. "Oh, you'll find out. You'll find out very soon."

CHAPTER SIXTY-FOUR

Rita sat on the chair Yusuf had carried in for her. It was light, easily lifted so it wouldn't scrape on the floor; institutional, orange and black like the chairs in the centre.

She stared at the window, trying to assess how much time had passed. It felt like hours.

From time to time she heard sounds outside; voices, footsteps. She cowered against the door, terrified someone might open it. She had that key, clutched so tight it left its impression on her palm. Was it the only copy? Wouldn't a janitor hold a master key? What if they didn't believe Yusuf's story about the blocked toilet; might they try and break in?

She stared at the door, half expecting an emergency plumber to come crashing in at any moment. If they found her here, what would happen? Could she pretend to be Maryam Gandhi again? Or did they keep a list of recent arrests, people they didn't want here?

She heard a noise behind her and spun her head round,

her breathing shallow. She gripped the chair seat under the fabric of the jeans Jennifer had lent her.

Outside, silhouetted in the obscured glass, was what looked like a pigeon. It slammed into the glass then made scrabbling sounds as it found a perch. She stared, desperate for distraction. Then she realised.

The window might open.

She crossed to it. It was a sash window. The paint was flaking. The wood had swelled over time.

She gripped the handle and heaved upwards. With a jolt, the frame went up about a centimetre. The pigeon flew away.

She tugged again. A few more centimetres, far enough to get her arm through. She looped it around the bottom of the frame and rested her palm on the glass outside.

She heaved with her shoulder. It moved again. Now there was enough space for her to push her face out.

She twisted her neck and peered out, gulping in the fresh air. The window overlooked a brick wall and a rooftop below. It was covered in felt, a heating unit on top. On either side of her were walls. One of them had a window at her level.

She gave another heave. She grunted at a sharp pain in her shoulder.

The window didn't budge. She tried again, more gently this time. Her shoulder screamed at her.

The window didn't move.

She fell into the chair, her shoulder throbbing. She ran her fingers over it and widened her eyes. It felt wrong, bulging and twisted.

She plunged her head between her knees and gulped in breaths. At last the dizziness passed and she felt able to touch her shoulder again.

She looked back at the window. It wasn't going to move any further, and even if it could, she didn't have the strength. She'd never squeeze through that gap.

She stiffened. A knock at the door. Just two this time. She flicked her head round, wincing at a snag from her shoulder.

Who was it? Did they have a key?

She gulped down bile.

Then there were more knocks. Four this time. She allowed herself to breathe again.

"Hello? It's me." Yusuf's voice.

She slumped into the chair, regaining her breath. Her heart was galloping in her chest.

"Let me in?"

"Sorry."

She opened her palm to reveal the key then slid it into the lock. Her shoulder burned as she moved.

"Take it easy coming in. I'm hurt."

She drew back and waited for him to see the state she was in.

CHAPTER SIXTY-FIVE

JENNIFER FOLLOWED MAGGIE ALONG THE THIRD ROW IN the Strangers' Gallery. As they shuffled past journalists and visitors, she heard whispers rise up around them. She allowed herself a smile.

"Out of the way, folks," Maggie urged. She pushed her way through, not caring whose feet she trod on.

From their seats, Jennifer surveyed the room.

Around them, people were nudging each other and whispering. They glanced at Jennifer and Maggie, their eyes dark.

She looked ahead, her expression neutral. Beyond the bulletproof glass was the familiar Chamber of the House of Commons. She clenched her fists, remembering the last time she'd been here.

John Hunter entered, surrounded by MPs vying for his attention. She smiled. John loved this; the networking, the chat. She'd always envied him his ease at this aspect of the job, something she'd struggled with.

But then, she had her own skills. When Hayley Price had killed herself with a coat hanger at Bronzefield Prison,

Jennifer's words in this room had saved her own skin. They'd resulted in reforms to the prison system that had, as far as she knew, meant no suicides since.

John would have been all bluster in a similar situation. He had a habit of saying what he thought. His bluntness was refreshing, especially after Michael Stuart's guile, but sometimes he took it too far.

She didn't care how he played this today. Bluntness would be just fine. In fact, it would be perfect when weighed against Catherine's aloofness.

Tom Hamilton, the MP who had replaced Jennifer, had found his way to a seat immediately behind John. She smiled; *well done, that man*. He looked up at the gallery then laid a hand on John's arm.

John turned, puzzlement crossing his face. Then he followed Tom's eye. He looked at Jennifer. He gave her a quick smile.

She grinned back.

CHAPTER SIXTY-SIX

"That looks bad. What happened?"

Rita felt stupid. "I was trying to open the window. I pushed too hard."

Yusuf looked towards the window. The pigeon had returned. It stared in at them. "Can't blame you," he said. "Stuffy in here, I imagine."

"Yes. Thanks."

He frowned. "It's dislocated. You'll need me to put it back in."

She felt the blood drain from her face. "To do what?"

"Don't worry. I've been trained. We've had a few service users turn up with dislocated shoulders. I've popped – ooh, three, maybe four – back in. I'm a pro."

How could he be so confident?

She pulled away from him. The pain bit at her shoulder again, continuing to chew its way down her upper arm. She felt faint.

She nodded.

"That a yes?"

Another nod.

"Say it, Rita. Please."

"Yes," she breathed.

She closed her eyes.

She felt his hands on her arm, large and firm.

There was a wrenching sensation in her shoulder and a crunch. A moment of intense pain was followed by the realisation that the pain was fading.

She brought her fingers up and touched her shoulder, screwing up her eyes. It felt like a shoulder again.

She opened her eyes and forced herself to breathe. Her shoulder ached still but it was nothing like it had been.

"Thanks."

"No problem. You need to go easy on it for a bit. I'll bring you up a sling. But first there's something you might want to watch."

"Watch? Downstairs?"

What had happened? Had the police arrived? Was there trouble, because of her?

"I'm sorry, Yusuf. If my being here is—"

"No. No, it's not that. It's live, on TV. We can watch on the computer in my office."

CHAPTER SIXTY-SEVEN

CATHERINE WAS ON HER FEET NOW, DELIVERING THE standard speech that kicked off Prime Minister's Questions. Innocuous stuff for the most part, but then she threw in a grenade.

"This House will be aware of the government's pilot programme of British Values Centres. I can announce today that we will be conducting a thorough review of their effectiveness in reducing recidivism rates as well as limiting recruitment to extremist organisations in prisons. The Home Secretary will report on this review in due course."

Words, thought Jennifer. Words that meant nothing. Pilot studies, reviews, reports. All mealy-mouthed nothingness. Was she going to close them down, or not?

Around her, the Strangers' Gallery was hushed. Journalists scribbled in notebooks or tapped the screens of phones or tablets. Occasionally someone would glance her way.

Catherine sat down and the Speaker stood. He waited for the MPs' responses to subside; the shouts and accusations. From above, it looked more like a sport than the business of government.

The Speaker cleared his throat to call John.

Catherine turned to look at the Strangers' Gallery. She scanned the rows for a moment then stopped as she reached Jennifer. Her expression was impassive, her eyes blank.

Jennifer stared back, mirroring her expression. Beside her, Maggie chuckled.

"Oh, she's a one."

Jennifer turned to frown at her. Catherine was more than *a one*.

John stepped towards the dispatch box. He patted his top pocket. Jennifer felt her breathing slow.

The Speaker glared around at the MPs and they quietened. If Rita was watching this, she'd say they reminded her of a class of naughty children.

John looked across at Catherine. He smiled. She stared back, not returning the smile.

"I have a question for the Prime Minister," he said.

"Get on with it!" someone called. There was a laugh. The Speaker focused his glare on the Tory benches.

"The Prime Minister has already referred to the British Values Centres in her statement," John continued. "Which is fortunate, considering my question regards a former member of this house who so recently was held in one of those barbaric places."

He paused, still watching Catherine. She kept her gaze steady. Maggie grasped Jennifer's hand.

"My question is about Jennifer Sinclair. The Prime Minister may have noticed she is here today, watching proceedings. Having won her freedom."

Catherine straightened her back. She blinked.

The shouts started: *Bloody Jennifer Sinclair! What you on about! Close them down!*

"Order!" cried the Speaker, rising from his gilded chair. The shouting dropped.

"This House will recall that Ms Sinclair – Jennifer – was arrested for hiding her son. Who was under suspicion of being a member of a prohibited group."

The Speaker stood up. "The Right Honourable Member needs to ask a question."

"Apologies, Mr Speaker. Can the Prime Minister tell us how it was that Jennifer knew her son was under suspicion? How did she know she had to hide him?"

Maggie's grip on Jennifer's hand tightened. "What?" she whispered. "What's he on about?"

"Keep listening," Jennifer replied.

She looked at Catherine, that blush creeping up her neck. She smiled, remembering the first time she'd seen it, the way she'd been impressed how Catherine learned to control it as she rose through the ranks.

She glanced at Jennifer, steely eyed, stepping to the dispatch box. John gave her a smile that to the uninformed observer would look friendly. He sat down.

Jennifer held her breath. He wasn't stopping here, surely?

"The Right Honourable Gentleman will probably have more idea than me of the answer to that question, given that he was such a close friend of Jennifer Sinclair and her family."

MPs jumped to their feet, waving order papers and shouting. Jennifer twisted a thumbnail into her palm.

Catherine retreated. John advanced. He was shaking his head and smiling.

"I find the Prime Minister's response most interesting." He dipped his fingers into his top pocket.

Catherine paled. She glanced up at Jennifer, her eyes wide with accusation.

John continued, his fingers still inside his pocket.

"Can the Prime Minister deny that it was she, in fact, who knew about Samir Hussain, Jennifer's son, being under suspicion? Can she deny that she warned Jennifer about this..."

He leaned forwards, his eyes shining. Jennifer felt her heart skip.

"...in a note that she delivered to Jennifer's office on the sixth of September last year. A note that I have in my possession."

CHAPTER SIXTY-EIGHT

JOHN PULLED THE NOTE FROM HIS POCKET AND HELD IT aloft. Catherine looked from him to Jennifer, her mouth open.

"Order!" cried the Speaker. The MPs were in turmoil now, shouts and accusations peppering the air.

"Was that you?" Maggie whispered in Jennifer's ear. Jennifer nodded.

"Good girl."

John leaned further over the dispatch box. "I have another question. Is the Prime Minister aware that by doing this, she broke the Official Secrets Act?"

The House erupted. Jennifer felt the floor beneath her shift as journalists shuffled in their seats, trying to get closer to her.

The Speaker cried out, his face reddening. He was ignored.

At last the noise died down. The Speaker was glaring at John, his hair damp with sweat.

John stared at Catherine. The note was in front of him, on the dispatch box.

The Speaker cleared his throat.

"The Right Honourable Member needs to retract his statement."

John turned to him. "I apologise, Mr Speaker. But I can't do that."

The Speaker shook his head. "Accusations of this nature are contrary to Parliamentary rules. I ask the gentleman to retract his statement at once, or face censure."

Voices rose up. A journalist leaned around Maggie and looked at Jennifer.

"Can you confirm what he's saying?" she asked.

Jennifer glanced down at Catherine, who was staring up at her. John's eyes were locked on the Speaker.

"Yes," she said, not dropping Catherine's stare.

Catherine looked from her to the journalist. She turned to Robert Trough behind her, her Shadow Home Secretary. She spoke to him and he looked up.

The Speaker's voice was lower now. Firm.

"The Right Honourable Gentleman is subject to the censure of this House. He should leave the Chamber."

John grabbed the note and stuffed it in his pocket. He looked up at Jennifer and started walking in her direction, towards the St Stephen's exit. She'd expected him to go the other way, but that would mean passing the Speaker.

She had to get to him. She had to make sure this was carried through.

She stood up.

Maggie stood with her. "Right, everyone. Out of the way. We need to get through."

They pushed through the packed gallery, Maggie elbowing journalists out of their way. Questions were fired at them, voices raised. Jennifer stared at Maggie's back as they headed for the exit.

As she reached the doorway, she looked down. Catherine had gone. MPs were thronging the space, shouts and gestures traded across the floor. The Speaker was almost purple, straining to be heard.

She hurtled down the stairs. Behind her, the rumble of footsteps followed.

The stairs spat her out into St Stephen's Hall. It was already filling up.

"Jennifer!"

She turned to see John waving at her. MPs crowded round him. The noise engulfed her.

She pushed through the crowd towards him. He was in the centre of a tight group of Labour MPs. His face was red.

"John."

"Jennifer. Sorry I wasn't able to do more."

"I think you've done enough."

Jennifer turned to see Catherine standing behind them. The crowd fell silent, pulling back to let the Prime Minister through. From the corner of her eye Jennifer saw a BBC cameraman approach.

She smiled.

"Catherine."

"Jennifer."

Jennifer said nothing. She waited for the cameraman to come closer. She wondered if Yusuf was watching.

The skin on Catherine's neck was raw. Her nostrils flared. "I don't know what you're trying to achieve by encouraging the Leader of the Opposition to slander me in the Chamber."

John snorted. Jennifer heard muttering; MPs were jostling each other, trying to get closer again. They'd been joined by more journalists.

She ground her thumbnail into the palm of her hand and took a deep breath.

"It's not slander and you know it. We have evidence."

She thought of the safe at home. Suddenly it occurred to her that Catherine could send the police, or the security services, to seize it. Would she go that far?

"That pathetic note you've been bandying about. It's nothing."

John pulled his copy from his pocket. "I don't think so."

Catherine glared at him. "I think it's best if you keep out of this."

The muttering around them grew. "Show us!" somebody cried.

Jennifer looked at John then took the note from him. She turned to face the camera.

She held it up, with the text facing the camera.

"The Prime Minister sent me this note when she was a Home Office minister, in September 2021. A week before my son was arrested. She warned me that he was under suspicion, and encouraged me to go into hiding."

Voices rose around them.

Catherine pushed in front of her, grabbing the note. Jennifer gasped and reached for it but Catherine had it in her pocket. John looked lost for words, a rare sight.

"This note means nothing," Catherine said. She was addressing the crowd of MPs but her gaze kept flicking to the camera. "It has no names on it. Not mine, not hers. Not her son's."

"How do you know that?" asked John. "Have you seen it before?"

The blush spread to Catherine's lower jaw. "She came to visit me. Right here, only an hour ago. She showed it to me and tried to blackmail me. So yes, I've seen it."

A journalist turned to Jennifer. "Is that true?"

"Yes. I showed it to her. I wanted to warn her that it would be revealed today, in the Chamber."

"Rubbish!" cried Catherine.

Jennifer stared at her. Was she going to do this again? Was she going to throw this back at her, turn it into an accusation of blackmail?

"Look, everyone," said John. "Let's just calm down." He turned to an aide and took something from him. "I have another copy here. Be prepared, eh, Prime Minister?"

Catherine twisted her face into a frown that made her look ten years older.

John passed the copy to Jennifer. "This is yours, I believe," he muttered.

The cameras advanced on her, pushing Catherine out of the way.

"Ms Sinclair, can you hold it up?"

Jennifer held it towards them. John's aide started moving through the crowd, distributing something. More copies!

Bless you, John, she thought.

"You can all have your own copy," she said. "The original is in a safe place. I will be handing it over to the police. Meanwhile, you have plenty of examples of the Prime Minister's handwriting to compare this to. Call in your experts."

She felt breath on the back of her neck. "I was trying to help you." Catherine's voice.

For a moment she felt her legs weaken; had she brought herself as low as her former friend, by betraying her like this?

No. This was for Samir, and Rita, and everyone else.

She felt a hand on her shoulder. She turned, ready to

face Catherine. But it was the same woman who'd arrested her, right here, less than six months earlier.

She felt her heart skip a beat.

"We need to talk to you," the woman said. "My name is Detective Inspector Johnson."

"I know."

She turned to see another officer, this one in uniform, guide Catherine away. The MPs surrounding them were shouting now, cries of *liar*, *traitor*, *bitch*. She didn't know who they were aimed at. She didn't care.

DI Johnson cocked her head. "I need you to come with me."

"Yes," she said. "Of course."

69

APRIL 2022

THE SUN WAS APPEARING OVER THE HORIZON, ITS LIGHT filtered by the tall fence next to Jennifer's car.

Yusuf sat in the passenger seat, blowing on his hands.

"I wish this didn't have to be at dawn," he said. "It feels so unwelcoming."

She shrugged. "More secrecy. Less Press."

She'd spent the last three weeks dodging journalists, when she wasn't hunkered down with the police going over her evidence. The case was complicated; she wasn't only the main witness in the case against Catherine, but she was a convicted criminal and the mother of a convicted terrorist sympathiser.

Until, suddenly, she wasn't. She had no idea whose doing it was, but two days earlier she received a letter from the Home Office saying that Samir's conviction had been overturned. No explanation of when, or where, or why. But she wasn't about to argue.

Which meant her conviction was now null too. You couldn't harbour a suspected terrorist if they were officially no longer a suspected terrorist.

Yusuf had asked her if this meant she'd go back to Westminster, find herself another Parliamentary seat. She'd said no; she was too tired. Too worried about the boys. Not yet, anyway.

She heard the squeal of metal on metal and turned. Behind them, a gate was opening.

Yusuf put his hand on her arm. She'd stopped breathing.

Blinking away tears, she pushed her door open and looked at the gate. A prison guard stood inside it, his gaze on the building behind him.

Yusuf grabbed her hand. She squeezed back and approached the gate.

"No closer," the guard said. They stopped.

She heard a clang as another door opened, unseen. A shadow emerged from around the corner of the building. Tall, thin. Gangly.

She gasped and put her hand to her mouth to keep from crying out. She stepped forwards.

The guard glared at her. She held her ground.

The shadow stepped into a pool of light. Samir was blinking, rubbing his eyes. He looked tired. Thin. Five years younger than his now seventeen years.

"Samir!" she cried.

He turned to her, his eyes widening. They were stark, ringed by dark circles. She hoped he hadn't been hurt in there.

Yusuf cleared his throat. "It's so good to see you."

Samir approached them. He stopped as he reached the guard and gave him a questioning look. The guard waved him through.

Samir stepped through the gate and looked up at the

sky. He laughed, a high-pitched cackle that spoke of despair as much as joy.

Jennifer stepped forwards, her hands outstretched. He hadn't let her hold him in years.

She waited.

He all but fell forwards, into her arms. She felt herself breathe again.

"Welcome back, love. Welcome back."

Yusuf wrapped his arms around them both.

"Where's Hassan?" Samir asked. His voice was strained.

"At home," said Yusuf. "With Grandma."

Samir pulled back to look at each of them in turn. His eyes were as wet as Jennifer knew hers were.

"I'm sorry, Mum. Dad," he said.

Jennifer pulled him in again. "Don't be. Don't be."

70

MAY 2022

Mark watched Yonda. She was packing books into a brown cardboard box. Her jacket – dark blue today – hung over the back of her chair.

"You betrayed me," she said, not meeting his eye.

He said nothing.

She looked up. Her eyes were rimmed with purple and her cheeks were blotchy. "Not going to explain yourself?"

"You don't need me to tell you why I did it."

"Hmm. Look at where you got us."

"I don't think that was me."

She threw the second of the porcelain dogs into the box. Mark widened his eyes, waiting for a crash.

She slumped into her huge chair. "I suppose this'll be yours now."

"What d'you mean?"

"Come on, Mark. You don't have to be coy with me. They'll have offered you the job."

"They might have."

She stood up and grabbed her jacket. She slung it over

her shoulders. She muttered to herself as her hand caught in the sleeve.

She moved to the side of the desk and gestured at the chair. Behind her, beyond the window, two vans made their way up the driveway. Delivering supplies for the new psychiatric unit that was to be housed here. NHS, not Home Office. Or Forval.

"I said no," he told her.

"No? What d'you do a stupid thing like that for?"

He shook his head. "I'm going to Canada."

"Canada? Why the hell are you doing that? Stay here, you'll be like a pig in shit."

He laughed. Suddenly Yonda looked ridiculous, and not scary. Now that she'd had her power stripped from her. Strictly speaking, it wasn't fair that she'd lost her job. She was only following orders, after all. But they needed their scapegoats.

"My wife – ex-wife – and son are out there."

"Oh. I'd forgotten about them."

She looked at the box as if waiting for him to pick it up. After a moment's silence, she heaved it up herself.

"So you're not going to track Meena down then?"

"I think Meena's got her own fish to fry."

"Ah." She put the box back on the desk and wiped her hand on her skirt. She held it out.

"Good luck, Mark."

"Thanks. And you."

When she'd left, he crossed to the window and watched the workmen unloading the vans. He wondered who'd be working here in a few days' time. Who the patients would be.

His phone rang.

"Hey."

"Hey," he replied, feeling his pulse pick up. "How's things?"

"OK. He's nervous."

"I know. It's been almost three years."

"He's not the baby he was. You'll need to get to know him again. Take things at his pace."

"And us?"

"What about us?"

"You know what I mean, Vee. What pace should I take *us* at?"

"Let's work that one out when you get here, huh?"

71

OCTOBER 2022

"Can you get that, love? I'm just icing the cake."

"Yeah."

Jennifer looked up and watched her son stroll towards the front door. He was showing signs of being a teenager, despite everything he'd been through.

"You've spelt my name wrong, Mum."

"What?" She looked down at the icing, her spirits falling. "No I haven't."

"It should be Hass."

She flicked his arm. "No, silly. That's just what your brother calls you."

She pushed the cake away and surveyed her handiwork. She wasn't the world's best baker, was probably the world's worst cake decorator, but it was the thought that counted. Hassan's name, wrapped around the best drawing of his new kitten that she could manage. The kitten was growing, but still liked to climb curtains then leap off them onto the tops of cupboards.

Samir called from the front door.

"Mum?"

She frowned. "What is it?"

She stepped into the hall. He looked worried.

"Who is it?" she asked.

"Er, she says she knows you. He doesn't."

Jennifer gave him her most reassuring smile. She shouldn't have asked him to answer the door, he was still scared of the police knocking. Yusuf was in the living room, blowing up balloons. Balloons Hassan had objected to – *but Dad, I'm thirteen* – but would love once they were ready, she knew.

She wiped her hands on her jeans and opened the door further.

"Jennifer!"

She stepped forwards and wrapped their visitor in a hug. Next to her, a young Asian man hopped from foot to foot. He was tall and slim, with a deep dimple in his chin. He reminded her of a young Yusuf.

"This must be Ash?" she said.

Rita pulled back and grabbed the man's arm. "Jennifer, meet Ash. Ash – Jennifer."

"Pleased to meet you," he said, offering his hand. Jennifer took it, then leaned in and put her arms around him. Today felt like a day for hugs.

"Where are the candles?" Hassan was next to her now, his voice straining. It had started breaking, his vocal register veering from bass to falsetto within each sentence.

"Sorry, sweetheart."

Hassan screwed up his face at her.

"I mean, I'm sorry *Hass*."

He nodded. That was better.

"They're in the drawer in the kitchen, next to the cooker."

She turned back to Rita and Ash. "Come in. Take off your coats."

They followed her in and she closed the door. It was chilly today, none of the sunshine there'd been on Hassan's tenth birthday.

Yusuf appeared from the living room. He looked out of breath. "Hey, Rita."

"Hey."

"And this must be Ash?" He held out his hand, gripping Ash's arm as they shook. "Good to meet you at last."

Ash smiled nervously. Next to Yusuf he looked young and awkward. Rita leaned into him, twirling her finger into his sleeve.

"Dad, where are— Oh."

"And this is Samir."

Rita's face lit up. "Samir. It's an honour."

Samir lowered his head. He frowned at Yusuf.

"Don't worry," said Yusuf.

There was movement behind him, in the living room.

"Meena!" Rita cried.

Meena eased around Samir, smiling. "Hi Rita. Good to see you."

Rita leaned forward, a question in her eyes. Meena laughed and hugged her. She drew back to Samir, who snaked his arm around her waist.

Rita clapped her hands together. Her cheeks were pink and her eyes bright. "Oh, it's so good to see you two together."

Samir blushed. He bent to mutter in Meena's ear and they retreated into the living room.

"Have you got a present?" Hassan asked.

Jennifer laughed. "Oh, some things never change!"

"Yes," said Rita, pulling a parcel out of a bag. "Of course."

"Hang on," said Jennifer. "My phone's buzzing. It might be another guest."

She darted into the kitchen and grabbed her phone from next to the cake. "Hello?"

"Jennifer."

"John?"

"You sound surprised."

"I thought you'd be too busy to remember Hassan's birthday."

"Hassan's what? Oh hell, I've forgotten again, haven't I?"

"It's OK. You can make it up to him another time."

"Well, it's you I want to make it up to."

She looked into the hall. Hassan had told a joke and Rita was laughing at him, her eyes dancing. An engagement ring flashed on her finger.

"I have to go, John. Can we talk another time?"

"Don't you want to hear what I've got to say?"

"What? It's not the best time. Can you—"

"I want you to be my Home Secretary."

She laughed. "Nice joke, John."

"I'm serious, dammit. I want you back in the government. Deborah's resigning. Illness. There's a vacancy."

Deborah, the former shadow education secretary in the same shadow cabinet Jennifer had served in, had been Home Secretary for six months now.

"I know," said Jennifer. "She called me, last week. It's rough."

"Yes," said John, after an awkward pause. "But anyway, the job."

"Are you sure that's a good idea? Everywhere I go, governments seem to topple."

"Well, I can thank you for this last one."

"Fair enough. But no, I don't think it would be a good idea."

"You did this to me once before, remember. When I offered you Shadow Home Secretary."

"That was different."

"Home Secretary. You're not even tempted?"

"Oh John, I'm very tempted. Very tempted indeed."

"So why not join us? You don't have to worry about that bitch Catherine Moore anymore, she'll be behind bars for a while. The party loves you for what you did."

"Well, I appreciate that. But I'm not even an MP."

"That's what the Lords is for."

"No, it's not. And besides, I've accepted another job."

"Oh?"

"The new body, to regulate the prisons service. I'll be heading it up."

"You're going to be spying on me?"

"No, John. I'm going to be making sure you and your government don't let things get out of hand. That you don't keep secrets."

"Fair enough."

Hassan ran in, brandishing his present. A LEGO model of Big Ben. Jennifer had been puzzled when he'd asked for it. She could only hope he didn't harbour political ambitions.

She gave him a playful punch on the arm. He swatted at it and laughed.

"Sorry, John. I've got to go. Party."

"Party?"

"The other kind of party. Birthday party." Silence. "For Hassan, remember?"

"Oh. Yes. Tell him Happy Birthday from the Prime Minister."

"He'll like that. Especially as it's you this time."

"Thanks. I guess I'll be seeing you on the other side of a Parliamentary inquiry at some point."

"No time soon I hope. I need to help Samir recover from what he went through in the detention centre. I need to watch over Hassan better than I did his brother."

"Makes sense."

"See you around, John. Be the best Prime Minister we ever had, eh?"

"I'll try, Jennifer. I really will."

Did you enjoy the Division Bell trilogy? You can read the companion stories for free and find out more about the author at rachelmclean.com/bookclub.

Terror attacks have hit London and Birmingham.

Seven people's lives are torn apart. Their world will never be the same again.

In this set of interwoven stories, learn more about the events of the opening day of *A House Divided* and meet some of the characters who feature in the Division Bell trilogy.

Download for free at rachelmclean.com/bookclub.

Printed in Great Britain
by Amazon